DRIVEN BY DESIRE

Also available from Headline Liaison

True Colours by Lucinda Chester
Spring Fever by Lucinda Chester
Vermilion Gates by Lucinda Chester
The Challenge by Lucinda Chester
Portrait in Blue by Lucinda Chester
Course of Pleasure by Lucinda Chester
The Journal by James Allen
Love Letters by James Allen
The Diary by James Allen
Out of Control by Rebecca Ambrose
Aphrodisia by Rebecca Ambrose
A Private Affair by Carol Anderson
Voluptuous Voyage by Lacey Carlyle
Magnolia Moon by Lacey Carlyle
The Paradise Garden by Aurelia Clifford
Hearts on Fire by Tom Crewe and Amber Wells
Sleepless Nights by Tom Crewe and Amber Wells
Dangerous Desires by J J Duke
Seven Days by J J Duke
A Scent of Danger by Sarah Hope-Walker
Private Lessons by Cheryl Mildenhall
Intimate Strangers by Cheryl Mildenhall
Dance of Desire by Cheryl Mildenhall

Driven by Desire

Lucinda Chester

First published in 1998
by HEADLINE BOOK PUBLISHING

A HEADLINE LIAISON paperback

10 9 8 7 6 5 4 3 2 1

All characters in this publication are fictitious and any resemblance to real persons, living or dead, is purely coincidental.

ISBN 0 7472 5760 4

Typeset by CBS, Felixstowe, Suffolk

Printed and bound in Great Britain by
Mackays of Chatham plc, Chatham, Kent

HEADLINE BOOK PUBLISHING
A division of Hodder Headline PLC
338 Euston Road
London NW1 3BH

For Sandra and Steve (and their handcuffs!)
with love from the Cook and the Curtain-twitcher

One

'Yes!' Liza clenched her fists in the classic sign of victory, not caring that several passers-by were staring at her in surprise. The news she'd just been given was incredible. In fact, she thought, it was the best thing that had ever happened to her. She still found it hard to take in, but the more she thought about it, the better she felt.

'Good old Gramps,' she said softly. 'You've really come up trumps for me, this time.' She knew that she'd always been Sam Hargreaves' favourite grandchild; she'd been the youngest by nearly twenty years, because her father – Sam's middle son – had come very late to parenthood. Sam had been captivated by the two-year-old Liza's big blue eyes and blonde ringlets, and had adored her every since. Even throughout the tortuous stage of her teenage years, when she'd rebelled against her parents and dyed her hair black, worn a nose-ring and dressed in clothes which had shocked her father, Sam had indulged her, standing up for her and encouraging her to broaden her horizons.

The clashes between them had only started when Liza decided to go to university. Sam wouldn't have minded if she'd taken an arts course, and then gone to work in some nice charity – as befitting a woman in her position, being the youngest in a well-to-do family – but because she'd chosen to take a business studies course with French, he'd been annoyed, not seeing the point of it. He'd been even more annoyed when Liza had found herself a job in the City, in the market research department of a multinational company. As far as he was concerned, Liza should have been on the lookout for a husband in the City and starting the next strand of the Hargreaves dynasty, not actually working there.

Liza had been equally stubborn. Even though she'd known within two weeks of starting her new job that she'd made a huge mistake, and she was going to hate it, she couldn't bear the idea of her grandfather gloating and saying, 'I told you so.' So she'd gritted her teeth, and simply got on with her job, gradually rising through the firm to become the assistant manager of her department.

Sam had suspected that Liza hated her job. Although it exasperated him that she wouldn't admit it, he respected her for sticking to her principles and not whining about it. And now, Liza thought, he'd given her the chance to escape from the rat-race, with her dignity intact. He'd left her fifty per cent shares in an upmarket taxi firm called *James*, and it was worth quite a bit of money. She could cash it in, and use the money to do what the hell she liked; or she could even take the chance to switch careers and work for herself.

Her perfect cupid's-bow lips pursed. She had a feeling that Sam had had ulterior motives in leaving her the shares – like encouraging her to throw in her job, and start the next generation of the Hargreaves-whatevers (because, of course, she'd be expected to double-barrel her surname with her new husband's). However, Sam had been too shrewd to put any caveats on the inheritance, like the need for Liza to be married within the next few months. He'd left it entirely up to her what she did.

And he'd known what she'd do in the circumstances. Resign.

Liza's eyes glittered with pleasure as she thought about it. She could be her own woman at last. She'd done well enough in the City firm she'd worked for, becoming the Assistant Market Research Manager, but her job was beginning to bore her silly. All her innovative ideas had been blocked by her narrow-minded boss, under the guise of 'lack of funds', and she wanted something that would stretch her more – something that would tax her brain, and something that she could enjoy. She was sufficiently honest with herself to know that she wasn't ambitious enough to fight her way through the glass ceiling and make it to the very top of the firm; she really wasn't that interested in what they – or she – did.

Over the previous few months, she'd had daydreams about

giving it all up and going to Paris or maybe the South of France, where she could learn to paint and spend her days idling under hot Mediterranean skies, drinking local wine, and walking barefoot to the nearest farm to buy large slabs of Brie and jugs of fresh milk. Where she could spend her nights making love under the stars with a handsome young French farm-hand, knowing that there were no strings attached.

She spoke fluent French, thanks to her degree and the fact that she dealt with the French branch of their firm, so it wouldn't have taken a great deal to make the dreams become reality. Only her sense of responsibility had stopped her doing it. Though, now . . . She grinned again, and took her mobile phone from her handbag. Now, she could do what the hell she liked. Starting right this minute. And that was precisely what she was going to do. 'Thanks, Gramps. I really owe you one,' she said, lifting the phone in silent tribute, and pressed a quick-dial button, waiting for the call to be answered.

Three phone calls later, her smile was even broader. She'd half expected some parental opposition to her plans, and she'd got it. Her mother had said that she was completely mad – that her grandfather had left her the assets for security, not to chase some half-baked dream. And why throw up all her business qualifications? Why couldn't she just talk to her boss, take a few weeks' sabbatical to think about things, and be sensible?

But Liza had had enough of being sensible. She'd spent nearly ten years being sensible, working hard at her job and buying herself a flat and doing what people expected of her. It was time for a change. Which was why her second call had been to her boss, to announce her resignation and tell him that she would be in the next day solely to clear her desk. She'd skip the month's money in lieu of notice, and they could call it quits. He'd been too flabbergasted to argue with her.

Her third call had been to the other half of *James* – Bryn Davies – to make an appointment to see him. She'd given him the impression, on the phone, that she was a client. When he found out what she really wanted, no doubt he would be as shocked and angry and surprised as the rest of them. Well, he'd just have to learn to live with it, Liza thought crisply.

She'd made her decision, and that was that. She was going to work for *James*, and no-one was going to stop her.

An exclusive chauffeur service, the solicitor had called it. Liza wondered what he'd meant. Was it just a glorified taxi service, running expensive and newish cars rather than battered and elderly Cortinas? Or was it limo hire? *James*. The name conjured up liveried footmen, proper chauffeurs with peaked caps and deferential manners – though, for all she knew, it could be just a bog-standard taxi service, and the name was just clever marketing.

Then there was her co-owner, Bryn Davies. What was he going to be like? He had a Welsh name: no doubt he was tall and muscular, the rugby-playing type, with dark hair, piercing blue eyes, long eyelashes, and fair Celtic skin. Handsome in a rugged kind of way, like the tenor Bryn Terfel, though without the glorious voice: though he probably had an ear for music. She caught herself fantasising, and laughed at herself. How ridiculous. Why romanticise him, think that he was the typical stereotype Welshman? He was probably short, balding, middle-aged and running to fat. She'd soon find out. She was seeing him in an hour and a half.

She glanced at her watch. It would take her about forty minutes to reach the firm by tube, she thought. If she went early, she would catch him off guard – the real Bryn Davies, not the face he put on for customers. That would give her some idea of whether she'd done the right thing, or whether she'd be better off with her original idea of selling her half of the firm and using the proceeds to escape to France.

Bryn was working on one of the cars when Steve came over to him. 'There's a woman in reception for you,' Steve said laconically. 'She's not bad. I'd give her eight out of ten.'

Bryn couldn't help smiling at his mechanic. Steve saw every woman who passed the doors of *James* in terms of how much he'd like to go to bed with her. His taste ranged from dyed-blonde airheads to mature and sophisticated women, so what 'not bad' meant was anyone's guess. His face tightened for a moment. It couldn't be Jane. Steve knew what she looked like, and even if he did fancy her, he'd have given Bryn some warning. Like saying 'trouble in reception'. Everyone knew that the ex-Mrs Davies meant trouble – for the firm, as well as for Bryn. Thanks to her, the whole thing had nearly gone under, five years before.

He straightened up, wiping his oily hands on a rag, and walked out to the front office. His eyes widened as he saw the woman sitting in reception. She reminded him of someone. He wasn't quite sure who, but there was something in her blue eyes which was very familiar. Yet he knew that he'd never met her before. She was the kind of woman that you simply wouldn't forget.

His gaze travelled appraisingly across her. Whoever she was, she was obviously in business. Her dark suit was pure power dressing, her jacket's sharp tailoring emphasising her feminine curves. Her skirt was short and straight, showing off her good legs. She was wearing black opaque stockings – he knew instinctively that she was the sort who'd wear stockings, rather than tights – and high-heeled black leather court shoes, which looked Italian and handmade. Teamed with hair the colour of winter wheat which was held back by a black velvet Alice band, generous breasts under a demure white shirt, and a mouth that made him suddenly itch to kiss her, the effect was devastating.

He knew damn well that he couldn't afford to indulge in any fantasies about clients. 'How can I help?' he asked, his voice slightly abrupt.

'Bryn Davies?' He nodded. She smiled and stood up, extending her hand. 'Liza Hargreaves,' she said.

He frowned. 'I wasn't expecting you until half past four.'

'I'm sorry.' Her words didn't match the slightly challenging look in her eyes. Liza Hargreaves wasn't in the slightest bit apologetic. 'I'm a little early.'

He nodded. 'What can I do for you, Ms Hargreaves?'

Perfectly politically correct, she thought, with an inward grin. No checking of her left hand to see if she wore a wedding ring; and no 'Miss', which always seemed either insolent or patronising. She'd give him ten out of ten for first impressions. 'I'm Sam Hargreaves' grand-daughter,' she said quietly. 'So I think that it's more like what I can do for you.'

So that was why she looked familiar. He should have made the connection earlier. His face sobered instantly. 'I was sorry to hear about Sam.'

'Me too. Gramps and I didn't always see eye to eye, but I miss him.' She coughed. 'Look, is there anywhere that we can talk – somewhere a bit more private?'

He nodded. 'My office. This way.'

He ushered her through a narrow corridor into a small room. The place looked as though it could do with a good dusting, and it didn't look as if he'd done any filing for months. But at least there weren't dirty coffee cups everywhere, or any tacky topless girlie calendars hanging on the yellowing walls.

Bryn Davies was a surprise, Liza thought. So much for the short, fat, balding and middle-aged man she'd told herself that he'd be in real life, or the Celtic charmer of her fantasies. Bryn was neither. He was just under six feet tall – a good five or six inches taller than her – with dark intense eyes, dark wavy hair which was slightly over-long for her taste, and almost Mediterranean good looks. She would have said that he had Italian blood, maybe Spanish: certainly not Welsh. He wasn't much older than she was, either. He had to be thirty-five, at the most. And, despite his ancient green boiler suit and dirty hands, she found him attractive. Disturbingly so. It would be oh, so easy to turn to him, slide her fingers under the edges of the green material, pull the fastenings apart and then undo his shirt . . .

'Can I offer you a cup of coffee?' he asked, interrupting her thoughts.

'Thanks. Milk, no sugar, please.'

'Coming up.' To her surprise, he actually made the coffee himself, returning with two steaming mugs. 'It's instant. I hope that's okay.'

Liza almost never drank instant coffee – even at the office, she used a cafétière – but she smiled politely. 'That's fine. Thank you.'

'So. What's the story?'

She was impressed with his directness. 'Gramps owned half of *James*.'

He nodded. 'That's right. He was my partner.'

'Though he didn't know that much about cars.'

Bryn smiled. 'He enjoyed tinkering with engines, actually, so he used to spend a bit of time here, if that's what you're asking. The rest of the time, he left me to get on with the business. He was a sleeping partner.'

'Right.' She nodded. 'Well, I saw his solicitor, today. Gramps left me his share in *James*.'

'He what?' Bryn's face betrayed his shock.

'Don't worry, I'm not intending to change things too much.'

He chose his words carefully. 'So you'll be taking the same role that Sam did?'

She shook her head. 'Oh, no. I want to be a full part of this firm.'

'I see.' Bryn sipped his coffee thoughtfully. 'And you know a lot about cars, do you?'

'I can drive.'

'I mean the maintenance side. Engines, gearboxes – even washing the things.'

Her laugh was mirthless. 'Very funny.'

'If you want to be part of this firm, Ms Hargreaves, you'll get your hands dirty. Not to mention your expensive Armani suit.'

Liza's eyes widened. Had that been a lucky guess, or did he know something about clothes, too? His next words confirmed that it was the latter. 'And those soft Italian leather high-heeled shoes aren't remotely suitable for driving our clients around. Look, Ms Hargreaves, I appreciate that you're interested to see what sort of return your investment will give you, and I'm more than happy to give you the last set of audited accounts, and our day-book, so you can check all the figures. But if you think that I'm going to let you tinker around here, forget it. You'll distract my staff, and the money this place brings in isn't enough to keep you in your standard of living.' He scowled. 'I wish I could offer to buy you out, but my dear ex-wife was the reason why I had to sell half of *James* in the first place. I needed cash for her divorce settlement. I might be stuck with you as a business partner, but I don't have to put up with you swanning around the office.'

Liza's mouth tightened. 'You might think that I'm some

sort of spoilt rich kid indulging myself on a whim, Mr Davies, but that isn't the case. I have a degree in business studies – including French – and two sets of professional exams.'

'Then stick to whatever your profession is,' he informed her tartly, 'and let me get on with mine.'

'Small problem. I resigned, early today.' She sat back on her chair, folding her arms. 'So *James* is now my profession – well, fifty per cent of it, anyway.'

'You resigned? Why?'

'Because, among other things, I was sick of being pushed around by middle-aged men who wouldn't give me a real chance to prove myself. And I don't intend to let that happen in *James*, too.'

'Touché.' He lifted his mug. 'Though I don't consider thirty-five as quite middle-aged.' He paused. 'Well, Ms Hargreaves—'

'Liza,' she corrected.

'Liza.' His voice was warm and caressing as he said her name, and it didn't take much imagination to guess how he'd sound if he said a woman's name in passion. It sent a shiver of pleasure running down Liza's spine. 'I take it that you don't know much about the firm?'

She shook her head. 'The solicitor merely said that it was an exclusive chauffeur service.'

'That's more or less it.' He spread his hands. 'We provide a confidential and comfortable service for those who want it. Businessmen, people in the entertainment world, that kind of thing. The rule is, no gawping, no eavesdropping – just a friendly face and an efficient, discreet service. We have a fleet of six cars; I usually book out five of them, and the sixth is in for overhauling or emergencies.'

'Right.'

'And there are various jobs to be done. We're a small outfit – five drivers, a mechanic, and me.'

'So where do I fit in?' Liza asked.

He spread his hands. 'I built the business up from scratch – so I know everything about it, from the clerical side through to driving, routing, and being a mechanic. If you want equal shares in the business, I suggest that you do the same. Learn the business inside out.'

If he was expecting her to cave in now, Liza thought, he was very much mistaken. 'That's fine. I can drive, and I shouldn't think there's that much to routing. Obviously, I'll need someone to show me how your office system works, but as I've worked in an office before, I'm sure I'll soon pick it up. And I can take a course in car maintenance. I think that that just about covers it – don't you?'

Bryn laughed. 'You're stubborn, I'll give you that. Look, let's be sensible about this.'

Another person telling her to be sensible. God. What was it with people today? Was there no-one left in the world who took the occasional risk – or, at least, appreciated that maybe someone else wanted to take the risks they were too scared to take, themselves? She lifted her chin and stared at him coldly. 'You set the challenge. I'll meet it.'

'Right. Let's give it a month. If it doesn't work out, either you agree to be a sleeping partner, or I'll try sweet-talking my bank manager into lending me enough to buy you out.'

'And if it does work out?'

'We'll see.'

Another bloody negative man, Liza thought, expecting her to fail. Just like her ex-boss, Mark: on the rare occasions when he had let her act on one of her marketing ideas, he'd waited for it to go wrong, not believing in her. Well, she'd show him. 'We'll see,' she agreed, a saccharine-sweet smile on her face. She held out her hand, and he shook it.

'I'll see you tomorrow morning, then, at eight o'clock sharp,' he said.

'Eight o'clock,' she agreed.

'Oh – and make sure that you wear something a bit more suitable for working here.'

Liza smiled sweetly at him, only just resisting the temptation to slap his face, hard. 'Don't worry, I will.'

She took the phone from her bag as she walked back to the tube station. There were two people who'd be pleased for her; unfortunately, her best friend, Sally, had the day off, and there was no way that Liza could contact her to tell her the news. But there was someone else who'd appreciate it . . .

She pressed another quick-dial button; the line the other end was answered almost instantly.

'Rupert Walsh.' Abrupt and business-like.

She grinned, picturing her lover. He'd be sitting at his desk, leaning back in his swivel chair, watching the line of figures on his PC and tracking the share prices of his current deals. He looked every inch the City dealer, in his dark suit, crisp shirt and silk tie; his floppy dark hair fell over his forehead, and he was forever flicking it back in a gesture of upper-class arrogance. Rupert Walsh was very nice-looking, and he knew it; although it annoyed Liza, she could put up with it, because his sexual prowess was as good as his looks. He kept her more than satisfied in bed. 'Hi. It's me.'

'Liza.' His upper-class voice softened to a purr as he recognised her voice. 'Baby, how are you?'

'Fine. I had an interesting afternoon.'

'Oh, yes?'

She hadn't told him about her meeting with the solicitor. This was going to come as one hell of a surprise to him, she thought. 'Maybe we can talk about it, later tonight.'

'Over dinner?'

Liza chuckled. 'I was thinking more . . . in bed.'

'Right.' He coughed. 'Well, you have the key to my flat – unless you'd rather I come over to yours?'

'Your place is fine. And be home early. I've got exciting news.'

His voice was suddenly wary. 'Exciting as in what, exactly?'

She suddenly caught his thoughts, and smiled. 'I'm not pregnant, if that's what you're panicking about! No – I just want to tell you about my new career.'

'You've been head-hunted? Liza, that's great!'

'Sort of.'

'Champagne, then?'

'Okay, I'll get some on the way to your place. Oh, and I'll cook dinner. See you later.'

She went straight to Rupert's flat, not bothering to stop off at her own flat and change. On the way, she picked up the champagne and nipped into the nearest Marks and Spencer's food department to buy dinner – which was the nearest Liza ever came to cooking. She'd never really been the domesticated sort. She decided to feed Rupert first, then tell him the news when he was feeling mellow; at least then he'd react a bit better than everyone else had, even if he wasn't convinced that it was a good idea.

She had just put the tarragon chicken in the oven, when Rupert came in.

'Hi.' He slid his arms around her waist, pulling her back against him, and kissed the curve of her neck. 'Mm. Something smells good. I feel spoilt.'

'I just hope that you're worth it,' she said.

He grinned. 'If you want proof . . .' She'd already discarded her jacket, and the buttons of her crisp white cotton shirt were little barrier to his fingers. He licked her earlobe as he undid the buttons, stroking her skin as he revealed it. 'Mm. Shall we finish dinner, later?'

'What about your champagne?' she protested, half-heartedly.

'Later. And if dinner's ruined, we'll get a takeaway.' He fiddled with the oven, turning down the temperature, then waltzed her through to his bedroom. 'Mm. I've been thinking about you, ever since you called me. I couldn't get you out of my head.' He slid her shirt from her shoulders, letting it fall to the floor. 'And I nearly lost a deal, because I was concentrating more on how you taste, how you feel . . . I was fantasising about coming over to your office, and fucking you over your desk.'

Liza rubbed her nose against his. 'That would have been a bit difficult, seeing as I wasn't there, today.'

'Even so,' he said huskily, 'I like the idea.'

'I work in an open-plan office,' she reminded him.

'Then we'd have given a few people the show of their lives.' He eased his fingers under the white lacy cups of her bra, pushing the material down so that her breasts were bared and pushed up and together by the material. 'Mm.' He dropped to his knees, burying his face in her breasts, then drew his tongue over her areolae, breathing gently on her moistened skin so that her nipples grew hard. Then he drew one nipple into his mouth, sucking hard on it and rolling its twin between his thumb and forefinger.

'God, you taste good,' he said, lifting his head again. He pushed up her short skirt, revealing her knickers, then stroked the skin above the welts of her stockings. 'You look good, too.' He hooked one finger under the gusset of her knickers, and slid it along her quim, testing her arousal. 'Mm. And you feel good. Warm and wet.'

Liza reached behind her to undo her skirt; Rupert shook his head. 'I don't think I can wait this long.' He stood up, taking her hand and pressing it against his groin. His erection throbbed, long and thick; Liza's fingers curled round it automatically, and she began to frot him gently through the material of his trousers.

'Oh, hell,' he said hoarsely, pushing her hand away, and walking her over to the bed. He kissed her hard, his tongue pushing against hers and exploring her mouth; Liza rubbed her pubis against his cock, and he groaned. 'Liza, I can't wait!'

'Neither can I,' she said. That was one of the reasons why she put up with the young dealer's arrogance – Rupert was very good in bed. Liza refused steadfastly to live with him, preferring to keep her independence, but they usually ended up staying the night at each other's flats. And they were long nights, filled with orgasm after orgasm; Rupert was five years younger than she was, and had the staying power of a younger man.

She wasn't sure whether she liked it most when Rupert used his mouth on her, when he made her come with his hands, or when he slid his cock deep inside her. At the moment, she wanted all three. She knelt on the bed, sliding her hand between her legs so that she could push the gusset of her knickers aside, then wiggled her bottom at him. The sight of the lewdly-dressed woman on his bed, her breasts hanging free, her skirt rucked up around her waist, and her quim bared, was too much for Rupert. It was his favourite position, too – and the idea of filling his lover so completely made his cock twitch. His cock brushed along the length of her quim, once, twice, feeling her wetness: then he pushed, sliding deep inside her.

He drew his hands gently down her arms, urging her to

rest her forearms flat on the bed; she gave a small sigh of pleasure, and rested her head on her forearms. Then he began to thrust, tilting his pelvis slightly for maximum penetration. As the tempo of his thrusts increased, Liza began to pant, and finally to moan with pleasure as he pushed deeper and deeper. Her voice grew deeper as her excitement grew; the way his balls slapped against her quim made her almost howl with pleasure. She knew that he was enjoying it, too, and the extra friction of her knickers against his cock was driving him insane.

And then she felt the familiar pleasure of orgasm, starting in the soles of her feet and rolling up her calves, gathering momentum until it exploded in her solar plexus. Her quim flexed hard around the thick length of his cock; she gave a cry, half-muted by the duvet, and closed her eyes. A split-second later, she felt his cock throb inside her, and it felt as though he were trying to pour his whole body into her . . .

When both their heart-rates had calmed down, Rupert withdrew, slapping her buttocks affectionately. 'Wanton wench,' he teased.

'You wanted it as much as I did.' Liza climbed off the bed, and began to restore order to her clothes, intending to finish the meal she'd been cooking.

Rupert shook his head. 'No. I like seeing you like that.'

Liza raised one eyebrow. 'Your little totty, panting and flushed after a quick shag?'

Catching the edge in her voice, he winced. 'I don't mean it like that.' He let her pull her skirt down and push her bra back to normal, and restored order to his own clothing. 'So, what's this exciting news you've got for me, then?'

Liza bit her lip. Now that she was with him, she wasn't sure if he'd share her excitement. In fact, she knew that he wouldn't react well to it. No-one else had, and Rupert had more or less the same expectations of her as everyone else had. She sighed inwardly. Hopefully the sex would have mellowed him enough to avoid a row. 'Well. You know that I haven't been happy in my job, for ages.'

'You haven't thrown it in?' He was aghast. 'Bloody hell. I can't afford to support you, you know!'

Yes, you bloody could – if you really wanted to, Liza thought, annoyed. 'I'm not expecting you to support me,' she said coldly.

'So you haven't thrown it in, then?'

'Actually, yes. I resigned, this morning.'

Rupert missed the clipped note in her voice, and the cold sparkle of anger in her eyes. 'What the hell did you do that for? That's good money you're throwing away, Liza. Decent salaries aren't that easy to come by, you know.'

'Did it occur to you that I might possibly have something else to go to?'

He suddenly remembered their telephone conversation. 'Oh, yeah. You were head-hunted.'

'Actually, that's not quite it. My grandfather left me half of a firm. And I'm joining it, as from tomorrow.'

'Stock broking?' Rupert knew that Liza came from a rich and dynamic family. It was half the reason why he'd first started seeing her – because he was ambitious, and wanted the chance to further his career. Liza's lively personality and her skill in bed had helped to cement the relationship; but Rupert didn't want any demands on him. He wasn't ready to settle down, yet.

Liza, who suspected that half of Rupert's interest in her was due to her family's influence and the fact that she had a well-paid job in the City, was annoyed at his assumption. 'No. I'm going to be a taxi driver.'

'You're what?' He stared at her in disbelief. 'You're joking.'

'I'm not. I went to see my partner, today, and it's all fixed. I start at eight, tomorrow.'

'A taxi driver.' He shook his head. 'God, if you were that bored with your job, you could have done anything else. There are a lot of firms in the City who would have snapped you up. You could even have worked in an arty place, some charity or something. But no, you have to go slumming it.'

Liza was so angry that she didn't enlighten him to the true nature of *James*' business. 'If I want to be a taxi driver,' she said sharply, 'then I'll be a bloody taxi driver. Okay?'

Rupert scowled. 'I don't see why you had to throw in a perfectly good, safe, office job, for that. For a start, the hours are unsociable hours. And what if you picked up—' He stopped, suddenly aware of just how furious his girlfriend was.

'What if I picked up some of your friends, and they discovered that you were screwing a cheap little taxi driver, instead of a fancy career-woman with a well paid job in a highly respected firm?' Liza knew from the way he paled that she'd finished his sentence accurately. He wasn't worried that she'd pick up some knife-wielding maniac who might hurt her; he was just panicking that his friends would find out what she did for a living. 'Well, if all you're worried about is how much I earn, then we'd better finish it here, hadn't we?' She glared at him, and stomped into the kitchen to fetch her shoes.

'Liza . . .' He followed her. 'Look, I'm sorry. It was the shock. Let's talk about this.'

'Fuck you,' she said, putting on her shoes. 'Find yourself another stupid little rich kid to shag, Rupert. And you can cook your own bloody dinner.' She suddenly remembered the bottle of champagne. He wasn't going to enjoy that at her expense. She went to the fridge, and extracted it. 'No-one's going to stop me doing this, Rupert. It's my chance to escape a dead-end job.'

'Liza – darling–'

She ignored him. 'Too late, Rupert. Too bloody late.' She threw the champagne bottle at the floor; it smashed, satisfyingly, into tiny shards. 'Goodbye,' she said, grabbing her jacket and handbag. She left the flat, slamming the door behind her, while Rupert stared at his kitchen floor in disbelief, too surprised to go after her.

Two

At seven fifty-five, the next morning, Liza stood outside the *James* office, wearing practical leggings, a sweater, and low-heeled ankle boots. The office was locked; she made a mental note to ask Bryn for a spare key. Or maybe she could get one copied in her lunch hour.

Bryn arrived, two minutes later. 'You're punctual,' he said approvingly.

Liza's hackles rose instantly. 'Don't patronise me.'

He coughed. 'Look, there isn't room for temper tantrums at *James*. We're a small team, and we can't afford ego-trips.'

She sighed. 'Sorry. I didn't sleep particularly well, last night.' Because she'd been so angry with Rupert – not that she was going to tell Bryn about that. She'd been wide awake at three in the morning, still fuming over Rupert's reaction, and the fact that she'd wasted so much time with him. 'I just need some coffee.'

'Right.' He unlocked the door. 'I'd better get one of these cut for you, today, so you don't have to wait for me to get here, in future.'

'Thanks.' She smiled at him, pleased that he'd anticipated one of her questions. 'Do you want me to get you a coffee?'

'That'd be nice. Mine's white, no sugar, please.'

'Where's the kettle?'

'In the kitchen.' He ushered her through to a narrow galley-style kitchen. 'The milk's in the fridge; the coffee, tea, sugar and mugs are in the cupboard. There should be some biscuits in there, too, if you want some. I'll see you back in the office.'

'Right.' She smiled at him, and filled the kettle. She rummaged in the cupboard, and grimaced at the state of what she found. First thing in her lunch hour, she thought, she'd buy a cafétière and some decent coffee, to replace the cheap instant coffee Bryn used. And a tin of decent biscuits, too, for clients, rather than the half-crumbled and soggy packet of digestives. Nice mugs, to replace the cracked, stained and chipped ones; and the fridge could do with a thorough clean-out, too, before the Health and Safety people saw it and threatened to close them down. Things certainly needed changing around *James*, she thought, and she was the one to do it.

She made two cups of coffee, adding milk to both of them, and took them through to Bryn's cramped office. He was already sitting at his desk, poring over some paperwork.

'I think we'll have to have a move-round in here,' she said.

He looked up, his brow furrowed. 'How do you mean?'

'So I can get a desk in here, too; it'd be better than having to share yours. A couple of filing cabinets wouldn't go amiss, either. And some shelving, for that lot.' She indicated the heap on the floor by Bryn's desk.

He shook his head. 'The business can't afford non-essentials, right now.'

'Then I'll buy them myself. Call it a golden hello to the firm, or whatever.' She looked at him. 'Perhaps you can show me where you keep everything. Where's the computer?'

'We don't have one. And we can't afford one, either, before you say it.'

'We can pick up a second-hand one cheaply enough – we don't need a top range model or flash gizmos. All we need is a good spreadsheet, an accounts package, a database and a word-processing program.'

'Oh, really?'

'Yes, really. You look as if you hate filing, so it'll save you a lot of time. Once you've mastered the basics, of course.' She gave him a wicked smile. 'We could trade off, if you like. You teach me the basics of car maintenance, and I'll teach you how to use the computer.'

'And who says that I can't use a computer?' he fenced.

She folded her arms. 'Well, can you?'

'Yes, as a matter of fact, I can.'

'Well. Maybe I can teach you the *advanced* features, then,

in return for a quick guide to car maintenance.'

'You don't give up, do you?' He smiled ruefully. 'All right. I'll get Steve to sort you out on the car maintenance side. But we really can't afford a computer.'

'We can't afford *not* to have one. How else are you going to analyse your customer base, decide where your profitable areas are and how you can save money? Or where your advertising would work best?'

'The best advertising is word of mouth.'

Liza rolled her eyes. 'I know that. Look, you're the expert with cars. I'm good with computers and marketing. I used to work in research, and I've done a lot of work on customer needs. The whole point of a partnership is that we both bring something different into the business.'

Bryn was amused. 'You're really taking this seriously, aren't you?'

'Yes.' She lifted her chin. 'I know you think that I'm just Sam's spoilt grand-daughter, here today on a whim, and gone tomorrow – but it isn't like that. I want this business to be a success. So either you work with me nicely—'

'Or?' He eyed her levelly, waiting for her to continue her threat.

'Or I'll make your life such hell that you'll be forced to work with me.'

He grinned. 'You ought to have red hair.'

'And that's a pathetic cliché,' she snapped back.

His grin broadened; Liza was suddenly aware of just how attractive Bryn was. He had a nice mouth: she could imagine it wearing that same grin for a shared joke, in bed. Or opening in passion. Or travelling down her body, licking her skin and nipping gently at her pleasure-spots . . . She shivered. She didn't have time to start fantasising about her new partner. She had a business to get in shape.

'Penny for them?' he asked, seeing the sudden abstraction in her face.

She bit back the words: *nothing you'd be interested in.* It wasn't his fault that she found him attractive – or that she was still furious with Rupert, and in just the right sort of mood to go to bed with the first man who took her fancy, to prove to both herself and Rupert that other men found her attractive and appreciated her qualities more than her ex-lover had. 'Just that I might as well sort out the extra furniture and the computer during my lunch break.'

'Lunch break?'

'Yes. I assume you do have breaks, here? As it's a legal requirement,' she added. Bryn stifled a grin, and nodded. 'Now, I need more time today, because I'm going to clear my desk out at Fitchett's – that's the firm where I used to work – but I'll work straight through, tomorrow, to make up the time.'

'Fair enough.'

'So, this morning, perhaps you could show me the paperwork. I'll think about how to organise it on the computer, while I'm on the way to Fitchett's; and then, this afternoon, you can test my driving skills, and see if I need to polish anything before I take any clients.'

'You've got it all worked out, haven't you?' he said.

Liza's eyes narrowed at the amusement in his voice. 'I can assure you, Mr Davies, I'm very efficient.'

'If your deeds live up to your words. And, seeing as you've just annexed half my office space, I think that we'd better stick to first name terms, don't you?'

'Hm.'

He patted the chair beside him. 'Come on, Liza. I'll take you through the paperwork.'

Two hours later, Liza's brain was buzzing. She could barely believe that her grandfather – efficient, razor-sharp Sam Hargreaves, whose mental arithmetic put everyone else's to shame, and who could read a balance sheet and spot any discrepancies within seconds – had let *James* be so slapdash. It would take her several days to sort out the office and get it into the sort of order she was used to, let alone setting up the computer system. For a brief moment, she wondered if she'd taken on a little more than she could cope with; then she lifted her chin. No way. If Bryn was trying to make her think that it was a hopeless task, she'd just prove to him that she could cope. No, more than just cope: she'd show him that she could make a real success of it. Even if she had to work for the whole weekend, she'd have that office in good shape by the Monday morning.

She was a little cross to find that Bryn treated her quite impersonally, as though she were just another of the lads. Steve, Mike, Paul, Rob, Joe and Ted, on the other hand, were all pleased to meet her, and she was flattered by the gleam of appreciation in their eyes.

She didn't understand Bryn. He'd been shocked, at first, to find that she owned the other half of the firm; then, when he'd had time to grow used to the idea, he had accepted it. She'd wanted him to treat her as an equal, as his partner; but, at the same time, she was piqued that he seemed completely uninterested in her. She knew that she wasn't unattractive. Men liked her shoulder-length blonde hair and sparkling blue eyes, and her regular work-outs at the gym meant that she was in good shape. So why did Bryn treat her so impersonally?

He'd said that he was divorced, but he definitely wasn't remarried. Even allowing for the fact that not all married men wore rings, he didn't have a 'married' air. He was more the workaholic bachelor type: and one who'd probably been put off women for life, judging by the look on his face when he'd mentioned his ex-wife. She sighed. Hell. There was only one thing worse than being attracted to someone you worked with closely, and that was when the attraction was one-sided.

Well, once she'd sorted out the office, she'd see just how immune to her he *really* was. A smile twitched on her lips. When Liza Hargreaves wanted something, she usually got it. As Bryn Davies would soon learn . . .

'Liza! Is it true, or is someone having me on?' Sally Reynolds sat on the edge of her best friend's desk as Liza rummaged through the drawers.

'Is what true?'

'That you've done the dirty deed, and resigned?'

Liza look up, grinned, and spread her hands. 'Well, why else would I be clearing out my desk – or be in the office, dressed like this?' She lobbed her blue stress-ball at Sally. 'Here. You could probably do with this.'

'Thanks. Apparently, Mark's been in a bitch of a mood, since yesterday afternoon. Judging from how he's been this morning, I'm glad that I had yesterday off.' Sally raked a hand through her short dark bob. 'So what's the story? Are you eloping with the gorgeous Rupert or something?'

'Mr Narcissus?' Liza's laugh held no amusement. 'No. We're history.'

'You're history?' Sally repeated, surprised.

'Yep. I finally decided that you were right about him.'

'That he's an arrogant little shit, who doesn't deserve you, and is probably on the make?'

Liza nodded. 'Spot on. And he knows that I think that, now.' She shrugged. 'Sure, he was good in bed, but I'm at the stage where I need a bit more than that from a relationship.'

Sally digested this. 'So what's happened?'

'I was going to ring you and tell you about it yesterday but you were swanning around town.'

'Spending a fortune in Heal's.' Sally grinned. 'You could have left a message on the answerphone.'

'I wanted to tell you myself. My grandfather left me half-shares in a taxi firm. With a choice of being a drudge in the City, Sal, or working for yourself, what would you do?'

'What I'd do is probably different from what you'd do,' Sally reminded her. 'But, knowing how you've been feeling for months, I guess you'd rather work for yourself,' she replied promptly.

'Exactly.'

Sally's blue eyes were thoughtful. 'Liza, I know you pick things up quickly, but you don't know the first thing about running a taxi firm.'

'Like you said, I can learn.' Liza shrugged. 'And I could do with a new challenge.'

'Right. Well, leave me one of your cards. I'll pass your number round the office.'

'Thanks, Sal.' Liza's grin broadened. 'Though it's more a chauffeur service than a taxi firm. I think people might find us a little expensive for running them from their flats to a party, or whatever.'

'I'll have a word with Richard in Accounts. Maybe he can set up some kind of corporate deal so that we use you rather than ring firms on an ad-hoc basis.' Sally raised an eyebrow.

'Chauffeur service. It all sounds very intriguing.'

'Cook me dinner, tomorrow night, and I'll tell you everything. Including why I smashed a bottle of champagne on Rupert's kitchen floor.' Liza finished tipping the contents of her desk into a carrier bag.

Sally whistled. 'It must have been one hell of a row.'

'If I'm honest, it's been coming for ages. I'm not really one for the yuppie lifestyle, and I got sick of him trying to compete with me all the time.' Her lips twitched. 'The sex was pretty good, yes – but I've been thinking for a while that it's not really enough to make me put up with everything else.'

'I'm all ears.'

Liza chuckled. 'Well, your curiosity will have to wait until tomorrow night.' She straightened up. 'Is about eight okay with you?'

'That's fine. Well, take care. And I'll miss you.'

'Hey, I'm only moving jobs. We'll still see each other.' Liza hugged her friend. 'You take care, too. And if Mark gets too much for you, dump his coffee in his lap.'

'The secretary's ultimate revenge, hm?'

'Yeah.' Liza grinned. 'Or you could try seducing him, instead.'

Sally pulled a face. 'Yeuch! If he looked like Antonio Banderas or Charlie Sheen, maybe. But I like my men dark and good-looking, not fair and balding.'

'You'd like my partner, then. Actually, now you mention it, that's who he reminds me of,' Liza said, frowning slightly, 'Antonio Banderas. He's got that sexy Mediterranean charm about him.'

Sally groaned. 'If I were in your shoes, I'd never get any work done! Still, I suppose he's married.'

'Divorced. And firmly off limits.'

'His view, or yours?'

Liza smiled wryly. 'You know me too well, Sal. His view.'

'Well, you can change that. Just wear your little red dress into the office.'

'I'm going for the subtle approach – after I've sorted out our pit of an office.'

'Subtle, you?' Sally laughed. 'I'd like to see that!'

'I'll give it a shot.'

'And if that doesn't work, you'll take the steamroller approach?'

'Something like that.' Liza hugged her friend. 'See you tomorrow, then. I've got some shopping to do.'

'Anything nice?'

'Office furniture.' Liza rolled her eyes. 'The joys of being your own boss . . .'

Bryn raised an eyebrow at Liza's bags. 'How big was your desk? Room-size?'

'That rather depends on the size of the room,' she said. 'My new desk is arriving tomorrow morning. That's new as in "new to me" – I went to one of the second-hand places, before you start carping about money. And I paid for it myself. The computer's arriving tomorrow, too, and maybe one of the lads could give me a hand in putting up some shelving.'

'I'm sure they could.'

'Good.' Liza extracted her cafétière. 'First, decent coffee. I can't put up with that muck of yours any longer.'

'Caffeine's caffeine,' was the lugubrious reply.

'Wrong. *This* is proper coffee,' she informed him. 'Once we've had this, do you want me to take you out for a drive?'

'Whatever you say, boss.'

Liza didn't take the bait; she simply made them both a coffee, and tea for Steve and Mike who were working in the garage, and began tidying the room. She finally managed to clear enough space for her desk, and smiled in satisfaction. 'That's better,' she said, pleased.

Bryn looked up at her, and burst out laughing.

'What?'

'There's a huge black mark across your face. Anyone would think you were about five, not in your twenties!'

'Actually, I'm thirty,' she told him stiffly, rubbing at her face.

'You're making it worse. Here.' He came over to her, taking a clean handkerchief out of his pocket, and wetted it with his tongue, wiping away the smear. It was a completely innocent act, but it made a shiver of desire run through her body, and her nipples hardened in response. She was sure, for a moment, that the he was going to kiss her; she almost put her hand up to caress his face, but then he turned away.

'Come on. We'd better go for that drive.'

Liza glanced quickly at his crotch; she was sure that she saw a slight bulge there. He wasn't quite as immune to her as he liked to make out, then. All she had to do was break his reserve with her. Though she had a nasty feeling that it wasn't going to be as easy as she'd expected.

Bryn handed her the keys to a large, shiny grey Jaguar. 'I want you to drive me to Docklands.' He named a road. 'Can you find that?'

'Either you can give me five minutes to find my own route in the A to Z, or you can direct me,' Liza told him. 'Your choice.'

'I'll direct you – on this occasion.'

'Okay.' She took one of the peaked caps from the hatstand, placing it rakishly on her head. 'Just to give the right impression.'

He stifled a smile as she opened the back door of the Jaguar, and he sat in the car. She closed the door behind him, and climbed into the driver's seat. Bryn directed her through various back streets, until he'd reached the road he'd named in Docklands; she pulled over to the kerb, then got out of the car, opening the passenger door and waiting courteously until he got out.

'Well?' she asked.

'Not bad. You need to be a bit smoother on the gear-changes – though I expect that that's because the car was new to you.'

'And it felt like a driving test,' Liza admitted. 'I failed mine, twice, through sheer nerves.'

He raised an eyebrow. 'You can't afford to be nervy with our customers.'

'I won't be. It's just . . . Well, this time, it's a bit different.'

'I suppose so.' He smiled at her. 'You also took some of the corners too fast. You're not in a race, and you're not working to time-limits. So slow down a bit, and keep it smooth.'

'Right.'

'You also need to get to know London a lot better. Most of

our clients won't be able to direct you.'

'That's why I said I'd do my own route from the A to Z,' she reminded him.

'Well.' He smiled at her, holding out his hand. 'Keys.'

'Why?'

'Because you're going to be the customer, this time. I want you to experience the same sort of service a *James* customer usually gets.'

'Meaning that I'm not up to scratch.'

'At the moment, no – but with a bit of practice, you could be,' was the swift reply.

Liza made no comment, but handed him the keys and climbed into the back of the car. Part of her was angry with him for criticising her driving, the other part of her was determined to learn whatever he could teach her and make sure that she made a success of her role in the business. The determined half won; she made mental notes about the way he drove, the way he waited for her to talk to him before engaging in conversation. He was, she thought, the perfect chauffeur. She could almost get used to this – being driven around London in a nice car, by an attractive man. A man who would be solicitous, who'd ensure that her every want was met – including, maybe, driving her to the edge of Hampstead Heath and taking her for a walk, then making love to her under a secluded tree . . .

She shook herself. She really had to get this sex thing off her brain. Bryn was her business partner, that was all. He'd made it very clear that he intended their relationship to be a professional one only. And yet she couldn't help a surge of desire running through her, every time she caught his eyes in the mirror.

What would he do, she wondered, if she stripped off in the back of the car? If she peeled her clothes off, very slowly, exposing herself to him? And then, if she let her hand slide between her legs, in an approximation of the way she wanted his hands to touch her . . . What then?

Probably, he'd tell her to grow up and get dressed, she thought wryly. So instead, she made light conversation with him, until they arrived back at the office.

'Okay?' he asked.

She nodded. 'Your driving's smoother than mine. I could barely tell when we were going round corners – but it didn't feel like you were dawdling, either.'

'This has been my business for nearly fifteen years,' he told her. 'Now, I have to leave early, tonight.'

She glanced at her watch. 'It's only four o'clock.'

'You can go now, too, if you like. Or you can ask Steve to teach you a bit about engines.'

'I'll talk to Steve,' she said decisively.

'Right. I'll see you tomorrow, then.'

'Yeah. See you, partner.'

He grinned. 'Talking of which, you forgot to take this with you, at lunchtime.'

'What?'

'The key to the office. I had a spare cut for you. Make sure you lock up properly.'

She smiled, and took the key. 'Don't worry, I will.'

She wandered through to the garage; Steve was busy working on an engine. 'Hi.'

'Hello, Ms Hargreaves.'

'Liza,' she corrected, with a smile. 'Bryn said that you'd teach me a bit about engines. Do you want a cup of tea, first?'

'Er – I think I'll stick to coffee, thanks.'

She grinned. 'My tea that bad, is it?'

'Yes,' he said, smiling back. 'It's like dishwater!'

'Well, I make good coffee. How do you take it?'

'Milk, two sugars, please.'

'Coming up.'

When she returned with the coffees, Steve sipped his gratefully. 'You're right, it's definitely better than your tea,' he teased. 'Now. I hate to ask you this – and I'm not being sexist at all, I just want to make the most of our time – but do you know the basics, like where to put the oil and water?'

Liza was impressed at how sensitive the young mechanic had been. He was probably a couple of years younger than Rupert, but he had a lot more tact. Rupert would just have assumed that she knew nothing, and used it as an excuse to inflate his ego even more. She smiled wryly. 'I used to know, but the mechanic at my local garage started sorting that for me a couple of years ago, so I've probably forgotten.'

'Right, then. We'll start from basics.' Steve patted the space beside him. 'Now, this little lever here is the dipstick . . .'

An hour and a half later, Liza was much better acquainted with the workings of the car engine. She'd learned about the fan belt and ignition systems, as well as topping up water and oil. She also had another smudge on her nose – this time oil, not grime. Steve grinned at her. 'We'd better get you cleaned up. And we'll have to order a couple of boiler suits, in your size!' He led her through to the little room opposite the galley. 'Hold still,' he said, dabbing a paper towel in a pot of grease-remover. 'That's better,' he said, wiping the oil from her nose.

Liza wondered how old Steve was. Not as old as she was. Twenty-three, at the most, she decided. He was good-looking, in a roguish sort of way, with blond curly hair, grey-blue eyes, and a ready smile. His shoulders were broad, as though he spent a lot of his spare time in the gym, but he wasn't an over-developed gorilla. In all, he was a very nice package, she thought; and no doubt he'd already carved quite a few notches in his bedpost.

'I'd better let you have the shower, first, while the water's still hot,' he said softly.

Some devil in Liza snapped. She'd spent her day with a man who could turn her on with a look, but hadn't laid a finger on her; and she was still mad at Rupert. And there was one thing that was a sure-fire cure for frustration and anger . . . 'I like having a long shower,' she said. 'And I'd hate you to have to use cold water.'

He eyed her speculatively. Since the first moment he'd seen her, he'd wanted to make love with Liza Hargreaves. Knowing that she was going to be his boss, he hadn't dared make a move. But unless he'd misjudged the light in her eye, she was interested in him, too. He smiled, tracing the curve of her jawline. 'Is that an offer, Liza?'

'What do you think?'

'I think,' he said, tracing her lower lip and widening his eyes in pleasure as she opened her mouth and nipped at his fingertip, 'that you're right. We should share it.'

Gently, he removed her sweater; he took a sharp intake of breath as he saw her large breasts. He drew his finger along the lacy edge of her bra; her skin was soft, and she smelled gorgeous. His hands slid round to her back, and he undid the clasp of her bra, letting the garment fall on the floor.

'God, you're so beautiful,' he said, cupping her breasts and pushing them up and together, deepening her cleavage. He dipped his head, taking one hardened rosy nipple into his mouth; Liza gasped as he began to suck, and tangled her hands in her hair, urging him on.

His hands slipped lower, and he tugged at the waistband of her leggings, pushing them down. She shivered as he rested the heel of his palm on her mons veneris, his fingers cupping her quim. He might be young, she thought, but he was very promising indeed.

She tugged gently on his hair, so that he brought his face up to meet hers, and kissed him, pushing her tongue into his mouth. He reacted instantly, helping her peel his clothes off; at last, they stood naked in front of each other.

'I'm oily,' Steve said. 'Let me clean up, first.'

'I've got a better idea,' Liza said, switching on the shower. 'Let me clean you.'

When the water had heated to a bearable temperature, she stepped into the shower, drawing him in with her. She soaped her hands, and slowly washed his body, cleaning the oil and grime from him. She deliberately left his cock until last; then she lathered her hands again, and set to work on him, rubbing his foreskin back and forth, until finally he tipped his head back, moaned, and came, warm salty liquid spurting over her body.

He kissed her, hard. 'Thank you,' he said softly. 'Time to repay the compliment.' He smoothed the silky fluid into her skin – 'The best skin cream there is,' he told her with a grin – and then lathered his hands, soaping her body and washing her clean again.

He dropped to his knees, rubbing his face between her thighs; his skin was slightly rough with end-of-day stubble, and Liza closed her eyes, imagining that instead of Steve, Bryn was with her in the shower. He would do exactly what Steve was doing: drawing his tongue the length of her musky furrow, then licking her with abandon, with long slow strokes that travelled from the top to the bottom of her quim, interspersed with short stabbing bursts over her clitoris.

She felt her insides melt, and then her quim contracted sharply round his mouth. He kissed her gently on her nether mound, then stood up again, kissing her hard so that she could taste her own arousal on his lips. His cock had hardened again while he'd lapped at her, and she felt his erection pressing against her, promisingly thick and long.

Without a word, he lifted her up, holding her weight easily against the tiled wall of the shower; he let her slide down his body, until his cock pressed against her quim. She put her arms round his neck, lifting her legs up to grip his waist; he slid one hand between their bodies, guiding the tip of his cock to fit against her entrance.

Liza gave a sigh of bliss as he pushed, his cock sliding deep inside her; he rested her weight against the wall again, and began to thrust into her, deliciously long slow strokes which had her coming in seconds. He felt her quim rippling around him, but he didn't stop: he kept going, bringing her to the brink of another orgasm, then another. As her body soared again, Liza felt his cock twitching inside her; he gave a groan, and buried his head in her shoulder. 'Oh, God, Liza . . .'

He held her close to him; then, when he slipped from her, he gently set her on her feet again.

Liza smiled at him, stroking his face. 'What a welcome to the firm,' she said softly.

'Yeah. Though I assume it was a one-off?' he asked.

She nodded. 'First rule of business: don't mix it with pleasure.'

'Rules are made to be broken,' he told her with a grin.

'Occasionally, yes.' She reached up to kiss him lightly on the lips. 'Though our next lesson really will be just car mechanics.'

'Whatever you say, boss. Whatever you say.'

Three

'So,' Sally said, 'how was your first proper day, then?'

Liza wrinkled her nose. 'OK, I suppose.'

'That tells me a lot,' Sally said wryly. She topped up their glasses. 'Let's change the subject, then, and start with something easy. You were going to tell me about your huge row with Rupert.'

'Him.' Liza pulled a face. 'There were half a dozen messages on my answerphone when I got in, this evening. But if he thinks that he's going to worm his way back into my life, he's a hundred per cent wrong.'

Sally whistled. 'Whatever he said, it must have been pretty bad.'

'I suppose part of it was my fault,' Liza admitted. 'I expected him to be pleased for me, that I'd finally found something I wanted to do – but first off, he panicked that I was pregnant. Then he said that he couldn't afford to keep me. He knows damn well that I'd never ask him to do that, anyway; but it would have been nice to know that I could rely on him, if I really needed to. I told him what I was planning to do, and he was more worried that one of his friends might find out that I'd become a taxi driver than pleased that I'd finally made the move. So I told him where to go. I'd bought a bottle of champagne, to celebrate, but I wasn't going to leave it for him to enjoy. I was so angry, Sal. I smashed it on his kitchen floor, and left him to clear up the mess.' She grimaced. 'I think that he's more in love with my family and my background than with me – if he's capable of loving anyone but himself, that is.'

'I think he does love you, in his way,' Sally said. 'Don't forget, he's younger than you.'

'Yeah, I know.' Liza took a sip of wine. 'But that doesn't excuse his attitude. I don't know why you're standing up for him, anyway. You never liked him.'

'True. Look,' Sally said, 'why don't you come into the kitchen, and tell me everything, while I fix dinner? I take it that Chinese is okay with you?'

Liza smiled. Sally was an extremely good cook. In fact, Liza often wondered why Sally continued to act as Mark's secretary, when she had so many other talents. She could have made a fortune running her own café. Liza had tackled Sally about this on more than one occasion, suggesting that Sally could do better for herself than being Mark's undervalued secretary, but Sally had always said that she didn't want to be tied down to a job with incredibly long hours which would wreck her social life. 'That's fine – more than fine.'

'Come on, then.'

Liza followed Sally into the kitchen. 'Is there anything that I can do to help?'

'No. Just talk to me.' Sally made herself busy, chopping mushrooms and mixing various sauces and spices together. Liza watched her friend admiringly. Although Liza could cook, she had none of Sally's flair – nor, if she were honest with herself, Sally's interest.

'So what do you want to know?'

'Everything,' Sally said with a grin, tipping walnut oil into the wok. 'Start from the beginning. You were a bit hyper when I saw you yesterday, so I don't know if I've got the full story or not.'

'Well,' Liza said, 'the solicitor told me that Gramps had left me half the shares in this firm. Anyway, it meant that either I could start a new career, or I could sell the shares and disappear to France.'

'Funny,' Sally said, 'I would have expected you to go for the French option. I mean, you've been saying for months that you fancy the idea of going to the South of France, living in a small cottage and spending your days painting.'

'There's one small problem with that idea,' Liza said. 'I can't paint.'

'Since when has that stopped you trying to do something?'

Liza pulled a face. 'I'm being realistic, Sal. It'd end up as a six-month holiday, spent reading and sleeping in the sun and drinking too much red wine – and as soon as I came back here, the whole thing would start again. I'd still have to decide what I really wanted to do with my life.'

'So you decided to go for the new career, in this high-class taxi firm. What's your role going to be?' Sally asked. 'Are you going to be a driver, or are you going to run the office?'

'A bit of both, I think,' Liza said. 'I bought a computer yesterday, and it was delivered today. Honestly, you'd never believe what a pit Bryn's office is! There's about six months' worth of filing in a huge pile, next to his desk. I'm surprised that Gramps didn't say anything about it to him. You know how organised he used to be.'

'Yes, that's where you get it from,' Sally teased.

'I still can't believe that Bryn was trying to run that business without a computer,' Liza said. 'No accounting package, no word processor, no spreadsheet, no customer database–' she ticked them off on her fingers '– well, it's like something out of the dark ages.'

'You're plotting big changes, then.' Sally paused. 'How did he take the news?'

'What, that I was his new partner? Or that I'm planning to modernise his office?'

'Both.'

Liza took another sip of wine. 'Pretty guarded. He's giving me a month's trial.'

Sally frowned. 'Hang on, I thought you were supposed to be equal partners?'

'We are. But he thinks that I'm just a spoilt rich brat, and I'll be bored with it, within a month. So he's agreed that in a month's time, if I'm still pulling my weight, we're equal partners. In the meantime, I'm learning about car maintenance, routing, and driving.'

Sally rolled her eyes, tipping the strips of chicken into the wok and stirring them. 'That's crazy, Liza – you're a good driver. At least, I've always felt safe in the car, when you've been behind the wheel.'

'Yes, but I'm not up to his standards.'

'In his eyes, or yours?'

'Both,' Liza admitted. 'Anyway, it's a new challenge.'

'This wouldn't have anything to do with the fact that you're thirty, would it?'

'How do you mean?'

'Well,' Sally said, 'think about it. You've changed your job, you've dumped your man – this sudden need to turn your life upside down smacks to me of a thirty-something crisis.'

Liza shook her head. 'You know I've been restless at work for ages. And things haven't been that good between me and Rupert for some time,' she said. 'I want more from a man than just good sex. And that's all we really had in common, when it came down to it. Most of his friends were so competitive, so materialistic; I found myself acting like them, towards the end, and I didn't like myself very much.' She sighed. 'I suppose I thought that it was better to have a man of my own than no-one. Anyway, I've come to my senses, now.'

'Fair enough.' Sally kept her voice light. 'So what are the other people like at the firm?'

'Very nice.' Liza flushed as she remembered what she had done with Steve in the shower.

Sally chuckled. 'You're not telling me everything, are you?'

'I think we'd better change the subject.'

Sally added the sauce to her stir fry. 'You get a reprieve until we sit down,' she said. 'And then you can tell me. If you want to make yourself useful, you can grab a couple of plates for me.'

Liza did as Sally asked, and also retrieved two pairs of chopsticks from Sally's cutlery drawer. 'Two plates, as requested.'

Sally served up the stir fry; she and Liza headed for the dining room, carrying their plates, glasses and another bottle of wine. Sally went back into the kitchen for some prawn crackers, then she rejoined Liza at the table. 'So,' she said. 'Have you made a move on Bryn, yet?'

'No.' Liza grimaced. 'He's really attractive, Sally. I think I'm going to find it difficult to work with him, in some ways. Every time I look up from my desk and see him, I find myself fantasising about him. What it would be like if he kissed me . . .' She shook her head. 'Oh, I'll grow out of it.'

Sally raised an eyebrow. 'There's something you're not telling me,' she said.

Liza flushed. 'Um.'

Sally's blue eyes sparkled. 'Come on, out with it.'

'Okay, okay.' Liza in took a mouthful of stir fry. 'This is really good, Sal.'

Sally grinned. 'You're not going to get away with it that easily! Come on, tell me.'

'All right, all right. I had my first lesson in car mechanics yesterday, with Steve. He's a nice kid.'

'Kid?'

'Yeah, he's about five years younger than me, I think. Maybe a bit more. Anyway, he was really sweet, and showed me what I needed to know – the basics, anyway. And then . . . well, we ended up having a shower together.' Liza had the grace to look embarrassed. 'It was a one-off, and we both knew it. It's unprofessional to mix business and pleasure, and you should never sleep with a colleague.'

'Especially if you happen to be the boss,' Sally agreed. 'Oh, Liza.'

'Yes, I feel bad about it now.' Liza licked her lower lip. 'Mind you, I enjoyed it at the time.'

'Does Bryn know?'

Liza shook her head. 'He had to leave early, for some reason.'

'Just as well,' Sally said.

'I'm not going to make a habit of screwing my staff,' Liza protested.

'I should hope not!' Sally lifted her glass in a toast. 'Well, here's to you, and your new career.'

'I'm glad that someone is pleased for me,' Liza said.

'I'm sure everyone else will be,' Sally said, 'when they're used to the idea.'

'My parents think that I'm totally crazy,' Liza said glumly. 'My mother said that I should just take a sabbatical, and then be sensible about things.'

'Well,' Sally said, 'considering how restless you've been at

Fitchett's, I think you're probably doing the right thing.' She grinned. 'Providing you manage to keep your hands off your staff, that is – and Bryn!'

The following week, Liza had settled in to *James*. She spent the weekend setting up a database, and Bryn was quietly impressed with the work she'd put in. Not that he was going to tell her, yet.

The phone rang. Bryn picked it up, and grimaced. 'I'm sorry,' he said, 'but I won't be able to help you on this occasion. One of my drivers has gone off sick, and we're booked out for the rest of the day. Perhaps you could try–'

At that moment, Liza stuck a piece of paper under his nose with a scribbled message on it. *Don't turn away business. We can't afford it. I'll do the driving.* Bryn looked at her, pulled a face, and shook his head. Liza glowered at him and pointed at the paper again. Bryn ignored her. She pinched him, hard, and stabbed her finger at the paper; he rolled his eyes and mouthed 'okay' at her. 'Actually,' he said, 'I think that we might be able to help you. We have a new relief driver, and I think she'll be available, then. She hasn't done much of this kind of work before, so I'll charge you a lower rate.' He smiled. 'Yes, ten thirty will be fine.' He replaced the receiver, then looked at Liza, his face dark with anger. 'Don't ever do that again.'

'What?'

'Interfere, when I'm on the phone.'

'You were just about to turn away some business! That's crazy. I know Joe's ill today, but you've got me in the office now. I can do it.'

Bryn thought about it. 'Maybe I should take this job, and you can do the one I was going to do, later.'

'What's so special about this job, then?' Liza demanded.

'Ever heard of Geoff Morton?'

Liza's eyes widened. 'As in the actor?'

'That's the one.'

'You mean, he wants us to drive him somewhere?'

'Well,' Bryn said laconically, 'that's why people usually ring us.'

'Less of the sarcasm,' Liza snapped. 'I'm not a child.'

'No, I know you're not.'

'Don't treat me like one, then.' She looked at him. 'What should I wear?'

Bryn eyed her tailored suit. It wasn't quite so *haut couture* as the Armani suit she'd worn when he'd first met her, but it was still very classy. 'I think you'll do as you are. Just take one of the caps – our clients like that sort of touch. Now, he wants to be driven to Brighton.'

She nodded. 'I might need a hand with the route.'

'Fair enough. I'll work something out for you.' Bryn looked at her. 'I'll man the phone while you're on this job. If you need me, there's a radio in the car.' He looked at her. 'Don't forget our motto. No fuss, complete discretion, and no gossip.'

'Like I said, I'm not a child.' Liza looked at him, unsmiling, then went back to her desk and continued working on the spreadsheet she was setting up. Bryn watched her for a moment, then turned back to his own work.

At ten o'clock, Bryn left the office, and came back to tell Liza that the car was ready for her. He gave her directions, which she wrote down carefully, and then smiled unexpectedly at her. 'Good luck,' he said.

'Thanks.' Liza was about to add, 'I think I might need it,' when she remembered who she was talking to. She couldn't afford to show any weakness in front of Bryn. 'I'll see you later, then,' she said, offhand, and went out to the car.

She drove to the street where she was supposed to pick up Geoff Morton. It felt strange, driving through London at that time of day, but she found that she enjoyed it. She parked the car carefully, then checked her notes for the number of the house where she was to meet her new client. It was three houses down from where she'd parked; she went to the door and rang the bell.

A few moments later, the door was opened by a rather rotund man with fuzzy grey-white hair, small round-framed spectacles, and a slightly harassed air. 'Yes?'

'Hello, I'm Liza Hargreaves from *James*. I'm here to pick up Geoff Morton.'

The man looked at her, then nodded. 'He'll be down in a

minute. I take it you don't mind driving to Brighton?'

'Our aim is to give our customers exactly what they want. If he'd wanted to be driven to Land's End or John O'Groats, that would have been fine, too.'

She wondered for a moment if she'd been a little too rude, but the man merely grinned at her. 'Touché. I'll go and get Geoff.'

Part of Liza felt that this was a dream. The actor Geoff Morton was renowned for his fast-paced, high-tension action movies. He was tall and good-looking in a classical way, with blonde curly hair, piercing blue eyes, and muscles which men envied and women sighed over. Most of her friends would have loved to meet him – particularly Sally, who'd lusted after him for years. And here she was, going to be his driver, and taking him down to Brighton.

She was suddenly glad that the Jaguar had specially darkened windows. She didn't think that she would be able to cope with any crowds who might spot him in the car and crowd round him. Unless Geoff was intending to travel with a bodyguard, that was, a muscle-man who would make sure that the actor wasn't bothered by anyone.

To her surprise, Geoff wasn't accompanied by a bodyguard. His companion was a very slender girl of around eighteen; Liza found herself thinking bitchily that her blonde hair was only too obviously a dye job, and not a particularly good one, at that. The girl was wearing dark glasses, so Liza couldn't see her eyes. No doubt it was her way of hiding dark circles from lack of sleep – because any woman who spent time with Geoff Morton would definitely not be spending her time sleeping.

Liza knew that movie stars often didn't look anything like they did on the screen, in the flesh, but Geoff Morton was an exception. He really was tall – about six feet, she guessed – and his body was perfectly toned beneath his chinos and dark sweater. His famed blue eyes weren't hidden behind dark glasses, and Liza was stunned at just how attractive he was.

She felt herself blushing as the rotund man introduced him to her. 'Geoff, this is your driver.'

She held out her hand. 'Liza,' she said, suddenly shy. 'Good morning, Mr Morton.'

'Call me Geoff.' He took her hand and drew it up to his lips; Liza shivered at the touch of his lips against her skin. God, not only was he a good actor; she had a feeling that he would be a good lover, too. 'Delighted to meet you,' he said softly. 'I've never had a woman driver before.'

'Well, there's always a first time for everything,' Liza said, trying to stop her voice from shaking. She opened the door for Geoff and his blonde companion, who was looking decidedly sulky at the attention that the actor had given to Liza, and waited politely until they'd climbed into the back seat. She closed the door behind them, then slid into the driver's seat, and switched on the ignition.

It was a sunny day, bright enough for Liza to need her sunglasses. She adjusted the mirror, signalled, and pulled out. She spent the next few minutes in virtual silence, while she concentrated on getting out of London; eventually, they were heading down the road to Brighton. She glanced in the mirror, and her eyes widened at the sight. No wonder Geoff Morton had been so quiet in the back: he was more than occupied. His blonde companion had stripped off her slinky black top, and pulled down the cups of her bra.

The blonde was quite skinny, Liza thought, her breasts small and her rib-cage showing. Perhaps that's how Geoff Morton liked his women. Which meant that someone like Liza, who had more generous curves, stood no chance. Not that she was going to vamp the actor, in any case. She was there for one reason only, and that was to do a job – and do it well. This was her first time out for *James* and she couldn't afford to blow it.

She continued trying to concentrate on the road, but it was difficult when she could see everything that was happening in the back seat. She was sure that both Geoff and the blonde knew that she could see them, too. Bloody exhibitionists, she thought, half amused and half annoyed. And yet there was another feeling mixed in, too. Arousal. Because she could so easily imagine herself in the blonde's position, with Geoff touching her intimately . . .

She tore her mind from the goings-on in the back seat, and concentrated on the directions Bryn had given her. All the same, she was aware of exactly what was happening. The blonde wasn't wearing her seat belt, and neither was Geoff. He was bending over towards his companion, drawing his mouth down to her breasts. He licked the areolae, teasing them with the tip of his tongue until the rosy flesh darkened and puckered beneath his mouth. Then he took each hard rosy tip in turn into his mouth, sucking and licking and obviously using his teeth, judging by the delighted moans from the blonde.

The girl was wearing a pair of tight black jeans; Liza's hands gripped the wheel more tightly as she saw Geoff's hand wander over the girl's abdomen, then undo the button at the waistband of her jeans, and slide the zipper downwards. The blonde lifted her buttocks clear of the seat, so that Geoff could pull her jeans down properly. To Liza's surprise and shock, the blonde was wearing absolutely nothing beneath the denims. She had also shaven her pubis, so that her vulva was clearly visible. Geoff removed his girl's jeans, throwing them onto the floor of the limo, and grinned.

Liza said nothing, concentrating on the drive, but Geoff caught her eyes in the mirror, and gave her a broad wink. Liza flushed. Was all this for her benefit? Was Geoff expecting her to join him and the blonde in Brighton, in his hotel room, and continue the show there in a more interactive way? The very idea made her feel angry, that he thought she was just another lackey who would do the great star's bidding. And yet, the way that he touched the girl . . . Geoff Morton was a professional, in more than just the sense of being a damned good actor. Making love with him would be a real pleasure.

Liza gripped the wheel, and tried desperately to concentrate on the road. It would be terrible if she managed to get lost on the way to Brighton. Bryn would never forgive her, and she'd blow her chances to do well at *James*. She had to ignore what was going on in the back seat. As Bryn had told her, she had to show complete discretion.

Geoff smiled, and parted the blonde's legs. The girl was still wearing her high-heeled patent leather black shoes; she lifted her feet up, putting them on the seat. Part of Liza was tempted to make a sharp comment about any damage to the car needing to be paid for, but she wasn't sure enough of herself to say anything. She merely gritted her teeth.

The blonde began to simper, and Geoff slid his palm along her inner thigh, widening the gap between her thighs. Her vulva was now on full view, a deep and glistening vermilion which betrayed her arousal. Her flesh was wet and glistening, and when Geoff ran an exploratory finger along her quim, his fingertip glided easily along the soft flesh. He smiled, and pushed one finger deep into her. The blonde moaned softly, and he began to move his finger in and out. He settled his thumb on the already erect nub of her clitoris, and began to massage it in a circular motion. She groaned, and lifted her hand to her breasts, plucking at her nipples.

Geoff continued working her with his hand, and the blonde's moans grew louder, more abandoned. Again, Geoff caught Liza's eye in the mirror. This time, instead of giving her that cheeky wink, he blew her a kiss. Then, he turned back to the blonde, and kissed her hard, his tongue sliding between her lips. She slid her hands into his hair, and he broke the kiss, trailing his mouth down her body. Again, he toyed with her nipples, nipping gently at them with his lips and tongue; then, he moved lower. He removed his fingers from the girl's quim, and lifted his hand to his mouth, licking the juices from them. Then he continued kissing his way down her body, nuzzling her abdomen, and finally jamming his face between her thighs.

The blonde still had her hands in his hair, her fingertips massaging his scalp. Her movements grew more frenzied as Geoff began to lap at her in earnest, flicking his tongue across her clitoris rapidly, and then licking from the top to the bottom of her slit in one smooth and easy movement. Her moans grew louder, and then she gave a cry as she came. Liza glanced in the mirror, and flushed; the blonde's pale skin was mottled with a familiar rosy colouring which betrayed her orgasm as much as her cry had done.

Liza's knuckles grew white as she gripped the wheel. She turned off the motorway, heading towards Brighton. God, would this journey ever end? She half expected the blonde to get dressed again, but she was mistaken. Instead, the blonde tugged at Geoff's hair, so that he lifted his face to hers. Then she kissed him lasciviously, licking the glistening juices from his lips. Her hands slid down over his sweater, to the waistband of his chinos. Liza's eyes widened. Surely she wasn't going to–?

But that was precisely what the blonde had in mind. She slid the zipper down, and Geoff lifted his bottom from the seat – just long enough for the blonde to pull his chinos down to the middle of his thighs, together with his boxer shorts. Liza swallowed hard. Geoff Morton was a big man, in all senses of the word. His cock rose hot and hard from the cloud of hair at his groin. He was longer and thicker than any of Liza's previous lovers, and she would have bet large sums of money that Geoff was endowed with quality as well as quantity.

The blonde ran her fingers over his shaft, smiling. She curled her fingers round his cock, then slowly began to masturbate him. Geoff gave a sigh and settled back on the seat, with his head resting back, relaxing as she continued to work him. Her technique was impressive, Liza thought, for one so young. She varied the rhythm and pressure of her strokes, bringing Geoff to the edge of orgasm, then squeezing just under the head of his cock to delay him. She masturbated him for a while, then slowly bent her head, so that the curtain of her dyed blonde hair fell over his lap. Liza could not see what was going on, but it was only too obvious what was happening. From the movements of the blonde's head, she was fellating Geoff rapidly.

The actor's eyes were closed, and there was an expression of bliss on his face. He slid his fingers into the blonde's hair, urging her on. She continued to suck him, until he gave a cry, and jerked towards her. The blonde remained motionless for a moment, and then sat up straight again, licking her lips. She kissed Geoff hard, sliding her tongue into his mouth so that he could taste himself on her lips.

Liza was hardly able to take her eyes from the mirror. She'd never witnessed another couple making love before, and it made her feel slightly uneasy. At the same time, she was aroused. Again, she could imagine herself so very easily in the blonde's position, feeling Geoff's mouth and hands bring her to a climax, and then repaying the compliment. She was aware that her labia were growing puffy, and she had a nasty feeling that her passengers would be able to smell her arousal, she was so wet. She forced herself to remember that she was only there to do a job. Geoff and his companion had been teasing her, flaunting their sexuality. In her position, she couldn't rise to the challenge. She had to play them at their own game and remain calm.

Just then, the blonde moved again. She shifted so that she was sitting astride Geoff, her back to him. Geoff was already hard again, to Liza's impressed surprise. He curled his fingers round his cock, and fitted its tip to the entrance of his companion's sex. Then, as she lowered herself onto the thick rigid shaft, his hands came up to caress her breasts, stroking the soft undersides and rolling her nipples between his fore-fingers and thumbs. The blonde began to move over him, raising and lowering herself and moving her body in small circles at the same time, to change the angle of his penetration and give them both more pleasure. Liza could see his cock, lubricated by the blonde's copious juices as she bounced up and down on him.

They were on a two-way road again, and Liza was very relieved that they had dark glass in the windows when she saw the police car heading towards her. Although what was happening in the back was nothing to do with her, she had a feeling that the police would not see it that way, and the last thing she needed was to have some kind of legal summons for indecency.

Geoff and the blonde's movements grew more and more frenzied until, at last, she gave a small cry, and slumped back against him. He buried his head in the curve of her neck, kissing and licking her skin, and pulled her hard against him as he, too, came. They remained there for a while, motionless, and finally the blonde shifted and dressed again. By the time that Liza pulled up alongside the Grand Hotel, both Geoff and his companion were fully dressed, completely decent, and no-one would have guessed what had happened on the journey down from London.

Liza climbed out of the front seat, opened the passenger

door, and waited politely for Geoff and his companion to leave the car. Geoff smiled at her. 'Would you like to come in for a drink, or something?'

Liza smiled back. She knew that he was offering her more than just a drink. Had they not been short-staffed, she might have taken him up on it. But she wasn't in the mood to face Geoff's companion, who had grown sulky again as soon as she realised that Geoff was paying Liza some attention. Besides, she really had to get back to the office. She shook her head. 'Thanks for the offer,' she said, 'but I'll have to say no. I'm needed back at the office.'

Geoff's eyes sparkled, and Liza knew that he thought her a coward. 'Well, thank you for the ride.' I'm not the one you should be saying that to, Liza thought, but she merely smiled politely. 'My agent will settle the bill direct,' he told her. He held out his hand. 'Thanks again.'

'My pleasure.' Liza shook his hand, then climbed back into the car as Geoff and his companion walked into the foyer of the Grand Hotel. No doubt, she thought, they were going to continue where they left off in the back of the car. She switched on the radio, to contact the office.

Bryn answered immediately. 'Liza. Are you okay?'

'I'm fine.'

'You sound a bit shaky. Are you sure there's no problem?'

'Like you said,' she retorted, 'we have to be discreet. I'm on my way back.'

'Drive carefully.'

'Of course. I drive for *James*.' She switched off the radio, and drove back to the office. To her relief, Bryn was already out on another job when she walked into the office. She sat down at her desk and continued with the work she'd been doing before she picked up Geoff Morton, and lost track of time, until someone tapped on her shoulder. She looked up. It was Bryn.

'Don't you have a home to go to?'

Liza glanced at her watch, and her eyes widened. 'God, is it that late?'

He smiled at her. 'Geoff Morton must have made quite an impression on you, then, if he made you forget the time.'

She shook her head. 'He was a client, that's all.'

'Very discreet,' Bryn said dryly. His eyes glittered. 'Whether you admit it or not, you sounded pretty shaky when you called in. So are you going to tell me what happened?'

'I picked him up, on time, and drove him to the Grand Hotel in Brighton.' She shrugged. 'His agent is going to settle the bill.'

Bryn regarded her. Something had definitely happened, but he couldn't tell what. And Liza was maintaining her discretion. 'OK,' he said. 'Well, I'll see you tomorrow, then.'

'Yeah,' Liza answered. She finished what she was doing on her file, saved it, then switched off her computer, left the building, and locked up.

She went home on the tube, as usual, but whereas she normally played a game of looking at the other passengers and guessing what they did for a living, she was lost in her own thoughts. She couldn't get the picture of Geoff Morton out of her mind, the way he'd so lewdly made love with his companion, in the back seat of her limo, knowing full well that she could see everything in her rear-view mirror. She couldn't help wondering what would have happened if she had taken him up on his offer of a drink. Or something, he'd said. Something meaning what, precisely?

Still, there was no point harping on about it. She'd made her decision. She only hoped that it had been the right one. A small suspicion nagged at her. Had Bryn set it up? She shook her head. Now she was being paranoid. Or course Bryn hadn't set it up. He wasn't exactly likely to be best buddies with an actor who was such hot property. They weren't even the same age, let alone anything else.

She smiled wryly. Besides, although she'd found Geoff Morton attractive, she found Bryn even more so. If she was going to make a move on anyone, it would be him. But God only knew when she'd get the chance.

[illegible]

[illegible] How [illegible]

[illegible]
If they want [illegible] our service [illegible]

Four

A month later, Liza had settled in to *James*. Bryn had finally admitted that yes, she was good enough to be his partner, and Liza was enjoying herself. She had already improved their business's efficiency, the rest of the staff all liked her, and she enjoyed working with their customers. Bryn, after his initial doubts, even seemed to trust her to drive some of their clients.

She was going through the monthly accounts when Bryn came over to stand next to her, resting his hand on the back of her chair. 'Liza,' he said, 'are you busy, this weekend?'

Liza's eyes widened. Had he finally noticed her as a woman, rather than as a business partner? Was he about to ask her to have dinner with him, or something? 'Not particularly,' she said, careful to keep her voice completely neutral. 'Why?'

He looked pleased. 'I wondered, would you mind doing a job?'

She fought to hide her disappointment. 'What kind of job?'

'We have a new client,' he said. 'He's French. I don't speak French, and nor do any of the others. And, as you were at such pains to point out that you have a business degree, with French, I thought that perhaps you might be the best person for the job. If you want it, of course,' he added casually.

As if he didn't know that she wanted to do it – to prove herself to him. Liza looked thoughtful. 'A weekend, you say. Entailing what, exactly?'

'Apparently, as part of a business deal, he's bought a place in the country. He wants to have a look at it.'

She frowned. 'How come he doesn't have his own car, then?'

'Don't ask me,' Bryn said. 'I don't tend to quiz my clients. If they want to use our service, that's fine by me.'

'Funny how it's your client, yet it's our service,' she remarked sourly.

He rolled his eyes. 'Okay, okay. Our client. So, do you want to do it?'

'It's a weekend,' she said.

'Well,' he reminded her, 'the job involves unsocial hours, you know. Everyone else takes their fair share of them, including me.'

She sighed. 'All right, I'll do it. But I want to know more about the client, first.'

'Sure. What do you want to know?'

'His name, where I'm taking him, the sort of car he wants, the itinerary – that kind of thing.'

He nodded. 'His name is Alain Joubert. He's French, and he wants you to drive him to a place in Derbyshire. I believe he has a couple of business meetings there, so you'll be driving around the Peak District. I can't give you a precise itinerary, but I'm sure he'll do that, when you pick him up from Gatwick. I'd suggest you take the Jag.'

'Fine. What time does his flight arrive?'

'Half-past three, on Friday afternoon.'

'Oh great. So I get the M25 in the rush hour.' Liza pulled a face.

'Well, if you don't feel that you're up to it–'

It was precisely the kind of comment that would annoy her, and make her determined to prove him wrong – and they both knew it. Liza was cross with herself for rising to the bait, but she couldn't help herself. 'Of course I'm up to it,' she snapped. 'Though you'd better get me a decent map. And the Jag had better be on its best behaviour.'

'It will be.' Bryn went back to his own desk, hiding a smile.

At half-past three on the Friday afternoon, Liza stood in the arrivals lounge at Gatwick, holding a placard which said 'Alain Joubert'. She felt faintly ridiculous, as though she were taking part in a film, but there were several other chauffeurs there, all holding placards. She supposed that it was a fairly common thing; no doubt plenty of people were picked up from the airport by drivers who didn't know them and couldn't recognise them. A placard was about the best solution.

A few minutes later, a man walked towards her. He was about five feet ten, with dark hair brushed back from his forehead and dark eyes, and a Mediterranean type complexion. He was wearing a dark grey serge suit, teamed with a white silk shirt, and an understated silk tie; Liza could tell immediately that the well-cut clothes were expensive designer label, as were his black, highly-polished shoes. He was carrying a briefcase and a small suitcase. He reminded Liza of a younger Sacha Distel, and he had exactly the same charming, white-toothed smile.

'Good afternoon,' he said. 'I'm Alain Joubert.'

Liza held out her right hand. Alain's grip was impressively firm as he shook her hand. 'Hello. I'm Liza Hargreaves, from *James*.' She smiled back at him. 'Did you have a good flight, Mr Joubert?'

'Fine, thank you.'

'Would you like me to drive you to Derbyshire now, or would you prefer to stop for a cup of coffee or something to eat, first?'

Alain smiled. 'I must say, your training does the firm credit.'

She decided not to tell him that she was actually one of the partners. 'Thank you,' she said. 'May I take your bags?'

He shook his head. 'I never let a lady carry my bags.'

She touched the peak of her cap. 'I'm your driver, sir, not a lady.' Her eyes twinkled. 'So really, as your chauffeur, I should carry your bags.'

'*Ma petite chauffeuse*,' he said softly. His lips twitched. 'I'll decline your offer, I think. But a coffee sounds good. Can you recommend anywhere around here?'

She nodded. She'd arrived early at the airport, anxious not to be late, and had ended up with a good half-hour to spare. The smell of freshly ground coffee had attracted her to one particular café, and she had been pleased to discover that the taste matched up to the smell. 'If you'd like to come with me?'

He murmured something in French, and Liza had to hide her grin. If he only knew, she could translate everything that he'd just said, and he'd just intimated that he would very much like to come with her. She pretended that she hadn't understood him, and led the way to the small café. 'How do you like your coffee?' she asked.

'The proper way – no milk, no sugar. Strong.' He looked at her. 'But it's my bill.'

She shook her head. 'It's all part of the *James* service, Mr Joubert.' She ordered two coffees, one as Alain liked it, and a *café au lait* for herself, paid, put the receipt in her purse, and took the two coffees over to where he was sitting. 'I haven't yet had your itinerary, I'm afraid,' she said. 'Your company didn't manage to fax it to me.'

'Well,' he said, 'I'd like you to drive me to Derbyshire, where I have a cottage. It's in a little place called Bakewell – do you know it?'

'Not personally, but I'll make sure I get you there,' she said.

'I have a business meeting tomorrow, in Sheffield, and I'm planning to spend the evening at the cottage. Then I have to be back at the airport for three o'clock on Sunday.' He paused. 'There will, of course, be a room for you at the cottage. I'm sorry that I need you over the weekend.'

She took a sip of her coffee. 'That's what we're here for – to drive you when you need us.'

He looked at her. 'You know,' he said, 'I was expecting a male driver.'

She smiled. 'I know what they say about women drivers, but . . .' She spread her hands. 'Bryn wouldn't have hired me, if I wasn't a safe driver.'

'I didn't mean to offend.'

'No offence taken.'

Alain tipped his head on one side. 'There's something about you, though . . .' He frowned. 'The way you're dressed, the way you speak. I . . .' He shook his head, impatient with himself. 'Forgive me. I'm being rude.'

'Not at all.' Liza's eyes held his. She decided to be honest with him. She had a feeling that he would appreciate it more than if she kept her act of being merely a driver. 'But you're right, I'm not an ordinary driver. I'm Bryn's partner. And we decided that I was the best person for the job, because I speak

French.' She grinned. 'I wasn't expecting your English to be so flawless, or your accent to be so good.'

He raised an eyebrow. 'So – what I said, on the way here–'

'I understood perfectly,' she told him, with a smile.

'I see.' His eyes flickered with interest, as he realised that she wasn't in the least offended or embarrassed. 'So, may I ask, why are you working as a chauffeuse?'

'I've spent the past few years in the City, in market research,' she told him. 'But I was never really happy there. I inherited my part of the business from my grandfather, and I joined the firm because I decided that I wanted to work for myself.'

'Very commendable.' Alain finished his coffee.

'Would you like another coffee?' she asked. 'Or would you prefer to set off?'

'Well,' he said, 'I'd quite like to go to Bakewell, as I haven't seen the cottage, yet.'

She smiled at him. 'Do you have directions?'

He nodded. 'They're in my briefcase. I'll get them out for you, when we reach the car.'

Liza led him to the car, and unlocked the boot, so that he could put his suitcase inside, next to her small valise. Then she opened the door, and waited politely for him to sit down. When he was settled comfortably in the back seat, she opened the driver's door and climbed in. She adjusted the mirror, then turned round to smile at him. 'Just in case Bryn didn't mention it before, our service is completely confidential. Any calls you wish to make in the car will go no further. As far as I'm concerned, I won't have heard a thing.'

He smiled back at her. 'Thank you.'

'If you need anything, just let me know.'

'I will.' He opened his briefcase, and extracted a sheet of paper, handing it to her. 'Directions,' he explained succinctly.

'Thanks.' Liza scanned the paper swiftly, then placed it on the front passenger seat and drove off, leaving the airport car park and heading for the M25. As she'd expected, they hit rush hour traffic, and it was a while before she could ease out into the fast lane, and let the Jag have full rein. Eventually, they turned on to the M1. Liza was so busy concentrating on the road that she paid no attention to Alain, who was sitting making phone calls on his mobile, and making notes on his laptop. She turned on to the A617 towards Chesterfield, then they headed into the Peak District.

'It's a beautiful area,' Alain said.

'Yes,' she agreed. She hadn't been to Derbyshire since she was a small child, and she'd forgotten how beautiful it was.

He switched off his laptop and sat back to enjoy the view. Liza didn't bother to make polite conversation; she had to concentrate on the directions, so she knew where she was going.

'Liza,' he said eventually, 'would you mind pulling off the road for a moment?'

She was a little surprised, but did as he asked, pulling off into a small wooded area.

'I just need to stretch my legs for a moment,' he said. 'That's no criticism of your driving, of course. I've just been sitting down for a long time; first in the plane, and then in the car.' He looked at her. 'Would you like to join me?'

She nodded. 'That would be nice.' She had been driving for several hours, without a break. Bryn had always told her to make sure she took a break to stretch her legs, on long journeys, but she had been so absorbed in the drive that she hadn't noticed the time. She climbed out of the car, opened the door for him, and then locked the Jag behind them.

He stretched luxuriously. 'That's better,' he said.

To her secret amusement, he took her arm, escorting her. She smiled to herself. Usually, it was an elderly and slightly tottery lady taking the arm of her chauffeur for support – not a virile and good-looking man in his mid-thirties taking the arm of his female driver.

'What are you thinking?' he asked.

She shook her head. This was something she couldn't share with him. 'Nothing in particular.'

He drew her deeper into the woods. 'I am,' he said softly. He stopped, and turned her to face him. 'Liza.' His voice was slightly husky; with the slight tinge of a French accent, it was very seductive. 'Liza,' he said again, taking off her peaked hat, so that her hair fell down to her shoulders. 'Ever since I first saw you, I've wanted to do this.' He slid one hand under the curtain of her hair, caressing the nape of her neck, and bent his head to kiss her.

His lips were firm and warm against hers and she found herself responding, opening her mouth so that he could slide his tongue inside. His other hand smoothed down her back, stroking her spine and settling on the curve of her buttocks. He pulled her gently against him, and she could feel the unmistakable bulge of his erection pressing against her. She shifted slightly, and his kiss grew more passionate; she couldn't help winding her arms around his neck.

Alain slid one hand between their bodies, so that he could undo the buttons of her tailored black jacket. He tugged her shirt from the waistband of her skirt, his fingers gliding over her midriff, caressing her skin and arousing her further. She arched against him, and he slid his other hand up from her buttocks, pushing under the hem of her shirt, and deftly undoing the clasp of her bra.

He was still kissing her, and she made no protest as he pushed the cups of her bra out of the way, his fingers curving round her breast and squeezing it gently. His thumb slid over her hardening nipple, rubbing it gently, and she gave a small moan of pleasure, which was muffled by his mouth. His other hand was working on the waistband of her skirt, undoing the button and then sliding the zipper downwards.

She pulled back, and he looked at her. There was a dark flush across his cheekbones, his lower lip was full and reddened with arousal, and his eyes were almost black. 'I . . .' He licked his lower lip. 'Liza. I want you.'

She was torn between being professional, and giving in to the desire which raged in her belly. 'Alain, I'm supposed to be your driver.'

'But you're not an ordinary chauffeuse, are you?'

She smiled wryly. 'No, I suppose you're right.'

'Liza. We're both adults. We have a choice.' He stroked her face. 'I think you feel the same attraction, *hein*?' He rubbed his thumb across her lower lip, and Liza couldn't help opening her mouth, drawing his thumb into her mouth and sucking gently on it. He chuckled. 'You're like me, Liza. You live for pleasure. Why deny ourselves?'

She caught his wrist, taking his thumb from her mouth and kissing the palm of his hand. She curled his fingers over the invisible imprint of the kiss, and looked at him. 'Alain, I can't mix business with pleasure. It's not professional.'

He smiled at her, a sensual curve to his lips. 'Oh, Liza. You're still very young, if you haven't learnt that mixing business and pleasure can give even great satisfaction.'

'Maybe, but it can also cause a hell of a lot of problems.' She thought of the time that Rachel, one of her friends, had slept with a senior colleague after an office party. In the end, Rachel's life had become so unbearable in the office that she'd had to change jobs.

'Don't you ever take risks?'

'Not where my business is concerned. There's not just me to consider. There's Bryn.'

'This has nothing to do with Bryn.'

His voice was low and husky, and sent a thrill through her. Making love with this man would be more than a pleasure, she knew. And she'd been celibate for a month. Since splitting up with Rupert, and that never-to-be-repeated episode with Steve in the shower, she hadn't made love with anyone. She'd tried to switch off her libido, because working with Bryn – when he so obviously wasn't interested in her – was torture. She'd concentrated on *James*, and making her role in it a success. And now, this so attractive man was offering her almost limitless pleasure. No strings. She bit her lip. 'Alain, it's not professional.'

'Liza, if you don't want me, all you have to do is say so. Tell me,' he coaxed.

Liza remained silent. She couldn't lie. She did want him.

'Tell me,' he repeated.

She shook her head. 'You're making this very difficult for me.'

'I want you. You want me. Where's the problem?'

'Like I told you, this is meant to be business.'

He bent his head and rubbed his nose against hers, kissing her very lightly on the lips. 'I admire your principles. Though I deplore what they're doing to me.' He took her hand, placing her palm against his chest and drawing her hand down, until it covered his groin. She swallowed, as she felt the length and girth of his erection. 'Would it help, if I recommended you to my friends?'

'As what, precisely?' she asked.

He chuckled. 'As a very efficient, very personal service. And I mean a chauffeur service only.'

She couldn't help smiling back. 'That's bribery.'

'Not at all. I was impressed by the way you met me; you made sure that I was comfortable, and you've done everything I've asked you to do – on a professional level.' Again, he stroked her jawline, tracing the outline of her face with the tip of his forefinger.

'And what precisely would it mean to *James*, having your recommendation?'

'Well,' he said, 'I have other associates in France, who come over here on business. I also have a few associates in England. Once they've tried your service, I'm sure that they'll be pleased to recommend it to others, too.'

'So you're saying that if I make love to you, you'll help my business?'

He shook his head. 'I'll recommend you, anyway. If something happens between you and me, then that's just between us.'

She nodded. 'That's fair enough.'

He bent his head, nibbling at her lower lip. She opened her mouth, letting the kiss deepen; he broke it, with an effort. 'I want to make love with you, Liza. Now.'

'Here?'

He nodded. 'This seems to be a very private place. I don't think we'll be disturbed.' He tipped his head on one side, giving her a boyish and engaging grin. 'Dare I ask if you have a rug in the car?'

'As a matter of fact, I have.' She returned his grin. 'I believe it's to place over the laps of elderly businessmen.'

He chuckled. 'I imagine I could give you about six or seven years. That makes me elderly, does it?'

'Perhaps,' she said softly, 'I'm about to find that out for myself.'

He restored some semblance of order to her clothes, then

slid his arm around her shoulders. They walked back to the car, and she opened the boot of the Jag. Alain tossed her peaked cap into the boot, and fished out the checked rug. Liza locked the car again, and put the keys into her handbag. Then, still with his arm around her shoulders, he led her back into the woods.

He stopped in a clearing, and spread the rug on the grass. Then he turned to Liza. 'Now, where were we?' he whispered. 'Here, I think.' He pulled her into his arms again, sliding his hand under the hem of her shirt and stroking her skin. She shivered, and lifted her face up to his.

Alain kissed her gently, nibbling at her lower lip and teasing her until she gave a muffled groan of impatience, slid her hands round his neck, and jammed his mouth to hers, sliding her tongue into his mouth and kissing him passionately.

The next thing she knew, he had removed her jacket, placing it gently on the ground, and was unbuttoning her shirt. He gave a sharp intake of breath as he saw her. '*Chérie*, you are so beautiful,' he murmured. Her bra was still undone, and he finished removing it, cupping her breasts in his hands and lifting them up together to deepen the shadowed vee of her cleavage. He bent his head, then dropped to his knees in front of her, burying his face in her breasts and breathing in her scent. Liza slid her hands into his hair as he took the hard rosy tip of one breast into his mouth and began to suck. Her fingers dug into his scalp, urging him on, and he began to suck harder, using his teeth against her skin in a way that sent shivers of desire running through her, and staying just the right side of the pleasure-pain barrier.

Liza moaned, and he transferred his attentions to her other breast, using the tip of his tongue on her areola and breathing on it, making her arch her back and shiver. Then he took the hard crest into his mouth, and sucked. All the time, he caressed her other nipple with his thumb and forefinger.

Then he slid his hand down her sides, resting them lightly on the waistband of her skirt. Deftly, he undid the button and zipper at the back, and slid the skirt over her hips. The skirt was lined, so the material slid down easily. His eyes widened in pleasure as he saw that she was wearing black lace-topped hold-up stockings. He ran the tip of one finger across the welt of her stockings. 'Beautiful,' he breathed. 'So very, very beautiful.'

He kissed his way down over her abdomen. Liza tensed, waiting to see what he was going to do next. She ached for him to remove her knickers and put his mouth to her already swollen sex, kissing and sucking her to a climax; but Alain seemed to have other ideas. He left her knickers exactly where they were, though he pulled the gusset to one side. She widened the gap between her thighs, resting her hands on his shoulders for balance, and he dipped his head, licking his way across the soft white skin above the welts of her stockings. She gasped, and he breathed on her quim, making her wriggle with anticipation.

'Alain, don't tease me,' she pleaded.

She felt him smile against her skin, and then, at last, she felt the long slow sweep of his tongue along her quim. She moaned as he made his tongue into a hard point, flicking it rapidly over the swollen bud of her clitoris. At the same time, he curved one hand round her buttocks, kneading them, and slid the other hand between her legs, stroking his finger along her perineum. She gave a small moan as he pushed one finger against her sex, sliding it deep inside her. He began to move his hand back and forth, and Liza's fingers tightened on his shoulders.

It felt so good, so very good. Abstinence certainly makes the heart grow fonder, she thought wryly; then she stopped thinking at all as the familiar inner sparkling rushed through her. Her internal muscles contracted sharply round his fingers, and when Alain lifted his head, she could see that his face was glistening with her musky juices.

He pulled her down on to the rug beside him, and lifted his hand to her mouth, slicking the musky nectar along her lower lip. She licked her lower lip, then kissed him deeply. 'Thank you,' she said softly.

Alain looked at her. 'You've obviously been working too hard, lately, and you've neglected yourself.'

Liza frowned. 'How do you mean?'

'Your reaction to me.' His eyes glittered. 'I don't flatter

myself that I'm that good. Obviously, you've been working long hours, and your love life has suffered, as a result.'

She flushed. 'God, it's that obvious? How embarrassing.'

He smiled. '*Au contraire*. I find it charming, *chérie*,' he informed her huskily. 'But, right now, I need to be inside you.'

She needed no second bidding. She removed his jacket, placing it by hers, then undid his silk tie. The material of his shirt was smooth and slippery when under her fingertips, and she delighted in the luxuriant feeling. Slowly, she undid his shirt, revealing his chest. The contrast between the crisp hair on his chest and the smoothness of the material was intoxicating. She ran her fingers over his chest, delighting in the feel. His flat button nipples had grown hard, and he moaned softly as she touched him. This time, it was his turn to plead with her not to tease him.

'Liza, *chérie* . . .' His eyes were dark and pleading.

She cupped his face in her hands, kissing him lightly, and finished removing his shirt. She drew back for a moment, to look at him, and smiled appraisingly. His body was well toned, without a hint of fat. At the same time, he was no muscle-bound gorilla. Just very nicely built. 'Mm,' she murmured approvingly. Her hands slid to the buckle of his leather belt. She unclasped it, then undid the button of his trousers, and zip. Alain kicked off his shoes and shifted on the rug, helping her to remove his trousers properly. Then he lay back against the rug, clasping his hands behind his head, and giving her a seductive look. '*Chérie*,' he smiled at her, 'I'm all yours. Do with me what you will.'

Liza smiled back, and hooked her thumbs into the waistband of his silk boxer shorts. The outline of his cock was clearly visible through the thin material, and she liked what she saw. Alain lifted his buttocks, letting her pull his boxer shorts down over his hips; with a grin, she finished removing them, taking off his socks at the same time.

He chuckled, knowing what she'd been thinking. 'Yes, a man wearing only his socks is hardly erotic.'

She straddled him, resting her quim lightly against his cock. She was still wearing her knickers, but the thin gusset was little barrier. She cold feel how hard and heavy his cock was, and he could feel how hot her quim was, too. She rested one hand on each side of his shoulders, then dipped her head to rub her nose against his. Her hair swung down in a curtain, its end tickling his skin; he tipped his head back slightly, and she took the hint, kissing him.

The hard tips of her breasts brushed against the hair on his chest, the light friction sending a thrill through her. Alain moved so that he could cup her breasts, squeezing them gently; she smiled at him, and moved so that she was sitting upright. She lifted herself slightly, pulling the gusset of her knickers to one side, then curled her fingers round his cock, rubbing it very lightly. He groaned. 'Liza, *maintenant, chérie, maintenant.* Do it.'

She fitted the tip of his cock against her sex, then slowly lowered herself onto him. As she sank down, Alain groaned. The feel of her quim, like warm wet silk wrapping itself round him . . . It was the feeling he loved best in the world, penetrating the body of a sensual woman who wanted him as much as he wanted her.

Liza had intended to watch his face, but the way he felt inside her, filling and stretching her, was too much. She closed her eyes, and tightened her internal muscles round him, so that her quim fluttered around his cock.

He continued to play with her breasts, sensitising her nipples, and Liza began to lift and lower herself over him, her hips moving in tiny circles. He let one hand drift down over her midriff, his fingertips moving in tiny erotic circles over her skin. He cupped her mound of Venus, and extended his middle finger between her labia, seeking her clitoris. As she continued moving over him, he rubbed the hard nub of flesh, making her writhe.

Their movements grew more and more frenzied; at last, Liza felt the familiar rolling pleasure moving from the soles of her feet, up through her calves, and finally exploding in her solar plexus. Her quim contracted sharply round the thick rod of his cock; Alain groaned, and tilted his hips, pushing even more deeply into her. At the same time, he cried out softly. She didn't quite catch what he said, being so far gone herself, but she knew that he, too, had come.

He moved to a sitting position, wrapping his arms round her, and pulling her against his body. She buried her face against his shoulder, breathing in the sharp tang of his masculine scent, and she felt him kiss the curve of her neck. They remained locked together, until he finally slid from her. Then he kissed her very tenderly. 'Thank you.'

'It was good for me, too,' Liza said softly.

He stroked her face. 'The first time. How I'm looking forward to the encore.'

She stood up, and Alain dressed her tenderly, in silence, kissing each breast in turn as he replaced her bra, and nuzzling her midriff as he did up her shirt. By the time he'd finished, no one would have guessed that she had done anything but walk in the woods with him – unless they noticed the febrile glitter in her eyes, and the slightly reddened swollen curve of her mouth.

She helped him restore order to his own clothing; then he folded the rug and draped it over his arm. 'To the cottage, I think,' he said. He looked at her. 'As neither of us really knows the way, would you like me to sit in the front and direct you?'

She shook her head. 'You don't have to do that, you know. If you have work to do, I can follow the directions you gave me.'

He linked his fingers through hers. 'I'd like to.' He grinned. 'I'd quite like to drive the car, too.'

She grinned back. 'No chance. It's not insured for you.'

Alain chuckled. 'And I thought it was men who were supposed to be possessive about cars . . .'

Five

In the end, Alain decided to sit in the front, next to Liza, and directed her to the cottage. It was just on the outskirts of Bakewell, and her eyes widened as she turned into the drive.

'I thought you said that it was a cottage?'

He shrugged. 'It is.'

Liza said nothing. It looked to her as though it had at least six bedrooms. When Bryn had mentioned a cottage in the Peak District, she had expected it to be a tiny two-up, two-down, chocolate-box kind of place. She hadn't been expecting the large stone house which sat at the end of the long gravel drive, surrounded by shrubs and trees.

She pulled up outside the house, and climbed out of the car. She opened the door for Alain; he smiled at her, bowing his head to acknowledge her courtesy, and, together, they took the bags from the boot. Alain opened the front door, and sniffed. 'I have a part-time housekeeper,' he said. 'She knew that I was going to arrive here today. It smells like she's made us a meal.' He looked at Liza. 'I would offer to give you a tour, but this is the first time I've been here – so I'm not sure which rooms are which.'

She raised an eyebrow. 'You're very brave, buying a house that you haven't even seen.'

He chuckled. 'By brave, you mean foolish, don't you?' At her silence, he continued, 'It was part of a business deal. An associate of mine who's in property gave the place a thorough going-through first, so I knew there were no structural problems with the cottage. And I believe that the Peak District is one of the prettier places in England. It's in the middle of the country, so access is easy to all your main business centres. It seemed like a good idea at the time.'

'Did your colleague decorate it for you, too?' she asked, curious.

He shook his head. 'I hired an interior decorator. I gave her full rein – to make me *un petit paradis Anglais.*'

And the designer had certainly succeeded, Liza thought. The decor was faultless, the carpets thick and lush, and the whole house had a light and airy feel about it.

'Shall we take our bags upstairs?' he asked. Catching the expression on her face, he added, 'You do, of course, have a separate room. But if you would wish to share my bed for the weekend, I have no complaints.'

It was a tempting offer. One which Liza decided there and then to accept. She smiled. 'If this is how you usually do business,' she teased, 'then yes. I will.'

He laughed, and ruffled her hair. 'On very rare occasions. And I usually find it worth my while when I do mix business and pleasure.'

He ushered her up the stairs. Liza gave a sharp intake of breath when he opened a door, and she saw the oak four-poster bed in front of them. 'Wow. I've never slept in one of these before.'

'Neither have I,' he said, 'but there's a first time for everything. I believe the bed itself is an antique, but I can assure you that the mattress is new – and French. I've heard too many tales about lumpy English mattresses, and I prefer comfort.'

'Hence the blanket, earlier?' she teased.

He smiled. 'Something like that. Would you like a bath before dinner?'

She nodded. 'Yes, please. Travelling always makes me feel grubby. Though I'm glad we're eating in, tonight. I didn't bring anything dressy with me.'

He pulled her into his arms. 'As far as I'm concerned, *chérie*, I'd be happy to sit opposite you if you were wearing nothing but a string of pearls.' He kissed her lightly.

She chuckled. 'Apart from the fact that I don't have a string of pearls with me, it's not my style to sit down to dinner naked.'

He smiled. 'I'll leave you to have your bath in peace, then. If you need me, I'll be downstairs.'

He left the room. Liza swiftly unpacked her bag, then stripped off her chauffeur's outfit, and walked into the bathroom. It was as luxurious as the bedroom, with all the modern conveniences, although it was decorated in a Victorian style, and the bath itself had claw feet and a rolled edge. The old-fashioned chrome taps on both the bath and the washbasin matched the shower, and all the rest of the fittings were solid mahogany, the darkness of the wood in sharp contrast with the pale patterned walls.

It was the kind of bathroom she'd only ever seen in designer magazines; the tastes of the more well-to-do people she knew ran more to marble sunken baths and Jacuzzis, and her friends tended to have plain, modern fittings. This, she thought, was going to be a real treat. The kind of bathroom where you could spend hours, lying in deep suds and listening to chamber music and drinking champagne . . .

She ran herself a bath, adding liberal quantities of the expensive French bath oil which stood on the shelf behind the taps. She tested the water, added a little more cold water, then climbed into the bath, closing her eyes and letting the water soak away the aches in her body.

This weekend was turning out to be nothing like she'd anticipated. She had been expecting Alain Joubert to be several years older, perhaps a little patronising towards her – as she was both female and English – and that she would spend most of the time on her own, waiting in the car and wishing she'd brought a good book with her, when she wasn't driving him somewhere. Her lips curved. Instead, she'd found a bright, attractive and very personable man, who had a good sense of humour, liked the same sort of things that she did, and who was looking forward to sharing her company. This was definitely going to be more pleasure than business.

Eventually, she climbed out of the bath, dried herself on one of the thick fluffy bath-sheets, hung it over the mahogany towel rail, and then padded back into the bedroom. She dressed in a pair of tailored trousers and a loose shirt, and pushed her hair back with an Alice band. She half wished that she'd brought a little black dress with her; but then again, she hadn't expected to need one. She looked at herself critically in the cheval mirror, decided that she passed muster, and went downstairs.

The first room she came to was the lounge. Alain wasn't in evidence and, as none of the cushions on the over-stuffed sofa had been moved, she realised that he hadn't even been in there. The next room turned out to be the dining room – again, deserted – and the third room was obviously a study, with a large desk, a half-empty bookshelf which contained several legal texts in both French and English, and a docking station for a portable PC. He wasn't there, either.

Liza smiled to herself. That left just the kitchen. Either Alain was a good chef, as well, or maybe he was just making himself some coffee. As he'd said that his housekeeper had made them dinner, it was probably the latter.

She was right. Alain was sitting at the scrubbed pine table, with a newspaper spread across it, and a cafétière of coffee in front of him. He looked at her, and smiled. 'You look very nice,' he said.

'Thank you.'

'Would you like a cup of coffee?' He indicated the cafétière.

She nodded. 'I must say, I like your bathroom.'

'I should try it, myself,' he said. 'From Mrs Bowe's note, the casserole and jacket potatoes will be ready in about another twenty minutes. Do you mind amusing yourself, in the meantime?'

Liza chuckled. 'I'm your chauffeur, not your guest!'

'You're staying under my roof. That makes you my guest, *en mon avis.*'

She noticed that he was slipping into the odd French phrase, here and there. Obviously, he was getting tired, too tired to concentrate a hundred per cent in English. She smiled at him. 'I'm sure I can. Is there anything I can do, to help with dinner?'

'You can lay the table for us, if you'd like.' He gestured to the open bottle of wine. 'I took the liberty of opening red, but there's a bottle of white chilling in the fridge, if you'd prefer it.'

Liza could read the label from where she was standing. Margaux – her favourite. She shook her head. 'Red's fine with me, thanks.'

'Put some music on, if you like,' he directed. 'I'll be down in about twenty minutes.'

Liza busied herself setting the table for dinner. From a rudimentary inspection of the fridge, she could see that the intended pudding was cheese. Alain obviously didn't have a sweet tooth. She took the cheese from the fridge, placing it on a plate so that it would be at room temperature when they were ready to eat, then poured herself a cup of coffee and added milk to it. Clutching the mug, she went into the sitting room, and knelt down in front of the small and very expensive-looking hi-fi.

There was a rack of CDs next to it. Some of them up were French ballads, and she smiled to herself. When she'd been a student, some of her friends had teased her about always putting a Johnny Halliday record on the stereo when she wanted people to go home. There were also several classical CDs, mainly Mozart. She picked out a CD of string quartets, and put the disc on.

There was also a small bookcase in the room, containing a mixture of French novels, poetry, and the complete works of Shakespeare. She picked out one of her old favourites – a copy of Rimbaud's poems – and curled up on the sofa.

Alain found her there, a quarter of an hour later. He leaned over her shoulder, making a small noise of surprise when he saw what she was reading. 'Don't forget,' she told him, 'my degree was in business studies and French.'

'Even so, this isn't to most people's taste.'

'True.' She closed the book, and stood up. 'I think dinner must be ready, now. I must say, it's nice to have someone cooking for you.'

'You don't cook, then?'

She shook her head. 'I've never really been the domesticated sort. At university, I had a deal with my flat-mate. She did the cooking, and I did the washing-up.'

Alain made no comment, and ushered her into the dining room. He came back, a couple of minutes later, with two plates of casserole and jacket potato. He poured them both a glass of wine. '*Salut*,' he said softly.

'*Salut*,' she echoed.

Dinner turned out to taste as excellent as it had smelled, and Liza enjoyed every mouthful. They chatted lightly throughout the meal, and Alain made them both some coffee, after the cheese. She watched him as he walked back into the dining room. He'd changed into more casual clothes – a black polo-necked sweater and a pair of stone-coloured chinos – and they suited him, highlighting his good looks. Alain Joubert had an innate sense of style, she thought.

Eventually, she yawned, and stretched. 'It's not the company,' she said apologetically. 'I think it's a mixture of the country air, and travelling.'

'Yes, travelling does tend to make me tired, too,' Alain said. He smiled at her. 'Let go to bed.'

'If you'd rather stay up a bit later–' she began.

He shook his head. 'I've had a long day, too. And I can't think of anything nicer than curling up with you in my arms, and going to sleep. We'll do the washing up in the morning.'

He stacked the crockery in the kitchen, then followed her up the stairs. Liza felt suddenly shy, undressing in front of him. She turned her back, and heard him give a wry chuckle. 'What?' she asked.

He walked over to her, sliding his hands round her waist and drawing her back against him. 'Merely that, in the circumstances, you needn't be shy with me.'

She smiled back. 'Yeah, I suppose you're right.'

'Here. Let me.' Alain turned her to face him, and unbuttoned her shirt, sliding the soft garment from her shoulders and hanging it neatly over the back of a chair. He undid the button of her trousers, and then the zipper, sliding her trousers down over her hips. She stepped out of them, and he picked them up, hanging them over the top of her shirt. He took her hands, drawing them up to his lips and kissing the tips of her fingers. A shudder of desire went through her. God, this man really knew how to make love. Although she was tired, she suddenly wanted him. Very badly.

He let her hands drop again, and began to tug at his sweater. Liza helped him, freeing it from the waistband of his chinos. He lifted his arms, and she pulled the sweater over his head. Following his example, she folded the garment neatly, placing it on top of her clothes. She undid the button and zipper of his chinos, helping him out of them. Slowly, keeping his eyes fixed on hers, Alain shed the rest of his clothes. Then he undid her bra, sliding it from her shoulders and placing it with the rest of her clothes. 'So beautiful,' he murmured softly. 'I love the way you look, the way you feel.'

She flushed. 'You don't look so bad, yourself.'

He inclined his head in acknowledgement, and then slowly peeled down her knickers. When she was naked, he picked her up, carried her over to the four poster and pushed the duvet aside with one hand. He laid her gently on the bed. 'Macho, maybe, but irresistible all the same,' he told her.

She shifted over and he climbed into the bed beside her. He left the bedside light on, and pulled her into his arms. His hands slid down her spine, relaxing her, and then he began to kiss her, with tiny little butterfly kisses which left her unsatisfied and wanting more. Eventually, she slid her hands into his hair, and pulled his face to hers, jamming her mouth against his and kissing him deeply.

He stroked the soft undersides of her breasts, and she arched against him. Slowly, his mouth drifted down over the curve of her neck; he licked the hollows of her collar-bones, and then let his mouth track downwards. Her nipples were already hard; he took one rosy peak into his mouth, and sucked gently. Liza wound her hands into his hair, urging him on, and he moved downwards, nuzzling her midriff, then shifting to kneel between her thighs.

Liza parted her legs, drawing her knees up and placing her feet flat against the mattress. Alain kissed the curve of her thigh, and Liza closed her eyes, blissfully anticipating what he would do next. At last, she felt his breath, warm against her quim, and then his tongue was parting her labia, sampling her musky nectar and then teasing her clitoris. He drew the hard nub of flesh into his mouth, sucking gently, and she groaned with pleasure.

'Oh yes,' she moaned, 'yes. Alain. Lick me. Lick me hard.'

Alain did as she demanded, making his tongue into a hard point and working her until she came, flooding his mouth with musky juices. Then he shifted again, fitting the tip of his erect cock against her sex, and slowly easing into her.

Liza wrapped her legs round his waist, gripping him tightly, and he began to move – slowly, at first, and then thrusting deeper, speeding up the rhythm as his excitement increased. He felt so good, she thought, the way he filled her. All the time, he was murmuring soft endearments to her, lapsing into French. No wonder French was often seen as the language of love, she thought. Words which might have sounded silly in English sounded so erotic in French.

She felt his body tense, and then she felt his cock twitch deep inside her, filling her. They remained locked together for a while; when he slipped from her, he rolled over onto his back, pulling her into his arms and cradling her against his shoulder. Liza closed her eyes and, within minutes, she was asleep, her breathing deep and regular. Alain remained awake for a little longer, just watching her, then switched off the light, and joined her in sleep.

The next morning, Liza woke to find herself still asleep in Alain's arms. She was lying on her side, and his body was curved against hers, spoon style, his arm round her waist. As if he'd been waiting for her to wake up, as soon as he felt her slight movement, his arm tightened, and he nuzzled her shoulder. 'Good morning, *ma petite,*' he said softly.

Liza shifted to face him. 'Good morning,' she said. 'What time is your meeting?'

'Not until half-past ten. How far is Sheffield from here?'

'About forty-five minutes' drive.'

He glanced at the bedside clock. 'Plenty of time for breakfast, then. There are some croissants in the fridge, unless you prefer a cooked breakfast?'

Liza shook her head. 'I'm not much of a breakfast person. Croissants will be fine, thanks.' She smiled at him. 'I think I ought to sort them out, though.'

He chuckled. 'Yesterday, you told me that you hated cooking.'

'Putting some croissants in the oven to heat through is hardly cooking,' she protested. 'And I make good coffee.'

He nodded. 'In that case, thank you.'

'I'll have a shower first,' she said. She felt much less shy with him, this morning, and slid easily from the bed, not bothering to cover herself as she headed for the bathroom. The shower was, as she'd suspected, a power shower, and the strong jets of water soon had her feeling wide awake. She returned to the bedroom, dressed swiftly, and headed downstairs to sort out breakfast.

By the time that Alain had come downstairs again, dressed in the dark grey suit of the day before, Liza had laid the dining-room table, made coffee, and the croissants were heating in the oven. 'Perfect timing,' she said with a smile. She went into the kitchen to take the parcels from the oven. They both ate hungrily, finishing two cafétières of coffee between them. Then Liza glanced at her watch. 'We'd better be going,' she said. 'Whereabouts in Sheffield do you need to go?'

'On the outskirts,' he said. 'I have directions.'

He insisted on doing the washing-up before they left the house, saying that he couldn't bear to come back to a pile of dirty dishes; when they'd finished, and left the house, Alain decided to sit in the front, next to Liza.

'This isn't the way that chauffeuring usually works, you know,' Liza told him. 'You're supposed to sit in the back, relaxing.'

'And waving at *les paysannes*?' he teased. He ruffled her hair. 'I don't care. Anyway, you don't know the area. It'd be easier if I directed you.'

She had to admit that he was right. She drove him through the Peak District to the outskirts of Sheffield. Alain's directions were near perfect, and she found the place easily enough. 'I'll wait for you out here, then,' she said as she parked the car.

He shook his head. 'No, come up to the office. I don't know how long I'm going to be, and I'm not having you sitting outside waiting, when you could sit in comfort and have a cup of coffee. I think there will be a buffet lunch, too.'

Liza grinned. 'If all our clients were like you,' she said, 'my life would be a hell of a lot easier – because my drivers would all want to work for nothing!'

It turned out that two of the other men in the meeting had also been chauffeured there. Their driver was sitting in the reception area, drinking coffee and leafing through a newspaper, looking faintly bored, when Alain and Liza arrived.

Alain went into his meeting, and Liza made herself a cup of coffee, grimacing at the fact that it was instant: but she could hardly make a fuss and demand proper coffee. She sat down next to the other driver, smiled politely at him, and picked up one of the business magazines from the coffee table.

She'd been reading for a while, when she realised that he was staring at her. She looked up, and met his green stare unflinchingly.

'You don't get many women drivers,' he remarked.

'No.' Liza decided not to tell him she wasn't just an ordinary driver. She wasn't in the mood for justifying herself; and the driver looked like the stereotype cabbie, a young man who was nice-looking and a bit too full of himself. She couldn't be bothered to waste her breath, arguing with someone like him.

'Are you local?' he asked.

She shook her head. 'I'm from London.'

He looked at her speculatively, then held out his hand. 'Greg Marshall,' he offered.

He had a slight Yorkshire accent, which she found attractive, with thick dark hair which was tied back in a neat ponytail, and cheekbones that a lot of male models would have envied. As he was sitting down, Liza couldn't tell how tall he was, but she suspected that he was only a little under six feet tall. Broad-shouldered, too; she would have bet money that he went to a gym, most nights, when he wasn't working. He looked the type. She took his outstretched hand and shook it. 'Liza Hargreaves.' She smiled at him. 'I take it that you're local, then?'

He nodded. 'You picked up the French guy, didn't you?'

'That's right.' She paused. 'Do you know how long the meeting's going to last, Greg?'

'No idea. A few hours, I should think.' He grimaced. 'And they don't have much reading material round here, do they?'

Oh yes, they do, Liza thought; she didn't disagree with him aloud, though, not wanting to make the point. She knew that not everyone appreciated business magazines – unless they were in the industry themselves, and even then, some people found the trade journals just too heavy-going. She merely shrugged, knowing that he'd take her non-committal answer as agreeing with him.

'Do you play cards?' he asked.

'Not for money,' Liza said, catching the gleam in his eye and reading it accurately. 'And I'm afraid I don't know how to play much more than snap.'

He smiled. 'I could always teach you. We could play blackjack, if you like.' He looked at her speculatively. 'They'll be at least two hours. Would you like another cup of coffee, before I explain the rules to you?'

Liza was secretly amused. Obviously, he was incredibly bored, and playing cards was the only thing he could think of to pass the time. He was obviously eager for her to join him, hence the offer of making her a coffee. She would have bet money that he didn't usually offer to make a woman a drink, unless it was alcoholic. 'Thank you.'

'How do you take it?'

'White, no sugar, please.' Though the coffee was foul enough for her to be tempted to add sugar, to mask the taste.

'Coming up.' A few moments later, Greg reappeared, carrying two cups of coffee. He handed one to her, then took a pack of cards from his jacket pocket. 'It's quite easy,' he said. 'I'm sure you'll pick it up very quickly.'

Liza listened attentively as he explained the rules to her. He dealt the cards, and won the first three hands. She won the fourth, and he smiled at her. 'I told you that you'd pick it up,' he said. 'It's easy, once you start.' He tipped his head on one side. 'I don't suppose you fancy playing for some stakes?'

She shook her head. 'Like I told you, I don't play for money.'

'How about something else, then?' he suggested.

'Such as?'

He smiled broadly. 'If you win, I take off an article of clothing. If I win, you take something off. And you have to take off the piece of clothing the other person tells you to.'

Liza chuckled to herself. She'd thought, a few minutes before, that he'd been trying to look up her skirt. Now, she knew it for sure. 'What you're suggesting, then, is that we play strip blackjack, then?' she asked.

He nodded.

'And supposing the meeting finishes early?'

He shrugged. 'I don't think it will. I've chauffeured for one of these chaps before, and I think they're all set for a long session. In fact, I think they have a buffet lunch prepared.'

'What about us?' she asked.

'There's some for us, too, in the kitchen.' Greg spread his hands. 'Look, if it makes you feel better, we could play in one of the offices, rather than in reception.'

Greg, she thought, needed a lesson. He was obviously convinced that he was going to win: hence his offer of playing in one of the other offices, to spare her blushes when he stripped her. She smiled to herself. What he hadn't realised was that she picked things up very quickly indeed. She'd already noticed that when he thought he had a winning hand, he had a habit of drumming the little finger of his left hand on his knee. 'Okay,' she said.

He beamed at her, and stood up. Liza appraised him briefly, as he beckoned to her to follow him. She'd guessed his height correctly, and she liked the way he moved with an easy grace. Very nice, she thought. And there were no strings attached. She was a free agent. So if anything did happen between them, she only had to answer to herself.

Greg opened the door to one of the offices. It was a typical office, anonymous and bland. Even the pictures hanging on the wall were evidence of corporate taste, rather than personal. This place obviously believed in a clear desk policy – and the occupant of this particular office stuck to it rigidly, not even having a photo frame on the desk. Even the plant in the corner, and the up-lighter, owed more to corporate decoration than anything else. No doubt all the other rooms on this floor looked identical, Liza thought. Boring and samey.

He pulled two of the soft leather chairs up to the desk, and shuffled the cards. Then he offered the pack to her. 'Do you want to deal?' he asked.

She nodded. 'That's fine by me.' She shuffled the pack again, and dealt the first hand. Greg won, and opted that Liza should take off her jacket. Three hands later, she was still losing, and had removed both shoes, and her skirt.

Greg was beginning to look more than confident. Liza dealt the cards, and won the next four hands in a row, to his surprise and discomfort. He removed his jacket, shoes and trousers. She won the next two hands, too, saying that a man wearing just socks looked terrible; he glowered suspiciously at her. 'Are you sure that you've never played blackjack before?' he asked.

'Quite sure,' she said softly. She won the next two hands, too, and informed Greg that she wanted him to remove his tie and shirt. She raised one eyebrow. 'Well, well. This is becoming interesting, isn't it?'

He looked slightly sulky. Obviously, this hadn't been part of his plan. She smiled at him, and promptly lost the next hand, removing her shirt at his request. He stared at her breasts, which were barely covered by her lacy bra, and Liza was half-amused at how the outline of his cock, through his boxer shorts, grew very obviously and very quickly larger. She won the next hand, and Greg, gritting his teeth, had to remove his boxer shorts. He looked good, she thought. His body was well toned, and he obviously worked out on a regular basis.

'Hm. Very interesting,' she purred.

Greg flushed. 'I don't know what you mean by that.'

Liza smiled, and dealt again. Again, she won the hand. She spread her hands. 'Well,' she said. 'Now what do we do? You don't have anything left to take off.' She linked her hands behind her head, and crossed her legs, leaning back in the leather chair. 'Perhaps,' she suggested, 'we could move on to playing for forfeits.'

'What kind of forfeits?' He was looking decidedly sulky, but she noticed that his cock twitched at her suggestion.

'Well,' she said slowly, 'perhaps you could do something for me.'

'Such as?'

She made her decision. Sitting there, looking at his glorious body and seeing how aroused he was, was also arousing her, making her sex pool. Her labia were warm and puffy; and, as she had told herself earlier, she was a free agent. True, she had slept with Alain, the previous day, and would be sharing his bed again, that evening, but he didn't own her. And as for Bryn . . . Well, he wasn't interested in her – or, at least, he would rather die than admit to being attracted to her. She smiled. She'd be a fool not to take advantage of this. Greg had a good body, and if he didn't know how to use it, she certainly did. She liked good sex, and the game of cards had put her in just the right mood for it. 'I want you to use your mouth on me.'

Six

He looked at her in shock. 'My mouth?'

'Yes.' Liza looked levelly at him. 'I assume you do know how to please a woman that way?'

His face tightened with anger. 'I should have known that you were a bitch.'

Liza gave him a cool look. 'As opposed to a bitch on heat, which you would have preferred?'

'I . . .' He suddenly looked very young, and very vulnerable. She felt almost sorry for him: but he had needed to be taught a lesson. Perhaps, in future, he wouldn't treat any woman driver he came across with such disdain.

'Greg, you were the one who suggested this game,' she reminded him softly. 'If you're not prepared to lose as well as win, maybe you shouldn't play.'

He licked his lower lip. 'I know.'

'And you owe me a forfeit,' she told him. 'That was part of the deal.' She uncrossed her legs, took her hands from behind her head, and placed her hands on her knees. 'I'm not going to bite you, Greg.' She was tempted to add, 'Unless you want me to, that is,' but decided against it. She didn't think that he'd appreciate it, somehow.

He flushed. 'Now you're taking the piss out of me.'

She shook her head. 'I'm perfectly serious. I want you to use your mouth on me. Now.'

He stared at her breasts. Her nipples were hardened, growing darker, betraying her arousal, and were very clearly visible through her bra. The mocking light in her eyes had gone, replaced with what he recognised as desire. Slowly, he dropped to his knees, and crawled the short space between their chairs. He knelt between her parted legs, and placed the flat of his palms against her inner thighs, stroking the soft flesh above the welts of her stockings.

He bent his head, trailing his mouth from her knee across her inner thigh. Liza closed her eyes, leaning back in the chair and widening the gap between her thighs still further. To her surprise, he didn't head straight for her quim; instead, he let his mouth drift upwards, over her abdomen. She arched her back, and he undid her bra, dropping the lacy garment onto the floor beside her. He licked the soft underside of her breasts, making her shiver; she gasped as his mouth closed over one nipple, drawing on the hard peak. His hand came up to caress her other breast, squeezing it slightly, and playing with the nipple.

She couldn't help a soft moan escaping her; it felt so good, so very good. She loved it when a man worked on her breasts, moving from the gentlest caresses to something fiercer. In response to her murmur of pleasure, he sucked harder at her nipple, grazing the soft tissues very lightly with his teeth. Her hands came up to tangle in his hair, massaging his scalp and urging him on. She felt him smile against her skin, and then he gradually moved lower again, settling between her thighs. He hooked his finger into the gusset of her knickers, pulling it to one side, and she shifted as she felt him breathe along her quim.

'Yes, oh yes, do it,' she murmured softly. 'Do it to me now, Greg. Lick me. Make me come.'

At last, she felt the slow sweep of his tongue against her musky flesh, parting her labia. He found her clitoris, and drew the small bud of flesh into his mouth, sucking it. She moaned, and he sucked harder; at the same time, she felt him slide a finger between her labia, pushing it deep into her sex. She flexed her internal muscles around his finger, and she felt him laugh against her intimate flesh – a laugh of pure pleasure. Then he began to work her properly, adding a second and a third finger, his hand pistoning rapidly back and forth, and his tongue flicking rapidly across her clitoris, until her orgasm splintered through her, taking her by surprise.

He lifted his head, and smiled at her. She stroked his face, and he took her hand, kissing the palm. 'Liza.' His voice was husky with desire. 'Let's do it properly. Let's go all the way, right to the limit.'

It was an offer she couldn't refuse. She made no protest as he pulled her gently from the chair, so that she straddled him. She could feel the length and girth of his cock against her quim; he smiled again, easing one hand between their bodies, and lifted her slightly, so that he could fit the tip of his sex to hers. Then he let her sink down gently onto the thick shaft.

Liza slid her hands around his neck, and began to move. It wasn't a position she'd ever used before – her lover kneeling, and her squatting over him, straddling his cock – but it was one she discovered that she liked, very much. Every time she moved, her already sensitised clitoris was stimulated even more.

Greg cupped her breasts, stroking them and kneading them, playing with her nipples, and bringing Liza nearer and nearer to another climax. She jammed her mouth over his, and his lips parted, letting her slide her tongue into his mouth. She kissed him hard, all the time continuing to move over him. His hands slid over her abdomen, then curved round over her hips, so that he could cup her buttocks. He began to help her move, urging her to move harder and faster over him. Her cry of pleasure was lost in his mouth as her quim contracted sharply round his cock; he held her close, kissing her gently, and then finally stroking her hair as she buried her head in his shoulder.

'What a forfeit,' he said softly as his cock slid from her.

Liza's eyes sparkled with a mixture of amusement and mischief. 'You knew that it was going to happen – or, at least, something like that. That's why you suggested playing strip blackjack, in the first place.'

He grinned. 'It was too good a chance to waste. A beautiful woman like you, and the afternoon virtually to ourselves. What would you have done, in my position?'

She chuckled. 'I don't think that you need me to tell you that.'

'Well, then.' He stroked her face. 'I'd like to see you again, Liza.'

She shook her head. 'I live in London, remember. You're in Sheffield. I don't think that our paths will cross again, somehow.'

'That would be a pity.' He regarded her closely. 'Was it really the first time you'd ever played blackjack?'

She nodded. 'But I forgot to tell you that I pick things up quickly.'

'You can say that again.' He kissed the tip of her nose. 'You're not a regular chauffeur, are you?'

'I don't know what you mean.'

'Oh come on. The way you talk, the way you dress – it's obvious your clothes aren't chain store stuff. You're pure class – more like the sort of women I drive to places than a driver yourself.'

She spread her hands. 'Do we have to talk about that, right now?'

'Got any better ideas, then?'

She chuckled, curling her fingers round his hardening cock. 'You could say that . . .'

A couple of hours later, when Alain came out of his meeting, Liza and Greg were sitting in the reception, chatting lightly. They had made love twice more: once in the office, with Greg seated comfortably in a chair and Liza straddling him, her legs draped over the arms of the chair and with Greg supporting her movements as she raised and lowered herself over him, and once in the washroom where they had gone to clean themselves up again, with Greg lifting her and balancing her weight against the wall.

Once they'd sated the rush of desire, and set their clothing back to rights, it was impossible to tell that anything had happened between them. To the casual observer, they were merely passing the time by talking, until their clients were ready to leave – unless you looked closely at the sparkle in Liza's eyes and recognised the smile of satisfaction on Greg's face for what it was.

Alain smiled at Liza. 'Okay?' he asked.

She nodded. 'Fine, thanks.' As Greg had mentioned, earlier, there had also been a small buffet prepared for the chauffeurs.

Liza, hungry after her exertions, had wolfed down the smoked salmon canapés and small parcels of filo pastry filled with camembert and redcurrants, while Greg had preferred the more traditional ham rolls and cheese straws. They had ended up feeding each other black grapes and slices of banana, and had nearly made love again – until Liza realised how late it was, making it more likely that they'd be caught in the act. That was something she wasn't prepared to risk.

'Well, I'm ready to go whenever you are,' Alain said.

Liza stood up, and stretched. 'Now's fine by me.' She turned to Greg, holding out her hand. 'Well, it was nice to meet you,' she said.

Greg took her hand, shaking it warmly. 'You, too,' he said. 'Take care.'

If Alain noticed the conspiratorial smile between them, he said nothing. He merely nodded politely to Greg, then left the building.

Liza followed him, replacing her cap on her head at a jaunty angle. 'Where do you need to go, next?' she asked.

'It was a good meeting. I've more or less finished my business for the weekend.' He smiled at her. 'We could go shopping, if you like, or maybe we could take a trip round the Dales, and go for a walk, or something.'

She nodded. 'Actually,' she said, 'I came to Derbyshire on holiday, when I was quite young. I'm pretty sure that there are some caverns, in a village not that far from Bakewell – ones where you can take a boat trip to see the stalagmites and stalactites. Do you fancy having a look round? There's an old castle in the village, too, built not long after the Norman Conquest. It's ruined, of course, but I remember being impressed with it when I was a child. It's at the top of a steep hill, and there's a sheer drop on at least two sides.'

'Yes, I think that I'd like to see your castle.' Alain reached over to remove her cap. 'And I'd prefer you not to wear this, when you're with me.'

'It's standard chauffeur uniform – at least, for *James*,' Liza told him gently. 'Our clients expect it.'

'Even so, I'd prefer this to be a trip as friends, rather than employer and employee.'

'Fair enough.' She grinned at him. 'Though you're still not driving the Jag!'

Alain laughed as she unlocked the passenger door for him, and slid into the seat, stretching out his legs. 'Let's go, then.'

Liza took the A625 from Sheffield and drove them to Castleton, parking not far from the castle itself. 'I thought we could look round the castle, first,' she said. 'Then maybe we can drive a bit further into the gorge, and see the caverns under the cliff.'

He smiled at her. 'Sounds good to me,' he said. They climbed the steep winding path to the castle, and both of them were out of breath by the time that they reached the top. The view was amazing, and they both were transfixed by it, for a while, sitting on the grass and simply enjoying their surroundings. Alain had bought a guide book and, when they'd recovered their breath, they looked round the ruins, peering at the architecture and trying to imagine what the castle had been like, nearly a thousand years before.

Eventually, he ruffled her hair. 'I think that I could do with a cup of your English tea, now,' he told her.

She nodded. 'Sounds good to me.'

They made their way back down the narrow path, avoiding the grazing sheep which scrambled up and down the slope, and walked into the village. It seemed natural for Alain to slide his arm round her shoulders, and for her to slide her arm round his waist. He shortened his stride slightly to match hers, and they wandered happily through the narrow streets, until they found a café.

'I think that this has to be a full blown English cream tea,' she told him. She ordered two full teas, choosing Earl Grey for both of them. He was delighted when their food arrived: tiny cucumber sandwiches, walnut cake, and homemade scones, topped with raspberry jam and thick cream. 'I can see why you get so excited about your traditional tea,' he said, after the first mouthful of scone. 'It's very nice.'

Liza smiled back at him. This, she thought, was turning out to be to one of the most enjoyable assignments she'd ever had – and that included attending the odd marketing jolly, in her previous career. The lack of politics was exhilarating. She could just be herself, without having to worry about acting in the way people expected her to.

When they'd finished tea, they went back to the car, and Liza drove them down through the narrow roads, flanked with steep forbidding granite cliffs and the ubiquitous grazing sheep. She parked in the small car park, and they headed for the cavern tour. Alain was enchanted, both by the fact that it was an underground boat ride, and by the sheer beauty of the natural limestone sculptures.

When the tour was over, and they were outside in bright daylight again, Alain took her hand. 'I'd like to take you out to dinner, tonight,' he said.

She shook her head. 'You don't have to do that.'

He smiled. 'But I want to celebrate,' he said. 'The deal went well, and there's no-one else I can take out.'

She chuckled. 'So I'm second best, am I?' she teased.

Alain recognised her chaffing for what it was, and laughed back. 'What do you think? Come on, let's go home.'

They drove back in companionable silence; when they returned to the cottage, Liza made some coffee, while Alain rang the local wine bar and booked a table for them.

'I haven't brought anything dressy with me,' she said.

'I don't think that the place is that posh,' he reassured her. He sipped his coffee. 'Mm, this is good.'

After they finished their coffee, she had a shower, and changed into a pair of leggings and a silk shirt. She half wished that she'd brought a pearl necklace with her, something to dress up her outfit; as it was, she surveyed herself critically in the mirror, and grimaced. She'd just have to do.

To her disappointment, Alain didn't join her in the bedroom while she was dressing; he waited until she'd come downstairs again, before going up for his own shower. While she was waiting for him, Liza listened to one of his Johnny Halliday CDs, and continued flicking through the book of Rimbaud's poetry that she'd been reading, the evening before.

Alain came down, dressed casually in chinos and another polo-necked sweater. Her eyes travelled over him in appreciation. All he needed was a long black coat and a pair of small round gold-rimmed glasses, and he would look like one of the cosmopolitan intelligentsia – the sort she'd always preferred, before her affair with the younger and slightly less sophisticated Rupert.

With the exception of a certain Bryn Davies, she thought wryly, who still remained a mystery to her. She'd known Bryn for over a month, now, and she still had no more idea of what made him tick – the kind of music he liked, how he spent his free time, even what he liked to eat. Bryn had never once suggested that she joined him for lunch, on one of the rare occasions when he had been in the office; he tended to eat a hastily grabbed sandwich at his desk, and she hadn't dared to ask him out to lunch, in case he thought that she was trying to come on to him.

Which, if she was honest with herself, she would very much like to do. Though she knew that she had no chance, so there was no point in even trying. She had to content herself with the occasional erotic dream about him which left her waking with her hand working between her legs.

'Penny for them?' Alain queried.

She shook her head. 'Nothing important.' Certainly nothing that he would want to hear.

Alain had already told her that the wine bar was in the centre of town, and it was a nice enough evening for them to walk the relatively short distance. He ordered a bottle of good Chardonnay, and they sat down at one of the small tables. The place was a cross between a conservatory and a barn conversion, with plenty of plants covering the beamed walls and winding up the wrought-iron trellises. Soft rock was playing in the background, which Liza recognised as early Dire Straits, one of her favourite albums; she smiled, appreciating the atmosphere of the place.

The menu turned out to be another surprise, offering an intriguing mix of cuisines. In the end, she chose an asparagus, smoked salmon and goat's cheese tartlet, followed by duck. Alain chose the hot buttered toast and paté, admitting to a real weakness for it, and sole stuffed with prawns, served with Thai rice and a lemon grass coulis. The food, when it arrived, tasted as good as it had sounded, and Liza enjoyed every last mouthful. They both finished up with a plate of cheese and tiny water biscuits, followed by strong dark coffee and bitter mints; Liza sighed in satisfaction as she pushed her coffee cup away.

'Thank you,' she said. 'That was delicious.'

'My pleasure.' He smiled back at her. 'Shall we take a stroll by the river, before going back?'

She nodded. 'That'd be nice.'

Alain paid the bill, with what looked suspiciously to Liza like a gold credit card, and then they wandered down to the river, their arms wrapped round each other. Neither of them felt the need to speak; Liza relaxed, enjoying herself.

Eventually, they headed back to the cottage. 'I haven't finished celebrating, yet,' Alain told her. He went to the fridge, and extracted a bottle of champagne, opening it expertly without spilling a drop, and took two glasses from the cupboard. His eyes glittered as he looked at her. 'Let's go to bed,' he suggested.

She nodded, and followed him up the stairs. He switched on the bedside lamp, and placed the champagne and the glasses on the bedside cabinet. Then he closed the curtains, and walked over to Liza, taking her in his arms. He bent his head, touching her lips very gently with his own; his kisses were light and gentle, and she couldn't help responding to him, opening her mouth to let him deepen the kiss.

Alain slid his hands under the hem of her shirt, stroking her back. 'Your skin feels as soft as the silk,' he told her huskily. He continued to rub her back, the pads of his fingertips moving in tiny erotic circles. She found herself growing more and more aroused, even though he hadn't yet touched her intimately. Her breasts were beginning to swell and her nipples were tightening, the hard rosy peaks of flesh almost hurting with desire. She wanted him to touch them, taste them, take away the ache with his lips and his tongue and his clever fingers.

She groaned, moving against him, and he chuckled, a deep throaty sound. 'Don't be so impatient, *chérie*,' he chided her gently. 'We have all the time in the world.' Even so, his hands moved round to the front of her shirt, and he began undoing the tiny buttons. He caressed every inch of skin as he uncovered it, and Liza's pupils grew larger with frustrated desire. She wanted to feel him touch her more intimately, bring her to a rapid climax and then start all over again.

Her eyelids felt heavy, and she closed her eyes. She tipped her head back, and lifted her chest slightly; Alain chuckled again, and traced the edge of her lacy bra with the tip of his finger. She couldn't help thrusting towards him, and he let his finger drift under the edge of one of the cups of her bra. She gave a groan as his hand slid round to cup her breast, and he caught her nipple between his middle and ring finger, squeezing it gently.

She lifted her hand, covering his and pressing it gently. Alain took the hint, and continued unbuttoning her shirt with his other hand, pushing it off her shoulders and onto the floor. He pulled the cups of her bra down to expose her breasts, her dark nipples in sharp counterpoint to the creamy lace. Then, he dropped to his knees, and pushed his face between her lewdly displayed breasts, breathing in her scent. 'Liza, *chérie*,' he murmured huskily, and took one nipple into his mouth, the tip of his tongue teasing the puckered skin of her areola. She arched against him, and he began to suck harder, making her cry out with pleasure.

He transferred the attentions of his mouth to her other breast, licking the skin and breathing on it so that she wriggled with a mixture of impatience and pleasure, and then drawing fiercely on it. Meanwhile, he continued to tease its twin with his thumb and forefinger.

Her quim felt as though it were on fire, and she longed to feel his mouth against her intimate flesh, cooling her. 'Please, Alain,' she begged. 'Please. I need you to lick me.'

He looked up at her, and smiled. 'Like I said, *chérie*, don't be so impatient.' He resumed his attention to her breasts, licking and stroking and sucking and pinching them gently, until Liza was almost beside herself. With shock, she realised that her internal muscles were contracting sharply. No-one had ever made her come before, just by touching her breasts. 'My God,' she breathed unsteadily.

From the look on his face, she could tell that he knew exactly what had just happened. He grinned at her, pleased with himself, and hooked his thumbs into the waistband of her leggings, drawing them down over her hips. She lifted one foot and then the other, so that he could help her out of her leggings. Then she reached down to him, urging him to his feet. 'You're wearing too much,' she grumbled.

'Do something about it, then,' he told her.

She tugged at the hem of his sweater, and he lifted his arms, letting her pull the garment over his head. She let it drop to the floor, and then she ran her fingers lightly over his broad chest. His chest was covered in a light sprinkling of hair, and the contrast between the crispness of his curly hair and the satiny smoothness of his skin was delightful. His flat button nipples had grown hard, and she teased them with her fingertips, tracing the areolae and then flicking her finger rapidly across their hard centres.

Alain laughed. 'Revenge, *hein*?'

'Something like that,' she said lightly.

She let her hands slide down over his midriff, stroking him and sensitising his skin. Then she undid the button and zipper of his chinos, easing them down over his hips. His cock was already hard, and she could see its thick rigid outline through the thin silk of his boxer shorts. She curled her fingers round his cock, through the boxer shorts, and squeezed gently.

Alain groaned, thrusting his pelvis towards her, and she gave him an impish smile. 'As you said a few minutes ago, *chéri*, don't be so impatient.'

She helped him out of his chinos, taking off his shoes and socks at the same time. Then she dropped to her knees, rubbing her face against his abdomen. His scent was clean, tangy and very masculine, and it turned her on even more. She was unable to resist him, and slowly drew down his boxer shorts. Alain stepped out of the thin garment, and stood before her in full glorious nakedness.

She sat back on her heels and looked at him for a moment, drinking in his body. Although Greg had been very attractive, she thought, he couldn't hold a candle to this man. Alain simply reeked of sophistication and sensuality.

She curled her fingers round his cock again, cupping his balls with her other hand, and bent her head. She made her tongue into a hard point, lapping at his frenum, and he groaned, sliding his fingers into her hair and urging her on wordlessly. She continued lapping at his frenum, then licked the clear bead of fluid which wept from the eye of his cock. He tasted sharp and clean, and she revelled in the taste.

He moaned softly, murmuring endearments which she could only half catch, and she opened her mouth, taking the head of his cock into her mouth, swirling her tongue over his glans. Then she began to suck, moving her head up and down rhythmically and continuing to massage his balls with her hand. A sudden idea struck her, and she smiled to herself, squeezing his cock gently and removing it from her mouth.

She stood up, and Alain looked at her, his dark eyes widening in surprise and concern. 'What's wrong, *chérie*?' he asked.

'Nothing. I'm just a little thirsty.'

She walked over to the bedside cabinet, picking up one of the glasses and taking a sip. The sharp creamy taste of the fizz revealed it to be an exceptionally good bottle. What she had in mind would complement it perfectly, she thought. She came back to join Alain, handing him the glass. He took a sip, and gave it back to her. She knelt down again, taking another mouthful. Unbeknown to Alain, she didn't swallow it; she merely bent her head and resumed her former position, ringing his cock with one hand and stroking his perineum with the other.

Then she opened her mouth over his cock again, bathing his glans in champagne. She pressed her tongue against his skin, bursting the bubbles; he cried out in a mixture of shock, surprise and pleasure. '*Mon Dieu,* Liza . . .'

She swallowed the remaining champagne, and lifted her head again, giving him a wicked smile. 'I thought that you might enjoy that.'

'And how,' he murmured.

She smiled, and took another mouthful of champagne, repeating the action. When the last of the bubbles had burst against his skin, she began to fellate him properly, varying the rhythm and the pressure as she sucked him. She could feel his balls lifting and tightening; then her mouth was filled with warm salty liquid. Alain cried out her name, digging his fingers into her scalp, and she remained where she was, until his cock had stopped twitching. She swallowed every last drop: then knelt back again, tossing her hair back and looking at him.

Alain sank to his knees and kissed her deeply, not bothered about tasting his own juices on her mouth. 'Thank you,' he whispered.

'Pleasure.' Her eyes glittered.

'*Et, maintenant* . . .' He stood up again, and drew her to her feet. Then he removed her knickers, caressing her skin, and unclipped her bra, before lifting her up and placing her on the bed. Her champagne glass was left, forgotten, on the floor; as his cock hardened again, he could only think of sinking deep inside her.

She leaned back against the pillows, and he knelt between her thighs, caressing her skin and moving her legs so that her feet were flat against the mattress and her knees were bent, revealing her quim to him in all its beauty. He stroked her inner thighs, and she shivered at the intense expression of desire on his face. She widened the gap between her thighs, and he parted her labia with the middle and forefingers of one hand, sliding the forefinger of his other hand down his musky cleft.

Liza gave a small murmur of pleasure, closing her eyes and tipping her head back against the pillows. Alain smiled, and continued to caress her, his finger working very gently and very slowly up and down her slippery intimate flesh. She wriggled impatiently, and he rested his thumb on her clitoris, moving it in small circles to arouse the hard bud of flesh still further. She tipped her pelvis up towards him, and he laughed, pushing the tip of his index finger against her sex.

She was still wet from her earlier orgasm and the way he'd just been arousing her, and his finger slid easily into her waiting channel. He began to move his hand very slowly back and forth, and she rocked with him, her rhythm matching his and increasing the friction pleasurably for her. He added a second finger, and a third. To Liza, it felt as though she were being fucked by a short and very thick cock; she revelled in the feeling, rocking even harder against him.

She could feel the beginnings of her orgasm coiling in the soles of her feet, then moving upwards to bubble through her calves, rolling through her thighs, and finally exploding deliciously in her solar plexus. She cried out, her internal muscles spasming sharply round his fingers; he stopped moving, waiting until the aftershocks of her climax had died away before shifting to lie beside her and pulling her into his arms.

He slid his finger along her lower lip, coating it with her own musky nectar; her tongue moved lasciviously over the soft flesh, lapping up the juices, and he smiled in approval. *'Ma belle, ma petite sensuelle,'* he whispered, leaning over to kiss her properly and tasting the muskiness on her lips.

He pressed against her body, and she could feel his renewed erection against her skin. Despite her recent climax, she still wanted to feel him inside her, filling her and stretching her. She slid her arms round his neck, and pressed hard against him; he murmured something, and shifted to kneel between her thighs again. Gently, he stroked his way up one leg, placing it over his shoulder, then followed suit with her other leg, so that she was reared up to accept him.

He curled his fingers round his cock, rubbing the round tip up and down the slippery cleft; Liza moaned, flexing her quim, and finally he fitted his cock to the entrance of her sex and pushed. Clasping her ankles, his thumbs rubbing the sensitive hollows of her skin, he began to thrust. It felt good, so very, very good; she couldn't help crying out as he thrust deeper and harder, the position he was holding her in meaning that he penetrated her more deeply than before.

He brought her to a rapid climax, and another; then, she felt him stiffen, and his cock twitched deep inside her. Gently, he lowered her legs back down onto the bed, and she wrapped them round his waist, holding him down inside her. He buried his face in her shoulder, kissing her lightly; they lay locked together for a long while, until he finally slipped from her and rolled over onto his side.

'The very best way to celebrate something,' he murmured softly, reaching over to pick up the other glass of champagne and handing it to her.

She took a sip. There was only one thing she could say to that: *'Salut.'*

She handed the glass back to him, and he echoed her toast, sipping the wine. *'Ma petite chou,'* he said softly. 'I think I'll use your firm whenever I'm in England.'

'Good. And recommend us to your friends, too.'

'But of course.' His eyes glittered. 'Though I'd rather reserve your more personal services for me alone . . .'

'You must have made quite an impression with our Monsieur Joubert,' Bryn said.

Liza looked up from her desk. 'How do you mean?'

'Well,' Bryn said, 'he's recommended us to three other firms. We've had quite an influx of work, thanks to him.' He tipped his head on one side, his eyes glittering with a light that Liza didn't quite trust herself to interpret. 'I don't know if I dare ask what you did to him.'

'I don't mix business and pleasure,' Liza said crisply. 'Like I told you, I speak French, which helped, and he was impressed with the way he was treated. And, by that, I mean with courtesy, discretion, and friendliness. I'm a professional.' She returned to her paperwork.

Bryn watched her closely before a moment. There was more to it than met the eye, he was sure, but Liza had more than taken the firm's motto to heart. There was no way that she would tell him if anything had actually happened between her and Joubert.

He wondered briefly if she had seduced Joubert. He hadn't actually met Joubert himself, merely spoken to the man on the phone, but he'd been left with the impression that the Frenchman was very cultured, and very sophisticated. The kind of man who would attract a woman like Liza. And if she had seduced Joubert, her lips travelling across his skin . . .

Bryn shook himself. These were the last kind of thoughts he should be having about his new business partner. He didn't want to get involved, in that sense. Not after Jane. He'd learned, the hard way, that women were trouble. Not that he was celibate – he was far from immune to the charms of an attractive woman, and he enjoyed making love – but he didn't go in for serious relationships any more.

He made a mental note to add bromide to his tea, the next time he thought of Liza undressing, taking off her prissy business suit and stripping off her silk and lace underwear for her appreciative male audience of one. He couldn't afford to have those kind of thoughts about her. Although he still couldn't help wondering what it would be like to touch her hair, to unbutton her shirt and touch her skin with his hands, his mouth . . .

Scowling, he shook himself and turned back to the paperwork on his own desk.

Seven

Liza looked through the books, frowning. Despite the influx of work from Alain's business associates, the finances of *James* were still a bit shaky. They could do with a cash injection. The main problem, she thought, was their cashflow. They'd had to pay out for some expensive parts for one of the cars, recently; they couldn't afford to keep the machine off the road but, at the same time, they also couldn't really afford to do the repairs. Not with their bank balance the way it was.

Everyone was working flat out, and there was no way that she'd consider letting any of the staff go. Apart from the fact that they had more than enough work to keep everyone busy, she knew that paying redundancy money wouldn't help their immediate problem. Far from it. She sighed. She was only drawing a small salary herself, living off her savings; she knew that Bryn was doing something similar, although she didn't think that he actually had much in the way of savings. He was just doing what he could to keep the business afloat.

'What's the matter?' Bryn asked, coming into the office and seeing the serious look on her face.

'Money,' Liza said grimly. 'I've just been going through our bank statement, and it isn't good news.'

He shrugged. 'It'll pick up. We've got plenty of work coming in.'

'Mm, but we can only consider it to be work if it's profitable. There's the small matter of marginal costs to take into account. If it costs us too much to take on a job, we'd be better off turning it down – unless it's a loss-leader, of course,' she said thoughtfully. 'A sprat to catch a mackerel.'

He chuckled. 'You know, I really didn't take you seriously at first. Now, I'm beginning to think that you're more obsessed with the business than I am!'

She didn't rise to the bait. 'Our real problem is cashflow,' she told him. 'Some of our clients just aren't paying up on time, and it takes three snotty letters before they pay their monthly account. That's taking time and money to write to them that we just can't afford – let alone the interest on our overdraft, when they don't pay on time. I think that we're going to have to change the way we do the accounts.'

'How do you mean?'

'We'll have to move back to giving fourteen days' credit, not thirty. And we'd better start charging late payment fees, as well.'

'Oh, that'll really please our best clients.' His voice was sharp with sarcasm.

She spread her hands. 'Okay, then we'll hit them with the big bill up front, and give discounts for early payment. It's the same thing, though I suppose that it might be more palatable to our clients. You're right – people like to think that they're getting a bargain.'

'And?' Bryn could see from her face that she was thinking about more than just adjusting their accounts payment methods.

'We need to negotiate an increased overdraft, in the meantime,' she said.

Bryn shook his head. 'The last time I saw the bank manager, we had a huge row. He halved our overdraft, the following day. So don't ask me to have a word with him, or we'll have to change banks!'

She smiled. 'I wasn't going to ask you to do it. I thought that I might try a bit of feminine charm.'

'You mean, you're going to vamp him?' He raised an eyebrow. 'I'd like to be a fly on the wall. Our dear bank manager is–' He stopped, suddenly remembering who he was talking to. Liza liked challenges, and it was beginning to sound as though he were offering her one. Besides, he might just have a personality clash with David Brennan. It wasn't fair to prejudice Liza against the man from the outset, and ruin their chances of maybe improving their relationship with the bank.

'Our dear bank manager is what?'

He grimaced. 'It doesn't matter. Let's just say that we don't exactly see eye to eye. He's not my favourite person, and I'm definitely not his.'

Liza shrugged. 'Maybe he might get on better with me. I'll book an appointment for tomorrow morning – if you don't need me to do anything else, that is.'

'No, that's fine by me.' He smiled wryly. 'I'll just wish you luck.'

He didn't need to add, 'You'll need it.' It was written all over his face. Liza wondered just what their bank manager was like, that he should rub her partner up the wrong way. Bryn got on well with the rest of their clients and suppliers; maybe he just had a hang-up about finances.

She rang the bank, and arranged a meeting with David Brennan. Then she swiftly typed a letter to confirm the appointment, adding the list of letters after her name. She rarely did that, but she had a feeling that if David Brennan was as difficult as Bryn had hinted, she'd need him to know her qualifications, so that he'd take her seriously.

The following morning saw Liza at the bank. She'd deliberately worn the kind of outfit that she used to wear at Fitchett's: an expensive tailored suit, teamed with a silk shirt, high-heeled handmade Italian shoes, a designer handbag, and understated but obviously expensive jewellery. She was also carrying her soft black leather briefcase, and she'd made sure that her make-up was flawless. She smiled to herself. If Bryn could see her like this . . . Her smile faded. It probably wouldn't make any difference, in any case. He regarded her as his business partner, and nothing more. Hell would freeze over before she could change that.

'Ms Hargreaves?' The receptionist's voice broke into Liza's thoughts.

Liza looked up. 'Yes?'

'Mr Brennan will see you now. If you'd like to follow me?'

She nodded, and followed the receptionist down the narrow corridor. The receptionist knocked on a heavy oak door; at the sharp 'Come in!', she opened the door. 'Mr Brennan, Ms Hargreaves from *James* is here to see you.' She smiled nervously at Liza, ushering her into the room.

Liza surveyed the room swiftly. David Brennan, she thought, was one of the old school: one who believed in status, judging by the leather chair with arms, the large desk, and the expensive-looking brass desklamp. He wasn't the kind who would be happy in a modern open-plan office, or in a non-status organisation where everyone had the same kind of desk and chair, regardless of their position in the firm. She appraised him briefly. He wasn't that much older than she was, so he must have been brought up with the same kind of business training that she had had. So his love of status had to stem from an inadequate personality, she thought wryly.

He was the archetypal nerdy bank manager, a comic stereotype. He was thin and not particularly tall, with small eyes hidden behind steel-rimmed round glasses, thinning blond hair, and what looked like a slight touch of dandruff on his dark suit. He was the kind who would never have been picked for a sports team, but she didn't think somehow that he'd have the sweet personality that often went with a more bookish disposition.

'Ms Hargreaves. Do sit down.'

He indicated to a chair in front of his desk; Liza had to stop herself laughing when she realised that the chair was deliberately lower than his. It would mean that she had to look up to him. Maybe he thought that it was clever psychology, having clients sitting in an inferior position; Liza, who preferred doing business on equal terms and with someone she could respect, didn't think that at all. But she made no comment, and simply sat down.

'You said in your letter that you wanted to discuss an overdraft facility.'

She nodded. 'That's right. I'm Bryn Davies' new business partner. My grandfather owned half of the firm, but left it to me, on his death. I've been looking for a new challenge for a while, so I thought that it was the right opportunity for me.'

He looked at her. 'And what makes you think that you need an increased overdraft facility?'

'Because I want to expand the business,' Liza said. 'One of the things I want to do is to change our cashflow position.

We'll be changing the way we do the accounts, offering a shorter credit period; in the meantime, we need to make repairs to our capital equipment – without which, we simply can't function. So I'd like an increased overdraft facility for three months, please.'

He rubbed his chin. 'And why should I grant that?'

'Because,' Liza said sweetly, wanting to hit him, 'I'm sure that you're a man who can recognise business enterprise.'

'There's a recession.'

She shook her head. 'Consumer confidence is rising. We're inundated with work – and it's getting busier.'

'It could be a temporary blip.'

'I don't think so.'

'And you're an expert in economics, are you, Ms Hargreaves?'

Her eyes glittered with anger. The supercilious little bastard. Who the hell did he think he was? 'Perhaps I should have sent you my CV,' she said quietly. 'Before I joined *James*, I worked for Fitchett's, as a market research manager.' David Brennan didn't need to know that the word 'assistant' had been in her job title. What she was telling him was true enough. 'I think that I'm more than qualified to comment on economic trends.'

'I see.'

'Well,' Liza said, 'if you're not going to give us the overdraft, then I'm sure that we can find a bank which has equal positive attitude to small businesses. One which will give us the financial backing we need.'

'Are you threatening me?'

Too late, Liza remembered what Bryn had started to tell her. She could see now why he hadn't hit it off with David Brennan. She gritted her teeth. This calls for charm, she thought – charm which she didn't particularly feel like using on a slimy, patronising jerk like Brennan. But she had to do it, for *James*' sake. 'Of course not. I believe in exploring all options – don't you?' She forced one of her warmest smiles to her face, hoping that he wasn't perceptive enough to see that it didn't reach her eyes.

'Naturally, we have to assess each risk on merit.'

'Naturally,' she agreed. To disguise her impatience, she

shifted in the chair, recrossing her legs; David Brennan watched her closely, his eyes flickering slightly behind his glasses. She registered with sudden shock that he was interested in her, in a sexual sense. The way she'd crossed her legs – although it had been perfectly demure, rather than a blatant come-on like the infamous Sharon Stone scene in the movie – had actually turned him on. She could almost see it in his face, how he was wondering exactly what she was wearing under her skirt.

Her mind worked quickly. It was an advantage, one that she could use to make him agree to help with the overdraft. She knew that she had the figures in her briefcase to back up her plans, so it wasn't as though she were trying to corrupt the bank manager to help with a scam. This was a genuine business deal, one which would be good for both them and for the bank. It just might need a little helping hand. Although the man set her teeth on edge, she was prepared to do whatever she had to do, to help the business. And a small hope flickered within her that this might be just the thing she needed to help her crack Bryn's defences.

She made the decision, and gave David Brennan her best come-hither smile. He shifted slightly in his chair, and she hid a smile. Obviously, he had an erection, and he was trying to get himself comfortable again. Well, when she'd finished with him, he'd be very uncomfortable indeed. She recrossed her legs, this time a little more blatantly, and leaned forward slightly. If only her shirt wasn't so demure; if only she'd left the top button undone, so that he could glance down the opening of her shirt and see the shadow of her cleavage. Still, he would get the message. 'Mr Brennan,' she purred. 'Or may I call you David? I'm much happier doing business on first-name terms. It makes things seem somehow more–' she paused deliberately, licking her lower lip '–civilised, don't you think?'

'Er – yes.'

His response was more a cough than speech; Liza smiled to herself. She was having just the effect she'd hoped for. She shuffled the chair forwards, so that she could lean on his desk. 'David. I have all the figures with me. I've done a cashflow projection for the next six months on three different bases: last month's work level, this month's work level, and the extrapolated trends. I think you'll agree with me that the figures are very . . . interesting.'

Again, he coughed; although Liza had been talking about figures on a piece of paper, she knew that he'd translated it as her own figure.

'Would you like to see them?' 'Them' meaning her papers; or maybe her breasts.

'Yes.'

She smiled. 'It's so warm in here. Would you mind if I removed my jacket?'

'Not at all.'

His face had grown redder; she hid her smile, and removed her jacket, hanging it neatly on the back of her chair. Then she undid the top button of her shirt, and sat down again. She bent down to open her briefcase and extract her papers, knowing as she did so that he would be able to see down the neck of her shirt, see the soft swell of her cleavage. Then, with another of those come-hither smiles, she sat up again, and placed the papers on the desk between them. 'Take a look,' she invited huskily.

He swallowed, and began to shift through the papers. Liza waited for a moment, then stood up, and walked round to his side of the desk. He looked up at her, his eyes widening.

'I thought that it might be helpful if we were sitting on the same side. It's so tiresome, trying to read upside down, don't you think?'

'I . . . Yes.'

'Exactly.' She smiled at him, and tapped one well-manicured nail on the top sheet of figurework. 'As you can see, if we're cautious and keep to last month's workflow and last month's accounting methods, we'll be in the red. If we use my proposed accounting methods, we'll just about break even.'

'I see.'

She turned over to the next sheet, and drew her finger along the bottom line. 'If we stay at this month's workflow, we'll be doing better.'

'Yes.'

His voice was strangled; Liza looked surreptitiously at him, then smiled to herself. Yes, this was going to work. She placed her hand over his, squeezing gently. 'David. Trust me. I know exactly what I'm doing. And I don't make mistakes.'

He looked up at her, flushing; she smiled again, and shifted to sit on the edge of his desk. She kept her hand over his, and removed his glasses with her other hand, deftly opening the drawer of his desk and placing the glasses inside. 'I'd hate these to be damaged,' she said softly.

'Ms Hargreaves–'

'My friends call me Liza,' she told him, her voice at its most sensual and husky. 'And I think we're going to be friends, David. Very good friends.' Luckily, the blinds at the window were drawn, she thought; she'd hate anyone to witness what she was just about to do.

'Ms Hargreaves . . . Liza . . . I–'

'Sh. This is just between you and me.' She pressed the top of her forefinger against his lips to silence him. She winked at him, then released his hand, climbing off the desk and walking over to his door. She locked it from the inside, then came back to stand in front of his desk.

She unzipped her skirt, letting it fall to the floor. Her shirt came down to the top of her thighs; she swayed slightly in front of him, smiling, then slowly unbuttoned her shirt, shrugging it off her shoulders. Then she walked round to his side of the desk, and stood in front of him, wearing only a white lace bra, a pair of matching knickers, and a pair of black lace-topped hold-up stockings. 'David,' she said huskily, running her tongue along her lower lip.

He was visibly shaken. 'I – I think that you should get dressed now, Ms Hargreaves. We – we'll both pretend that this hasn't happened.'

She let her gaze travel down his body. Despite his bluster, it was obvious that he was aroused. His eyes were glittering, there was a dark flush across his cheekbones, and the groin of his trousers was suddenly very tight, betraying his erection. She smiled again. 'Why? When we can enjoy ourselves?'

'This isn't the way the bank does business.'

It's not the way I usually do business, either, Liza thought, but she merely smiled. 'Business? No, this isn't business. We're merely oiling the wheels of commerce, getting to know each other a little better. Because I think that you'd like to get to know me, David, wouldn't you?'

He made a last-ditch attempt to be the pompous little businessman he usually was. 'This is completely unprofessional.'

'Honey,' she said silkily, 'I'm very professional, in everything I do.'

His eyes widened as he digested her words and their implication. 'This is a set-up, isn't it? Just tell me who paid you–'

'No-one paid me to do anything,' she said. 'I'm not a kissagram or a stripogram. I'm a businesswoman, I want an increased overdraft facility, and I want you to take my proposals seriously.'

'How can I take your proposal seriously, when–' He swallowed, silenced, as she reached over and removed his jacket, letting it drop to the floor, then undid his tie.

'When I'm undressing you? Oh, David.' Her voice was a caress that she didn't really feel. 'Let yourself go.'

'I—'

'Sh.' She let his tie drop on top of his jacket, then undid the buttons of his shirt, letting her fingers slide over his skin. He didn't feel as good as Alain, or Greg the chauffeur: in fact, he wasn't her usual type at all. She liked her men with brains and a little brawn as well; David Brennan probably took no more exercise than walking between his car and his desk, and his muscle tone was non-existent. His skin was pasty, almost, and his chest was virtually hairless; Liza swallowed hard, and pretended that Bryn was there, in front of her, and she was making love to him in the *James* office – which was still untidy, but which had a damn sight more character than the corporate and almost clinical office she was really standing in.

She finished taking off his shirt, and let it drop to the floor. She didn't care that it would crease; if anything, she thought, it would be amusing to see the reaction of the receptionist, seeing David Brennan so crumpled after his meeting with Liza Hargreaves. No doubt this was the first time that a client had had the upper hand with him; and, she thought, she was going to enjoy every minute of it.

She took his hands, then, pulling him to his feet, then slid her arms round his neck and pulled him across to her, jamming her mouth over his. He stood in complete shock, unable to move. It felt weird to be kissing someone who wasn't much taller than her, Liza thought. Though at least he didn't have bad breath, to go with the dandruff.

She thought of Bryn, and what it would be like to kiss him; letting her imagination run riot, and pretending that it was her business partner who stood in front of her, she began to nibble David's lower lip, taking tiny erotic bites from his skin which had him helplessly opening his mouth to her, letting her explore him with her tongue.

Almost nervously, he slid his hands down her back, pulling her into his body. She could feel his erection against her pubis; he wasn't as big as her previous lovers, but she knew that size was less important than the knowledge of what to do with it. And she knew exactly what she was going to do with David Brennan's cock.

She broke the kiss, holding his gaze with hers. Then, slowly, she brought her hands down to his belt, unbuckling it and then undoing the button of his trousers. As she eased the zip down, then drew the material over his hips, she let her hand graze against his penis; he shivered, his mouth opening and his tongue moistening his lower lip.

You want this, and you'll give me exactly what I want, when I want it, Liza thought, fighting to keep a triumphant smile from her lips. She didn't want to go too far and wreck this. Not now, when she'd had to work so hard.

Silently, she helped him out of his trousers, then pulled down his plain white underpants. She dropped to her knees, easing off his shoes and his socks; then stood up again, giving him a smouldering look. His clear desk policy was going to stand her in very good stead; she tucked her papers into the blotter on his desk, then dropped the blotter onto the floor.

David said nothing, as if he still couldn't believe what was happening: that he was standing in front of her, naked, while she was touching him. She smiled, and slid her fingers under the edge of her bra, pushing the cups down so that her breasts were revealed to him. She stroked the soft undersides, pushing her breasts together and up to deepen her cleavage, and rubbed her areolae until her nipples hardened, becoming dark rosy peaks. Then she hooked her thumbs into the elastic of her knickers, slowly pulling them down. She turned round, bending over so that he could have a clear view of her quim as she removed her knickers, and she heard his strangled gasp of pleasure.

If only, she thought, it were Bryn standing there. And if it had been her partner, she would have given him a show to blow his mind, before giving him the best sex he'd ever had in his life. She kicked her knickers across the floor, then hoisted herself onto the bank manager's desk, sitting with her legs wide apart. 'Sit down,' she commanded quietly.

He did so, his gaze fixed on her exposed crotch.

She smiled, thinking of Bryn, and slid one hand between her legs, resting the heel of her palm on her mound of Venus. Then she let her fingers fan out over her quim, hiding it from his view for a moment, and then let her middle finger dip between her labia. She rested her other hand on his desk, leaning back slightly, and began to rub her quim. Had she been concentrating on David alone, she wouldn't have been aroused; but thinking of Bryn had already made her wet.

What she was doing was the archetypal male fantasy. Masturbating in front of a man, pleasuring herself before her audience of one. She wasn't sure just how much further she'd have to go with David Brennan, to get him to see her viewpoint, but she was prepared to go all the way, if she had to. She continued rubbing herself, slicking the musky juices of her arousal over the hard nub of her clitoris, and tipped her head back, her breathing quickening as her excitement grew. Suddenly, her internal muscles contracted sharply, and she came, giving a small sigh of pleasure.

She opened her eyes again, looking at David; he was staring at her, mesmerised. He was just where she wanted him. A little further, and he'd agree to almost anything she said. 'Touch me,' she commanded softly.

For a heart-stopping moment, she thought that he was

going to refuse; then he stood up, sliding his hand between her legs and drawing one finger the full length of her musky slit. Then he drew his finger across her nipples, smearing them with her nectar, before bending his head to take one nipple into his mouth.

Liza's eyes widened with shock. She hadn't expected him to be so inventive. Either he was a better and more experienced lover than she'd given him credit for, or he'd read widely: she wasn't sure which. She held her breath for a moment, and then felt him stroke her inner thighs, gentling her. She closed her eyes. This was just what she could imagine Bryn doing with her.

Slowly, he pushed her back against the desk, widening the gap between her thighs. He caressed her midriff, moving up to stroke her breasts and roll her nipples between his thumbs and forefingers; then she felt him fit the tip of his cock to the entrance of her vagina, pushing deep inside her.

She had to make an effort not to cry out Bryn's name; she kept her eyes tightly shut, thinking of Bryn's handsome face and imagining what he'd look like in passion. David continued to push into her; she flexed her muscles around his cock, pulling in tight as he withdrew, and opening herself as he thrust back in. She wrapped her legs round his waist, drawing him closer to her, and he continued to caress her breasts, concentrating on one nipple and then the other. Then, at last, she felt the familiar rolling warmth of her climax spread from the soles of her feet to her calves, to her thighs, and then a glorious splintering explosion in her solar plexus. The contractions of her quim around his cock brought him to his own orgasm; he gave a cry, and his body stiffened as he poured his release into her.

When the aftershock of her orgasm had died away, Liza unlocked her legs from round his waist. As he withdrew from her; she sat up, and smiled. Had it been Bryn in front of her, she wouldn't have stopped, there. She would have changed places with him, pushing him back across the hard oak and straddling him, riding him to another climax; but she thought that she'd gone far enough with the bank manager.

Quietly, she slid from the desk, and dressed swiftly. Her

shirt was slightly crumpled, but she knew that no-one would notice it under her jacket. David looked slightly more crumpled, she thought, as she watched him knot his tie; she smiled to herself, wondering what the receptionist would make of it. But then, who cared, as long as David Brennan gave her what she wanted?

'Well,' she said softly, 'perhaps you could look at the paperwork, and fax me to let me know when we can have our extended overdraft.'

His eyes glittered. 'Your extended overdraft.'

She traced his lower lip with a forefinger, then rubbed the backs of her fingers against his cheek. 'I'm sure you'll see that all the figures add up.' She picked up her briefcase, and went to the door. 'I'll look forward to hearing from you,' she said, her voice still slightly husky. *'Au revoir.'*

David didn't reply; he merely watched her as she unlocked the door and left the room. Liza crossed her fingers as she walked down the narrow corridor. She hoped to hell that he'd give her what she asked for. She was sure that the papers she'd left him were good enough to state her case; but there was still the fact that he and Bryn didn't get on. Still, there was no room for sentiment in business. And she hoped that what she'd done with David, in the previous few minutes, would neutralise his hostility towards Bryn.

When she walked back into the *James* office, Bryn raised an eyebrow. 'Dressy today, aren't we?'

She gave him a haughty look. 'I had a meeting with the bank manager this morning, if you remember.'

He nodded. 'I'll make us a cup of coffee, and you can tell me all about it.'

'I'll make the coffee,' she said, 'and there's really not much to tell. He's looking at the papers I left him – the cashflow projections for the next six months – and he'll be in touch later today.'

'I just hope that he's not going to halve our overdraft again,' Bryn said grimly.

She scowled at him, and went to make the coffee. Although she still fancied him like mad, there were times when she could cheerfully have slapped him. Today was definitely one of those days. She made the coffee extra strong, then returned to the office with the two mugs, and sat at her desk, ostentatiously ignoring him.

Later that afternoon the fax rang. Liza made no move to get up and check the contents; eventually, Bryn stood up, and went over to the machine. He scanned the fax quickly, and raised an eyebrow. 'I won't ask what you did to him,' he said, 'but you've worked a bloody miracle. He's giving us the extension you asked for, and at a special low rate.'

Liza hid her smile of triumph. 'Well,' she said, 'obviously he recognised that I'm a professional.'

'Meaning that I'm not?'

'Meaning that I didn't have any macho male contest with him,' she said smoothly.

Bryn appraised her. There was no way that she would antagonise any man, dressed the way she was. She looked utterly delectable. He was almost tempted to go over to her desk, pull her into his arms, kiss her – and to hell with the consequences. But he couldn't afford to take the risk. He merely pulled a face at her, dropped the fax on her desk, and turned back to his own work.

Eight

A couple of weeks later, Bryn came over to stand by Liza's desk. 'I have a little job for you,' he said.

'What kind of job?'

'Well, you want to expand the business. We can certainly interview some drivers – but we'll also need more cars, for them to use.'

She frowned. 'So where do I fit into this?'

'Seeing as you're such a hot-shot negotiator–' Liza hid her smile. Bryn was obviously still sulking at the fact that she'd managed to succeed with their bank manager where he had failed '– you can go and get us another car.'

She nodded. 'Shall I take Steve with me, so he can check the engine and what have you?'

He shook his head. 'Steve's busy. You'll have to do this one on your own.'

She was surprised. 'And you trust me not to get stuck with a lemon?'

'You're supposed to be my business partner. If you're not capable of buying new equipment for the firm–' He let the sentence trail off insultingly.

She lifted her chin. If he was challenging her, she'd more than live up to it. 'Fair enough. What's the price range?' He named a sum, adding that he wanted something similar to the rest of their fleet, and she nodded. 'I'll start looking today, then.'

Four days later, after lunch, she returned to the office in triumph. 'I've found us something. It's being delivered on Monday,' she announced.

'Good,' Bryn said. 'I can start interviewing new drivers next week, then.'

'I reckon so.'

Her triumph was short-lived, however; when the car was delivered Bryn inspected it, then grimaced and shook his head. 'I thought you said that you got us a good deal?'

'I did.'

'Perhaps I should have let Steve go with you.'

She frowned. 'Why? What's wrong with it?'

'The bodywork, for a start. This car's been in a smack-up, and it's been resprayed. And not particularly well. Couldn't you feel that?' She was silent, not understanding what he meant. He rolled his eyes. 'Liza, if you rub your fingertips very lightly across the car's paintwork, you can tell if it's been resprayed. The paint isn't as smooth as when it's straight from the factory. There's also half a dozen spots of rust around the door frames and the wheel arches that you should have picked up. I'm not even going to bother looking at the engine. That car's a dud.'

Liza looked defiantly at him. 'Well, if you knew that I was going to make such a hash of it, why did you let me go on my own?'

He shrugged. 'Like I said, you're meant to be my business partner. I expected your judgement to be as good as mine.'

'So what are we going to do? Can Steve fix the problems?'

Bryn shook his head. 'He's too busy. I can't afford him to spend his time on tarting up that heap of junk.'

'So what, then?'

'You'll just have to take it back, and get our money back.'

'I see.' Liza gave him an icy stare, and stalked out of the office. She nearly collided with Steve, who put his hands on her shoulders to steady her.

'Hey, what's up? You look as if you want to kill someone.'

Liza was so angry that she told him. 'I do. Mr Perfect in there told me to buy a new car. I asked him if you could come with me to check the engine, and he said that you were too busy. Now he claims that I've picked a lemon, and he says that I have to go back and get our money back.'

Steve whistled. 'That wasn't very fair of him.'

Her lip curled. 'You can say that again!'

'Where did you get it from?'

'A place called L F J Motors.'

'Louise's place.' Steve grinned.

Liza frowned. 'Louise?'

'He's well known in the business. Louis Johnson. I suppose he's the original Arthur Daley.' Steve's lips twitched. 'They call him Louise, because the rumour goes that he likes wearing women's knickers.'

Liza looked at him in shock. 'You're kidding!'

'Apparently not.' He shrugged. 'Well, go and sock it to him. Do you want me to come with you?'

She shook her head. 'Thanks for offering – it's really sweet of you – but I got myself into this mess, and I'll get myself out of it. And then I'll wipe the smile of Mr Prissy's face through there.' She jerked her head in the direction of the office.

Steve chuckled at the sheer fury on her face. 'Go get 'em, tiger.'

Liza smiled despite herself. Steve's teasing was at least good-natured, unlike Bryn's sharp comments. 'Yeah. See you later.'

She climbed into the car, and headed for L F J Motors. The engine didn't sound too bad, and she'd already tried the old test of revving the car hard, and looking in the mirror to see if there was a cloud of smoke behind her. She wasn't that ignorant about cars. She really had thought that the car would suit them.

On her way, a sudden thought struck her. If Louis Johnson refused to give her her money back, what the hell was she going to do? She swallowed. She had to keep thinking positively. Of course Louis would give her the money back – or, if not, she could always persuade him.

She thought again about Steve's remarks, the way he'd called Louis 'Louise'. If Louis Johnson really did enjoy wearing women's knickers . . . Well, rumour was one thing, and something that he probably enjoyed – giving him a character that made him stand out from the rest of the secondhand car dealers – but fact was quite another. Facts that he wouldn't want to get out, with proof, because then he'd stop being a character and start being someone that people didn't really want to deal with.

A scowl crossed her face. The way she was thinking, it was like she had become some dirty-dealing East End tart. She didn't like this change in herself. At Fitchett's, she'd always been so scrupulously above board in her dealings. But then again, this was a completely different business. Dog eat dog. She had to do whatever she could to protect *James*.

Sighing, she pulled into a parking space, and locked the car. She headed towards a chemist, leaving the shop with a disposable camera, a pair of silk stockings, and an even deeper frown. Then she continued to L F J Motors. To her relief, the place was almost deserted; though there was a light on in the office, so she knew that someone was there. Hopefully it was Louis, on his own.

She walked up the wooden steps to the Portakabin, and rapped on the door. Without waiting for anyone to tell her to come in, she opened the door and walked into the office. As she'd hoped, Louis Johnson was there on his own, talking rapidly into the phone.

He was a typical East End dealer, she thought. The absolute stereotype of a car salesman. Dark curly hair, twinkling brown eyes, a ready smile, and a very well-cut suit. Though she knew damn well that the Rolex on his wrist was a fake, and that his gold bracelet was there more for show than anything else.

'I'll call you back, later, Mal. I've got a client here.' He replaced the receiver, and looked up at her. 'Hello, sweetheart. How's it going, then?'

Liza grinned, despite herself. He had the patter all ready. The best thing was, he was also aware that it was just patter, and he was playing a part. Even his accent had grown much more Cockney since she'd walked into the Portakabin. 'Hello, Louis.'

'Come back to get another motor from me, have you?'

She shook her head. 'Actually, I need to ask you to take the car back.'

He sucked in his breath. 'No can do, darling. Not at the price you paid for it. There's nothing wrong with that motor.'

'That's not what my partner says.'

He spread his hands. 'This is all above board, you know. I

don't sell dodgy motors. That is L F J Motors, you know, not Arthur Daley's place.'

'I know.' She gave him her most persuasive smile. 'I'm just saying that I made a mistake, and the car isn't suitable for what I need. Can't you help me out?'

He shook his head. 'I'd love to, darling, but unfortunately I can't. I've already spent the money. I bought new stock with it, this morning – so I can't do anything at all.'

Liza decided to try a different tack. 'As the saying goes, you scratch my back, and I'll scratch yours.'

He looked at her, his pupils expanding slightly with interest. 'Would you like to tell me a little more about that?'

'Let's just say that maybe I can make it worth your while to help me.'

He rubbed his jaw. 'I'm not quite sure what you mean.'

'Oh, Louis. I thought you were a bright boy. Do I have to spell it out for you?' A plan was forming in Liza's mind. A wicked, dirty and delightful plan. After several weeks of being so close to Bryn, and knowing that she couldn't touch him – and spending too many nights with only her own right hand to give her comfort – she was in the mood for living dangerously.

Louis Johnson, who was probably only a couple of years older than she was, was an attractive man. She liked the way he dressed, too. His shirt was pure Egyptian cotton, and perfectly ironed; no doubt he had a willing girlfriend at home, or he sent his clothes to a laundry. Judging by the gold bracelet and the fake Rolex, she had a feeling that it was the latter. If Louis Johnson enjoyed wearing women's knickers, there was no way that he'd have an understanding girlfriend who was domesticated as well as sexually tolerant.

He looked at her. 'If you're suggesting what I think you're suggesting . . .'

Liza smiled. He was about to find out. 'Let's sit down and discuss things, shall we?' She pulled the blind at the door, and switched the lock closed. Then she went to the windows of the Portakabin, closing the blinds there, too. Finally, she went to sit on the edge of Louis' desk, and beckoned to him.

He came to sit down in his swivel chair. Liza had already

noticed that it was leather, with arms: his idea of office luxury, perhaps. 'Louis,' she said softly, 'If I do something for you, perhaps you might change your mind about the car.'

'Like I said, sweetheart, I've already spent the money.'

She noticed that he'd dropped the barrow-boy accent again. 'But I'm sure that you always have a good cashflow,' she purred.

'And if I do?'

'A dealer with your reputation? Well. Let's just say that I don't think you'd miss out on an opportunity. A chance to . . . shall we say, enjoy yourself?'

A slight flush stained his cheekbones. Liza took advantage of his momentary discomfort, and leaned over to kiss him, cupping her hands round his face and nibbling erotically at his lower lip. As she'd caught him by surprise, his mouth opened, and she slid her tongue inside his mouth, exploring him. He tasted sweet, and a sudden flush of desire flooded through her.

Then he was kissing her back, standing up and moving between her thighs, sliding one hand under her hair at the nape of her neck and stroking her buttocks with the other. His groin was level with her pubis, and she could feel his erection pressing against her. His cock seemed long and thick, reminding her of Greg the chauffeur; suddenly wanting him, she allowed him to take control of the kiss, deepening it.

When he finally broke the kiss, he was shaking. 'My God, sweetheart–'

'Like I said, you scratch my back.' She left the rest of the sentence unspoken, spreading her hands.

He smiled, tugging her shirt from the waistband of her skirt, then unbuttoning it slowly. He pushed it just over her shoulders, then traced the edge of her bra, dipping one finger into the cups to stroke the swelling mounds of her breasts. Her hardening nipples were clearly visible through the lace of her bra, and he idly played with them, rubbing her nipples through her bra so that he created a delicious friction against her skin.

Liza gasped, and caught his wrists. 'This wasn't quite what I had in mind.'

'What did you have in mind, then?' His voice was low and husky.

'Sit down, and I'll show you.' Louis did as she said, sitting back in his chair and crossing his legs, tucking his hands behind his head. 'Put your arms down,' she commanded gently. He frowned, but did as she asked.

Liza took the hem of her tailored skirt, pulling it up and bunching it around her hips to reveal her thighs. She was wearing lace-topped hold-up stockings, and she bent forward, rolling first one then the other towards her feet. She removed her stockings, then slid her high heels back on, and smiled at him. 'Like I said, you have a reputation. So I think that you might rather enjoy this.' She wrapped her stockings around his wrists, tying him to the arms of the chair.

His eyes dilated. 'What the hell – ?'

'Sh.' She smiled at him. 'I haven't finished yet.' She knelt down in front of him, and undid the buckle of his belt. Then she undid the button of his trousers, and slid the zipper downwards. 'Hup,' she said. Obediently, he lifted his bottom, and she slid his trousers down to the middle of his thighs. Bingo, she thought, suppressing a grin. Steve hadn't been just teasing her. Instead of the flashy boxer shorts she'd been half expecting, Louis was wearing a pair of black silky lacy knickers. The kind that Liza herself would wear.

He looked at her, as though daring her to say something; she merely smiled, and curled her fingers around his stiffened cock, rubbing it through the silk knickers. He gave a small moan of pleasure, and she smiled at him. 'Mm, Louis. What a treat you have in store.'

She opened her handbag, extracting the pair of stockings she'd bought from the chemist, earlier, and tied his ankles to the base of the chair. His cock was swelling even more, straining against the black silk. She pulled his knickers down slightly, just enough to give her access to his cock. It sprang up, rigid, and she noticed the clear bead of moisture at its tip. She bent her head, stretching out her tongue, and lapped at the eye of his cock.

He moaned, and tugged against his bonds, but he could do nothing. She'd tied him tightly enough to hold him still, though not hard enough to cut off his circulation or hurt him. He was simply and very professionally tied, so that he was completely at her mercy. She rocked back on her heels, giving him a coquettish smile, and then leaned forward, curling her fingers round his cock and pressing the thick rod of flesh between her breasts. She held him there, moving slightly so that the lace of her bra rubbed against his skin; he moaned, and she pushed one bra cup down, running her hardened nipple along his frenum.

'My God,' he muttered hoarsely, 'I didn't know that you had an imagination like this!'

She grinned at him. 'I told you that you'd enjoy doing business with me, Louis, didn't I?'

'Oh, yessss.' His voice hissed with pleasure.

'I've heard a little more about you, since I bought the car from you. My source told me that you like . . . unusual things. So I figured that this would be right up your street.'

His pupils dilated, but he didn't speak. She bent her head again, making her tongue into a sharp point, and licked from the root to the tip of his cock, in one smooth and tantalising movement. He could feel her breath against his cock, and wriggled slightly in the chair; Liza smiled to herself. He was obviously dying for her to take him into her mouth; but she had no intention of doing so. Not just yet, anyway.

She cupped her hands round his balls, stroking the soft underside and letting her fingers drift along his perineum. He moaned, and she let her hair brush against his cock, teasing him.

'Do it, sweetheart, do it,' he moaned.

'I might. But that rather depends, doesn't it?'

'On what?'

'On whether you're a good boy. On whether you're going to do business with me over the car, the way I want you to.' Again, she dipped her head, licking his glans and blowing gently on it; he groaned.

'Oh, my God. Don't tease me.'

She lifted her head again, her eyes glittering. 'I could leave you here, just like this, you know. And what would happen if your next client walked in and saw you like this? Tied up, wearing a pair of women's knickers, and with a rampant hard-on?'

His face registered shock at her words. 'That's blackmail.'

'Not at all,' she lied. 'I'm merely making a suggestion, wondering aloud.'

His eyes narrowed. 'When I first saw you, I thought how sweet and innocent you looked.'

'And how easy it would be to rip me off?' she suggested.

He glowered. 'There's nothing wrong with that car.'

She moved her fingertips across his cock in tiny circles, arousing him still further. 'That's not what my partner says.'

'So what do you want me to do about it?'

'The way I see it, you have two choices, really. Either you give me my money back – which is what I'd prefer – or you exchange it for a car that really will suit my needs. A decent car – one that hasn't been in a smash and been badly resprayed. One that doesn't have a bad case of rust.' She dipped her head again, licking his glans and breathing on it; he shivered.

'And if I don't?'

'Then you'll miss out. On this.' She took the tip of his cock into her mouth, and slowly worked her lips down his shaft. She sucked him for a moment, then withdrew. 'So, Louis, what's it to be?'

She was still stroking his balls, teasing her perineum; he groaned. 'All right, all right. I give in.'

'So you'll give me my money back?'

'Yes.'

She nodded, and turned his chair round slightly. She pulled the black silk knickers up again, so it was blatantly obvious that he was wearing women's knickers and was in a state of high arousal, and then she took the small disposable camera from her handbag, and took half a dozen shots.

'What the hell are you doing?'

'Let's just call this insurance,' she said simply. 'In case you change your mind.'

His face tightened. 'You bitch.'

She grinned. 'I think you'll be saying something else, shortly. In fact, I think you'll be begging me to fuck you.' She put the camera back in her bag, then shifted to kneel between his thighs again. She bent her head, pulling the black silk knickers down to reveal his cock again, and resting her fingers on his perineum. She ringed his cock with the thumb and forefinger of her other hand, and began to move her hand up and down, arousing him still further. She took his cock into her mouth and began to suck rhythmically, moving her head in direct counterpoint to the way she was moving her hands.

He moaned with pleasure, and wriggled against the chair; she continued to work him, until she felt his balls lift and tighten; then she withdrew and squeezed just below his frenum, delaying his climax. When she judged that he was calm again, she continued her actions, this time wetting her finger before sliding it along his perineum and pressing it against his puckered rosy hole of his anus. He moaned more loudly, and she continued to stimulate him, pressing hard against the rosy flesh until it gave and she was able to slide her finger deep inside him. She began to move her hand in time with the way that she was fellating him, driving him to a higher and higher pitch.

Then she removed her hands, and moved back to sit on his desk.

'God, you can't leave me like this,' he moaned.

'Can't I?' Her voice was cold.

His eyes glittered. 'What do you want from me, Liza?'

She smiled. 'Like I said – I think you'll be begging me to give you relief.'

He swallowed. 'Never.'

She shrugged. 'Oh, well. If that's how you feel about it.' She spread her legs and pulled the gusset of her knickers to one side. 'Maybe I'll just make you watch me, then. Watch me make myself come, give myself the pleasure I'm going to deny you.' She slid her fingers along her quim; she was already wet, and her fingers glided easily along the soft flesh. She continued rubbing herself until her fingers were slick with her juices, and then she removed her hand, leaning forward and sipping the silky nectar along his bottom lip.

The scent of her arousal was too much for him. He couldn't help licking his lower lip, tasting her.

She laughed. 'Changed your mind yet, Louis?'

'I . . .' He swallowed.

She smiled again, and drew her fingers back down to her crotch. Again, she loaded her fingers with slippery juice, then dropped back to her knees in front of Louis. She slid her fingers along his perineum, and massaged his anus, plunging her finger in up to the knuckle. He cried out, writhing in pleasure beneath her hands.

'So what do you have to say, Louis?'

'Do it. Please.' His voice was hoarse.

'Do what?'

'Use your mouth on me. Suck my cock,' he moaned.

She smiled. He was almost at the point where she wanted him. 'I don't think I heard you properly.'

'Please. Please,' he begged.

'Please what?'

'Fuck me. Do what you want with me – but make me come. Please.'

'Good boy,' she said softly, and bent her head, taking the head of his penis into her mouth again. She began to fellate him vigorously, ringing his shaft with the thumb and forefinger of her free hand and setting up a deft rhythm in counterpoint to the way she sucked him, and continued massaging his anus with her other hand. At last, he cried out her name and came, filling her mouth with warm salty liquid.

Though she hadn't finished, yet. Not by a long way. She swallowed every last drop, then slowly began to work on him with her mouth, renewing his erection. His eyes dilated. 'Christ. I don't believe you're doing this.'

She finished licking him to hardness, and stood up again. 'Well, you didn't expect it to be all one way, did you?'

His eyes narrowed as he watched her, unsure what she had in mind.

She grinned. 'Oh, Louis. I'm going to fuck you, now. On my terms.'

'Aren't you going to untie me?'

'Not yet.' She rather liked the feeling of being in control, of having him completely at her mercy. She smiled, and turned her back on him. Ever since she'd seen Geoff Morton and his companion do this, she'd wanted to try it out herself. Now was her chance. She straddled his lap, still facing away from him, and slowly lowered herself onto his lap. She pushed one hand between her thighs so that she could position his cock at the entrance to her sex, and bore down on him, very slowly.

Louis gave a gasp of pleasure as he penetrated her; Liza smiled. Yes, this was going to be very good indeed. He'd just come, so this was going to last until she was ready – and then some. Slowly, she began to rise and lower herself on his cock, squeezing her internal muscles round him as she lifted herself, and then slamming back down again, grinding her pubis into his. The silk of her knickers rubbed against her thighs, and she felt his smooth belly against her buttocks, almost as silky as the flimsy knickers he was wearing.

She closed her eyes, and continued moving. Now, she was taking her pleasure from him, and there was nothing he could do about it. She lifted her hands to her breasts, pulling the other cup of her bra down so that she could stroke her breasts properly. Her nipples were hard and swollen, and her breath hissed sharply between her teeth as she pulled on them, increasing her pleasure. She began to move more rapidly, and let one hand drift down to cup her mons veneris, her middle finger stretching out to stroke her clitoris as she rode him.

Louis was barely able to move; she was aware of him trying to tilt his pelvis, penetrate her even more deeply, and she began to circle her bottom as she bounced over him. Yes, she thought, as she felt her orgasm rise through her. Yes. Her internal flesh quivered around him, and she remained still for a moment, delighting in the way it felt, her quim flexing while he filled her so well.

The movement of her internal muscles, like a hundred tiny fingers massaging his cock, was enough to tip Louis into his own climax; he groaned as he came. Liza smiled to herself, and stayed where she was, for a moment; then she climbed off him, bending forward and thrusting her buttocks back towards him. 'Clean me,' she said.

'What?'

'You heard. Clean me. Unless you really would like to stay there, like that, for your next customer.'

She didn't see the look on his face, but she knew that it

was a mixture of rage and rapture. Rage, because Louis was used to having the upper hand; and rapture, because what she was doing with him was way beyond what he was used to. Way beyond what she was really used to, too, but she was doing it for *James*. And then she felt his tongue against her, lapping her and cleaning the silky salty fluid of his ejaculation from her.

When he'd finished, she turned back to face him. 'So I'm still a bitch, am I?' she asked.

He looked at her. 'Yes. But I admire you for it.'

She grinned. 'And you're going to play things my way, now, are you?'

'Yes.' His voice was little more than a hoarse whisper.

'And you're going to give me my money back, now?'

He nodded. 'Cheque?'

'Cash,' she said firmly. It would be too easy for him to stop a cheque.

'You'd better untie me, then.'

'Tell me where the money is, and I'll get it.'

He smiled thinly. 'You don't trust me, do you?'

'No,' she said simply.

'All right. It's in the third drawer of my desk.'

She nodded, and went to the third drawer, as he had told her. There was a grey metal cashbox in the drawer; it turned out to be locked. 'Where are the keys?' she asked.

'I wouldn't be stupid enough to keep them in the same drawer as petty cash,' he informed her.

'Which is why I'm asking. Where are they?'

He hesitated for a moment, as if debating whether he should tell her or not; then, at the memory of her threat to leave him there, tied up, he swallowed. 'They're in the top drawer, at the back.'

She rummaged in the drawer until she found the keys, then opened the cashbox. She counted out exactly the amount of money she had given him for the car, then smiled at him. 'It's a pleasure doing business with you,' she said.

His eyes narrowed. 'I think I stand by what I said earlier. You're a hard bitch.'

'If you'd played fair with me, instead of selling me a car

that was full of rust and had a bad paint job, I wouldn't have resorted to this.' She stroked his face. 'But you enjoyed what I did to you, didn't you?'

'You know I did,' he muttered.

'That's all right, then.' Liza put the money in an envelope, and placed it in her bag. Then she put her bra back to its usual position, pulling her skirt down and tucking her shirt back in place, and untied Louis. He rubbed his wrists, then restored order to his own clothing.

'I'll see you around,' Liza quipped.

'Maybe.' Louis was still angry with her for getting the better of him.

'If I hear any comeback about this,' she said, 'I'll have these photos developed. I'm sure that some of the local papers would be most interested to see the negative – not to mention the trade press.'

'You wouldn't!'

'Try me.' Liza walked to the door, blew him a kiss, then unlocked the door and left the office. When she was back on the street, she hailed a taxi, and directed him back to the *James* office.

Bryn was sitting at his desk; she marched in, and flung the envelope in front of him. 'Money back, as requested. Every last penny.'

Bryn counted through the contents, and whistled. 'How did you manage this?'

'I asked.' Liza had no intention of telling him what had gone on between herself and Louis. 'Next time you want someone to buy a car, I suggest that you go yourself.'

'Fair enough.' His lips quirked.

'I'm going home, now. I'll work from home, for the rest of the afternoon.'

'I'll see you tomorrow, then.'

'Yes.' Liza scooped an armful of papers from her desk, and left the office.

Nine

'You've got the evening shift, tomorrow night,' Bryn told Liza.

'The evening shift?' She was surprised. Bryn had been adamant that she was only to have driving assignments during the day, despite her fight to be his equal; he'd loftily informed her that London could be dangerous at night, and she didn't have the physical strength to fend for herself in the way that he could. 'But I thought you didn't like me doing the evening run.'

'I don't. But this one's different. It's a client who specifically asked for a female chauffeur.' Bryn paused. 'You've probably heard of her, actually. Leila Swift.'

Liza shook her head. 'Sorry, doesn't ring a bell with me.'

'She's a writer,' he enlightened her. 'Pretty steamy stuff, I gather.'

'And how do you know what I read in my spare time?' she flashed at him, annoyed at his assumption about her reading habits.

His lips twitched. 'Just a lucky guess, I suppose.'

Liza glowered at him. 'As a matter of fact, I'm reading a book about quantum physics at the moment.'

'Smarty pants,' he teased. He walked over to her desk, dropping a piece of paper on it. 'These are the details. Let me know if there's a problem. I have to go, now – I have an assignment in about ten minutes, and I want to check something with Steve, first.'

Liza stared at the piece of paper. Why would Leila Swift want to have a woman driving her? Surely she'd feel safer with a man, in the evening – particularly if she was as famous as Bryn had suggested. The assignment was to pick her up from her house in Holland Park, take her to a party in the

West End, and bring her back again. Nothing too difficult.

A writer of raunch. Liza wondered what she looked like. Probably tall, with lots of flowing red hair, cut in pre-Raphaelite curls; Gothic make-up; and a very stylish dress sense. Either she'd be dramatic, wearing nothing but black, or she'd be outrageous, wearing something red, slinky and in silk.

She caught her thoughts, and smiled. It really didn't matter what the writer looked like. She was a client – to be treated with courtesy and utmost discretion. Liza smiled; then she read the rest of the instructions. The female driver was to wear a proper chauffeur's uniform: luckily, she had a pair of dark grey tailored trousers which matched one of her favourite jackets, a Chinese-cut affair which didn't need a shirt underneath it. Topped with the cap, she'd look the part exactly. Just why was Leila Swift being so specific about clothes, though? Liza couldn't think of a single reason; in the end, she put it down to being just a client's whim.

The following evening, she parked outside the house in Holland Park, and went to ring the doorbell. There was a long pause, and she was just about to ring the bell again when the door opened abruptly.

'Good evening,' she said with a smile. 'I'm Liza Hargreaves, from *James*, here to collect Leila Swift.'

'That's me. Thanks for being so punctual.' The woman standing in the doorway was nothing like Liza had expected. She was slightly shorter than Liza and very slender, with cropped copper-coloured hair and incredibly green eyes, which were emphasised with the minimum of make-up. Her lips were dark, and a perfect cupid's bow; and she was wearing an expensive-looking designer dress, made of black chiffon, with a black lace shawl thrown over the top. A dress which looked very demure, at first glance – until she moved into the light, when it was obvious that not only was the dress very sheer, but that Leila Swift was wearing absolutely nothing beneath it.

Liza was annoyed to feel a blush steal into her cheeks. She was thirty, for God's sake, and she'd hardly led a sheltered life. Some of the parties she'd attended in the past had been fairly wild; and she certainly hadn't been celibate since joining *James*. So why the hell should she be embarrassed that her client was wearing next to nothing?

'Would you like to go, now, madam?' Liza asked.

Leila grinned. 'Madam, eh?'

Liza inclined her head. 'Our clients expect to be given the deference they deserve.'

'I wonder,' Leila began; then she cut herself short. 'I'll just get my bag.'

Leila's evening bag was black satin, only just big enough for a set of keys, a credit card, and . . . Liza was cross with herself. It was none of her business what Leila's bag contained. She should just stop speculating, and get on with her job.

She waited quietly while Leila closed the door and locked up. Then she walked out to the car, opening the rear door and waiting politely for Leila to settle herself inside before closing the door again.

She slid into her seat, fastened her seat belt and, glancing in the mirror, pulled smoothly away. Her driving had improved immensely since she started working at *James*. Although she had classed herself as a reasonable driver before, now she felt more confident of her ability. Not least because she was beginning to know her way round London a lot more.

'Have you done this job for long?' Leila asked.

Her voice was low and husky; even if Bryn hadn't told her what Leila did for a living, Liza thought that she would have guessed. Leila Swift exuded sensuality. And even a polite and innocuous question, like the one she'd just asked, could be loaded with more than one meaning when she was the one to ask it. 'A couple of months.'

'Yes, Bryn said that you were fairly new.'

Liza was surprised. Bryn hadn't told her that Leila Swift was a regular – so obviously Leila would be paying by account, rather than at the end of the evening. It looked like Bryn hadn't told Leila quite what Liza's position was in the firm, either; she decided that now wasn't the time to explain to Leila that she was more than just a driver. 'Yes,' she said, as neutrally as she could.

Leila didn't bother trying to resume the conversation; the drive continued in relaxed silence, until Liza drew up in the road Bryn had told her about, and parked the car. She climbed out of the car, and opened the door for Leila. 'Would you like to ring us when you're ready for us to collect you?' Liza asked.

Leila shook her head. 'Didn't Bryn tell you? I wanted you to wait for me.'

'Of course.'

Liza's manner was professional, but her initial hesitation obviously gave her away, as Leila smiled. 'No, he didn't tell you, did he? Typical man.' She rolled her eyes. 'Well, come on, we don't want to be late.'

'You mean, I'm to wait inside for you?'

'Well, I wouldn't want you waiting outside.' Leila gave her a lazy smile. 'Besides, it's a party. Come and enjoy yourself.'

Liza locked the car, then followed Leila down the road. Leila gave her a sidelong glance. 'Don't look so worried.'

Liza coloured deeply. 'Sorry.' What the hell was it about this woman that made her feel so gauche? She wasn't sure if it was Leila's perfume, a rich and spicy chypre, or her manner, or what it was. And if she's having this effect on me, Liza thought, she must have one hell of an effect on men.

She followed Leila in silence to the front door of the house where the party was being held. Leila rang the doorbell, and they waited. At last, the door was opened, and a woman stood in the doorway. Her dress made Leila's outfit seem positively demure. She was wearing a very tight black silk sheath dress, and long black lace evening gloves; the sleeveless and backless dress left nothing to the imagination. There was no way she could possibly have worn any underwear with it; the neck of the dress dipped too steeply for a bra, her nipples were in sharp relief, and her groin was also highlighted in a way that meant that wearing even a g-string would have been impossible. Liza felt another betraying blush storm over her face.

'Dizzy.' Leila kissed the other woman – to Liza's intense embarrassment, it was neither an air kiss nor the genuinely warm kiss of a friend. It was full on the mouth, a lover's kiss with open lips, and it lasted considerably longer than Liza had expected. 'I've brought a friend with me. I knew you wouldn't mind.'

The woman – who was obviously the hostess – gave Liza a searching look, then held out her hand with a warm smile. 'Denise de Nerval, though everyone calls me Dizzy. Any friend of Leila's is a friend of mine.'

'Thanks.' Liza took her hand, shaking it. 'Liza Hargreaves.' She didn't add that she was actually Leila's chauffeur; she had a feeling that it just wouldn't be appropriate.

'Come in, come in. There's champagne on the table. Help yourself.'

Liza winced. 'Actually, I'm driving. Would it be possible to have something soft?'

Denise grinned. 'There's an answer to that,' she teased, making Liza blush even more. 'Of course. There's mineral water on the table, too, and some freshly squeezed orange juice. Just help yourself to anything you fancy.'

Liza had the decided impression that Denise meant more than just food and drink. Judging by her dress and Leila's, this was a wilder party than Liza had ever been to, and she felt way out of her depth. She followed Leila and Denise over to the table, and found herself some sparkling water while Denise and Leila helped themselves to champagne.

Leila touched Liza lightly on the hand. 'I don't expect you to stay with me all evening. Go and mingle, meet some new people.' Her eyes glittered. 'Like I said, I think you're going to enjoy this.' She reached over to tip Liza's cap to a rakish angle, downed her glass of champagne in one, picked up another glass, and swept out of the room in a swirl of chiffon.

Liza found herself a quiet corner, and sat down on a chaise longue, surveying her surroundings. The house was beautifully designed, with large airy rooms; the decor was perfect, and she guessed that it had been designed by a professional. The curtains were rich brocade, toning with the walls, and the carpet was thick velvet pile. The lighting was perfect, wall lights and uplighters giving a soft glow to the room, rather than the harsh glare of an overhead light.

She sipped her water, and cast her gaze over the other guests. They were all dressed more or less as Leila and Denise had been – some of them more demure, at first glance, until they turned round or were caught in the light, when their outfits were shown to be just as revealing. The men were less flamboyant than the women; most of them wore evening dress, black silk bowties and crisp white dress shirts.

Liza wondered what they all did for a living. Something in the media, perhaps; something glitzy and glamorous. Maybe some of them didn't need to work at all. The only thing that she could tell was that there were no City types among them: she could have told those ones a mile off.

She was suddenly aware that someone had sat down next to her, and turned round to face whoever it was. She had never seen him before; though, like all the other men in the room, he was very attractive. He was maybe a couple of years younger than she was; there was no hint of grey in his short dark hair, and his eyes were an incredible steel blue, fringed by thick lashes. His mouth was beautifully shaped, and Liza felt a sudden urge – which she suppressed – to reach out and trace its lower curve with her forefinger.

'Hello,' he said. His voice was rich and cultured; Liza felt a pulse begin to beat harder between her legs. This was just the kind of man she liked – someone who had a brain to go with his looks. And, judging by the half-amused smile on his face, he had the kind of personality she usually responded to: warm and open. Not the competitive type, like Rupert, or the arrogant type, like her ex-boss. 'I haven't seen you at one of Dizzy's dos, before. You came with Leila, didn't you?'

She nodded, suddenly tongue-tied, and furious with herself for acting like a seventeen-year-old.

'Jeremy Walker,' he said, extending his hand.

'Liza Hargreaves,' she replied, taking his hand.

'So this is the first time you've been to one of Dizzy's *soirées*, then?'

'Yes.' Liza wasn't sure whether she should tell him that she hadn't expected to be attending, that she was merely Leila's chauffeur for the evening; on the other hand . . . She decided not to.

'Are you an old hand at this, then?' she couldn't help asking.

He chuckled. 'I suppose you could say that. I've known

Dizzy for a long time. Actually, she's my cousin.'

'Oh.' Liza felt suddenly stupid. She didn't usually have a problem chatting with people, but what the hell could she say to this man? She'd never met him before, they had nothing in common, no friends or acquaintances or –

'Don't look so worried,' he said, interrupting her thoughts. 'I admit, Dizzy's parties can take some getting used to – but there's no pressure. Just go with the flow.'

She wondered quite what he meant by 'getting used to'. A party was a party – wasn't it? But then, there was the way that people were dressed. And Liza had the impression that there was a lot more to the party than met the eye.

'Perhaps you'd like me to show you round,' Jeremy suggested.

'I . . . Thank you.'

'Come on, then.' He looked at her half-full glass. 'Would you like a top-up?'

'Just mineral water, please. I'm driving,' Liza said.

'Pity.' He caressed her cheek with the backs of his fingers, sending a sudden tingle over her skin; then he found a bottle of mineral water, uncapped it, and topped up her glass. He took a glass of champagne from the table for himself, then put his hand under her elbow, drawing her gently to her feet.

Liza allowed Jeremy to escort her from the room. It was bizarre, having a guided tour by a man she didn't know, who didn't own the place, and who had only introduced himself a minute or so before; but that turned out to be less bizarre than some of the sights which met her in the other rooms. There were three other large rooms downstairs, each containing a table of drinks and a table of finger food. In one of them, music was playing, and people were dancing. But it wasn't like the dancing Liza was used to: this was more sensual, more sexual. She found herself looking away, blushing, when she realised that one couple were actually making love as they danced, the woman's dress pulled up at the front and her lover's hand buried between her legs.

The next room was slightly darker, the lights turned down to their dimmest; there were piles of soft cushions dotted round, and a man was leaning over one of them, his trousers round his knees and his bare buttocks raised. A woman, dressed in jodhpurs and a hacking jacket, and carrying a riding crop, was standing behind him; with shock, Liza realised that there were distinct red stripes across the man's white buttocks. She stared at Jeremy. 'You mean, she's –' She couldn't finish the sentence.

He nodded. 'It's entertainment, for those who like it.'

'Entertainment,' she echoed dumbly.

He took her hand, squeezing her fingers. 'You really are new to all this, aren't you?'

'Let's just say that I've led a rather more sheltered life than I thought,' Liza murmured.

'Do you want to go back?'

Liza swallowed. To say yes was to be a coward; to say no was to step into the unknown. She remained silent for a moment; then Jeremy made the decision for her, leading her into the third room, which was dimmer still – with the exception of a bright light which shone in the centre of the room, much like a spotlight. Music was playing, and a number of people were sitting, standing and lying in an approximation of a circle, watching what Liza realised was another form of 'entertainment'.

Two women were lying in the middle of the circle, their bodies clearly visible beneath the spotlight. Both were wearing stockings, and patent high-heeled shoes; the dark-haired girl was wearing a lace teddy, and the blonde was wearing a deep crimson teddy. The stretchy lace garments were pulled down to bare their breasts, the material acting as a kind of bustier to hold their breasts up.

They were lying facing each other, and the blonde was nuzzling the brunette's breasts, tracing her areolae with the tip of her tongue, which she had made into hard points. The brunette was stroking the blonde's hair, and arching her back, thrusting her breasts upwards. Her nipples were dark and heavy with arousal, and the blonde took one hard peak into her mouth, sucking hard. The brunette moaned, sliding one hand between their bodies and rubbing her abdomen, letting her hand drift lower to pull the gusset of her teddy aside.

The blonde took the hint: either that, Liza thought, or they had done this kind of thing in public before, and knew what their audience expected. Slowly, she nuzzled her way down the brunette's midriff, and lifted her legs up, bending her knees and spreading her thighs so that her quim was visible to the others in the room. She drew one finger along the musky furrow, and the brunette groaned with pleasure, pushing her pelvis upwards. The blonde continued to tease her lover, using long slow strokes and ignoring the way the brunette was circling her hips, pushing upwards and desperately trying to get her to rub her clitoris.

At last, she took some pity on her lover, and used her other hand to spread the brunette's labia, revealing the hard pink bud of her clitoris. She bent her head, stretching out her tongue, and flicked the tip over the apex of the brunette's clitoris, circling it rapidly and then finally taking the bud of flesh into her mouth and sucking hard. The brunette moaned again, and the blonde slid her finger into her sex, adding a second and pistoning her hand back and forth.

Liza couldn't tear her eyes away. She'd always considered herself to be strictly heterosexual, but this . . . She was ashamed to realise that it was turning her on, and her own sex was growing slick and puffy with arousal.

'I thought that you'd enjoy this,' Jeremy whispered in her ear, his breath fanning her skin and making her shiver.

Liza flushed. 'I don't know what you mean.'

He stood behind her, pulling her against his body and cupping her breasts. 'Even through your jacket, I can feel your arousal,' he said, rolling her nipples between his fingers and thumbs. Liza didn't know what to say. She swallowed. 'Admit it,' he commanded softly. 'This turns you on, seeing two women together.'

'I . . .' She choked, unable to answer.

He kissed the nape of her neck. 'Sh. There's nothing to be embarrassed about. Nothing in the world. Just relax, and enjoy it.' He held her against him, and she could feel his erection pressing against her buttocks; he continued to fondle her breasts, unbuttoning her jacket and giving a sharp intake of breath as he realised she was only wearing a bra underneath it. 'Oh, Liza.' He finished unbuttoning her jacket, and slid one hand under the cup of her bra, kneading her flesh and playing with her nipple.

Liza flushed. She knew that she should pull away and restore order to her dress – for God's sake, she'd known this man for only a few short minutes – but she couldn't help herself. The way he was touching her, combined with the sight in front of her, was turning her on too much.

The entertainment was having much the same effect on the rest of the audience; Liza glanced round, and realised that they were all too engrossed in each other, and in watching the show, to notice what Jeremy was doing to her. And what he was doing to her was mild, in comparison; some had their faces buried in their lovers' groins, licking and caressing their genitals, and others were engaged in mutual masturbation.

All the same, she didn't like the idea of being so much of a public spectacle. She pushed his hands away, and rebuttoned her jacket. 'Let's get out of here,' she muttered.

He followed her into the corridor, and spun her round to face him. His eyes were glittering with suppressed amusement. 'What's the matter, sweetheart?'

'What happened in there – it isn't me.'

'Isn't it?' he asked silkily.

She swallowed. 'Look, I think I ought to explain. I work for a chauffeuring firm; that's why I'm driving. Leila hired me.'

'Hm.' He looked at her. 'But you know what they say about women in uniform; and Leila swings both ways. You arrived with her, and you didn't say anything before about being her chauffeur. Besides, chauffeurs are usually male; and why would she want you to come to the party with her, unless you were – shall we say, her "friend"?'

Liza's eyes flashed with anger. 'Firstly, I'm wearing a uniform because she, as our client, requested a female driver with a proper chauffeur's uniform.'

'And you do this for your other clients?' he enquired.

'If they want me to wear a uniform then yes, I do. Secondly, she didn't want me to wait outside for her; and she didn't want to ring us when she was ready. She told me that I would be better waiting inside for her, and that's why I'm here.'

He chuckled. 'You're really on the defensive, aren't you? Why do I get the impression that you're hiding something?'

'I'm not,' she ground out through gritted teeth. 'For your information, I'm one hundred per cent straight. I've never made love with another woman.'

'But it turned you on, watching those two in the middle of the floor. You were imagining yourself there, in the brunette's place, having your nipples sucked and your cunt fingered.'

Her face burned. 'Don't be so coarse.'

'It's true,' he insisted. 'You wondered what it would be like, feeling another woman's hands caressing your body, her mouth working on you and bringing you to a climax.'

She glared at him. 'If you don't shut up, I'm leaving, right now.'

'You can't,' he reminded her. 'Not if you're really Leila's chauffeur. You have a job to do.'

'I thought that you were nice, at first. But that just shows how wrong first impressions can be.' She scowled. 'Why don't you just piss off and leave me alone?'

He chuckled. 'Don't be so aggressive. Dizzy's parties are always like this.'

'You said that you knew I hadn't been to something like this before. Why are you being so cruel?' She was near to tears with anger.

He mistook the glitter in her eyes for tears of shame and embarrassment, and stroked her cheek with the backs of his fingers. 'I'm sorry. I shouldn't have teased you.' He took her hand, bringing it up to his lips and kissing the tips of her fingers. Liza's eyes widened as he drew the tip of her middle finger into his mouth and sucked gently on it. 'I'd like to make it up to you,' he said huskily. 'Let me make amends.'

'You can make amends by leaving me alone.'

He shook his head. 'You and I both know that you don't really mean that.'

'I could scream.'

He nodded. 'True, but then you'd draw attention to yourself.'

'I could throw my drink over you.'

He grinned. 'Some people would say that that's your subconscious working.'

'Meaning?' she asked icily.

'Meaning,' he said softly, 'that if my clothes are wet, I'll have to take them off.'

'You arrogant bastard! What makes you think that I want you to take your clothes off?'

He bent his head so that he could lick her earlobe. 'Let's try this from another angle. I'd like to take my clothes off, in a private room, with you. Better still, I'd like you to do it for me. I'd like you to strip me, and then stroke my body, use your mouth and your hands on me to give me pleasure. To give us both pleasure.'

She pulled away. 'Go to hell.'

'So I was right, then. You do prefer women.'

'Just because I've turned you down, it doesn't make me a dyke, or frigid. It just means that I don't want to have sex with you.'

She turned on her heel, and would have walked away, but he wrapped his arms around her waist, pulling her back against him. 'And just as we were getting on so well,' he drawled laconically. 'Let's start again. Say I believe that you really are Leila's chauffeur, and I can see that you feel out of place here. At the same time, you have to admit that it turned you on, watching those women together. And even though you've never done anything like that yourself, part of you would love to know what it feels like. And part of you would like to know what it feels like to do that to another woman, too. How the texture of her flesh would feel, under your mouth; how she'd taste.'

It was true, and Liza nearly choked. How had he managed to guess the shameful secret she'd only just managed to admit to herself?

'Because,' he said simply, 'it shows on your face.'

Liza was shocked to realise that she'd spoken aloud. 'I . . .' Her voice trailed off miserably.

He turned her round to face him, and dipped his head to rub his nose against hers. 'Liza. Let's go somewhere quiet, and make things better – for both of us.' He touched his lips very gently to her own, in a kiss which was more coaxing than demanding; to her horror, Liza found herself kissing him back. What the hell was she doing? She hadn't even been invited to the party; she'd merely come in on Leila's coat tails. She'd had a row with this man, and he'd forced her to face up to a facet of her character that she hadn't even known existed; although she resented him for it, she was also very turned on still, and she found him attractive.

As she opened her lips over his, he slid his tongue into her mouth, deepening the kiss. His free hand smoothed down to cup her buttocks; Liza slid one hand over the nape of his neck, curling her fingers into the dark crisp hair.

When he broke the kiss and lifted his head, she was shaking. He traced the curve of her lower lip with the tip of his forefinger, and she shivered. The first time she'd seen him, she'd wanted to do that to him. But that had been before he'd shown her the 'entertainment', and she'd reacted so violently to it.

'Let's go somewhere quiet,' he repeated, taking her hands and dropping a kiss into the palm.

She allowed him to lead her up the stairs. He was obviously familiar with the house – she remembered that he'd said that he was Denise's cousin – and he went to a door at the end of the corridor, opening it and switching on the light. 'We won't be disturbed,' he said softly. 'This is my bedroom.'

Liza flushed. 'I don't think we should be doing this.'

He spread his hands. 'If you'd rather just go downstairs again, that's fine. No pressure, no strings. But wouldn't you like to–' he licked his lower lip '–relieve yourself of the ache? It could be a long time until Leila wants to leave. And it won't be very comfortable for you, sitting there feeling all hot and bothered.'

'I'm not hot and bothered.'

He took the glass from her hand, placing it on the bedside table with his own, and drew her back into his arms. He slid one hand between her legs, cupping her quim. 'Oh yes, you are. I can feel how hot you are, even through your trousers. And it bothers you, doesn't it?'

Liza closed her eyes in embarrassment. 'You're a bastard.'

'Perhaps.' He kissed her eyelids. 'But there's a nice side to me, too. I want to make love with you. Won't you let me?'

At her silence, he began unbuttoning her jacket, sliding the garment from her shoulders and hanging it neatly over the back of a chair. Then he undid the button of her trousers and the zip, easing the material over her hips. She lifted one foot and then the other, allowing him to take off her shoes and remove her trousers properly; then he pulled her into his arms, smoothing the curve of her buttocks and pressing her tightly against him.

He bent his head, touching his mouth to hers, the tiny butterfly kisses coaxing a response from her. When she opened her mouth, allowing him to deepen the kiss, he slid his hands along her spine, smoothing her skin and deftly undoing the clasp of her bra. He dropped the silk and lace garment on the floor, and cupped her breasts in his hands, lifting them up and together to deepen the cleavage. He stooped still further, drawing a trail of kisses down the shadowed vee between her breasts, and then took one hard rosy nipple into his mouth, sucking fiercely on it.

Liza tipped her head back, a small moan of pleasure escaping her as he began working on her other breast, teasing the nipple and grazing it gently with his teeth, while he rolled her other nipple between his thumb and forefinger, tugging gently on it. She closed her eyes, giving herself up to the sudden knot of sensuous feelings coiling in her belly.

Jeremy smiled, dropping to his knees, and nuzzled the soft undersides of her breasts, kissing and licking them in a way that made Liza shiver. Then he nuzzled her abdomen, breathing in her scent. 'Seashore and vanilla and honey, mixed with a dash of spice,' he murmured.

'What?' Liza hadn't heard him clearly.

'The smell of your arousal,' he said softly. 'It reminds me of honey and seashore and vanilla and spice.'

'You make me sound like some ancient cargo,' she quipped wryly.

He grinned. 'Not so much of the ancient – and I certainly don't think of you as cargo. You're all woman, all soft curves and perfumed flesh.'

That, she thought, was more to do with her workouts at the gym than anything else. The frustrations of working with Bryn, and knowing him to be untouchable, had made her go slightly overboard on the various weight and toning machines. Not to mention allowing herself to get into situations like this to assuage her raging libido.

'You're wearing too much,' she said simply. She dropped to her knees in front of him, unbuttoning his dress shirt. His bow tie was perfectly tied – not one of the fake ready-to-wear ones – and she tugged lightly on the ends, undoing it. Then she finished taking off his shirt, dropping it and the bowtie to the floor, and ran her hands lightly over his chest. His pectorals were good, she thought, though he could have done with a small amount of toning. She had a suspicion that the only exercise Jeremy Walker had was sexual.

She undid his trousers, and he helped her to remove them, balancing his weight on his hands while she pulled the material down over his legs. She could see the outline of his cock clearly through the soft material of his underpants; it was impressive, she thought. This was going to be a real pleasure . . .

Ten

Jeremy drew her gently to her feet, then led her over to the bed, pushing the covers back and sitting down on the mattress. He pulled her onto his lap, and she wound her arms round his neck, kissing him deeply. Again, he stroked her back and her midriff and her breasts, arousing her, before shifting their positions so that she was lying flat on the mattress and he was kneeling between her thighs.

She gave him an impish smile. 'A bit conventional, don't you think?'

He returned her smile. 'For starters, perhaps. Or maybe not.' He reached over to the bedside cabinet, opening the top drawer and extracting a condom from it. 'I assume that you'd prefer me to use one of these?'

Liza was impressed by his thoughtfulness. She nodded. He smiled, taking the top off the little packet and quickly rolling the latex over the shaft of his cock. Then he sat back on his heels, and slid his hands beneath her buttocks, lifting her onto his thighs. He curled his fingers round his cock, guiding its tip to the entrance of her sex, and pushed very gently, easing his way inside her. He slid his hands down her legs, moving her feet so that they were flat on the mattress, her back was arched, and she was taking her weight on her shoulders; then he knelt up again, and began to move.

Her eyes dilated. She should have guessed that he would be a connoisseur; although Rupert had been an inventive lover, he hadn't ever done anything like this. The angle of Jeremy's penetration felt incredible, and she had to clench her teeth together to stop a moan of lust bubbling from her mouth.

Jeremy continued to thrust, his movements slow and measured. Liza closed her eyes, curling her fists into tight balls, and gave herself up to the maelstrom of desire within her. For a moment, she could almost imagine that it was Bryn who was in bed with her, making love with her; then she pushed the thought from her. It wasn't fair to Jeremy. It wasn't his fault that she had the hots for her business partner – an unrequited passion, at that.

He moved his hips in slow sinuous circles, supporting her buttocks with his hands and driving deeply within her. Liza was shocked by the speed of her climax, but if he felt her quim rippling round his cock, he made no comment: he simply continued thrusting, taking her to a higher peak. At last, she felt him tense, and then he groaned as he reached his own orgasm.

He remained inside her for a moment, until their pulses had slowed down; then he withdrew, removing the condom and wrapping it in a tissue. He walked over to a door, disposing of the condom in what Liza realised was the *en suite*; then he returned to the bed, stretching out beside her and sliding his arm round her waist.

'Better?' he asked.

She nodded. 'Much.'

'Good.'

She curled into him, resting her cheek on his shoulder and her hand on his chest. He stroked her hair, and they lay in silence for a while. Eventually, he leaned over to drop a kiss on her forehead. 'Why were you so uptight, earlier?' he asked.

Her mouth set. 'Don't start that again.'

'I'm just interested. Someone who responds as well as you do – a born sensualist – just why would you get uptight at the suggestion of doing something a little different?'

She sighed. 'Look, this is all very new to me.'

He chuckled. 'The way you responded to me, I think that that's a teensy fib, isn't it?'

She rolled her eyes. 'I didn't mean that I was a virgin, or anything like that. Just that I've never been to a party like this before as a guest, let alone as a hanger-on.' A sudden thought struck her. 'God, Leila might be looking for me. She might be wanting me to drive her somewhere.'

He pulled her closer. 'I very much doubt it. At the moment

she's probably in one of these rooms upstairs, doing the same kind of thing that we've just been doing – though quite which permutation she'll choose, tonight, I don't know.' He grinned. 'Like I said, Leila swings both ways. She likes men – and she also likes women. And more than one, at the same time.'

Liza flushed. 'Isn't that a bit dangerous?'

'Not in a physical sense. Everyone uses protection.'

She digested his words. That hadn't been quite what she'd meant; from Jeremy's own considerate behaviour, earlier, she'd guessed that they would all use protection. They'd have to be extremely stupid, in this day and age, not to. 'But what about . . . I mean, supposing someone talked to the press?'

'Don't worry. Dizzy's guests are all carefully selected. You'll find media types here, yes, but they'd never breathe a word of what happens here. If they did, they know that they'd never be allowed in to another party. So it's in their interests to keep quiet, if they want to enjoy themselves. And as for the lawyers, accountants, MPs . . .' He shrugged. 'None of them will talk, either. They don't want any dirt dished on them to upset their careers. This is just a group of like-minded people, having a little fun with no strings attached.'

'But none of you have ever met me before. How do you know that you can trust me?'

He kissed her lightly. 'You came with Leila. That's recommendation enough.'

'But I've already told you that I'm merely her chauffeur.'

'Exactly. She wouldn't pick any firm that wasn't entirely discreet and dependable. Leila might write outrageous books and live an outrageous lifestyle, but she does it with discretion.'

'I see.' She felt suddenly restless. 'Hadn't we better – well, get up? In case someone misses you?'

'There's no hurry. The night is young – besides, anyone who wants to see me can always find me, later.' He smiled at her. 'My only regret is that I can't share a bottle of champagne with you.'

'I'm driving.'

'I know.' He stroked her cheek. 'If ever I need a chauffeur, I'll definitely contact your firm. Reliable, discreet – perfect.'

'I'll hold you to that.' She looked at him. 'So how did you

get involved with – well, all this?'

'I told you,' he said lazily 'Dizzy's my cousin.'

'Right.' That wasn't what she'd meant, but she had a feeling that he wasn't going to tell her any more.

Just then, the door opened, and Liza froze in shock. 'What the hell–?'

'Sh, it's all right.' He stroked her hair, and smiled at the person who had just entered the room. 'Hello, Celia.'

Liza turned round, and saw the brunette who'd been part of the 'entertainment', earlier. She was still wearing the white stretch lace teddy, with the front pulled down to reveal her breasts; but she was also wearing a pair of elbow-length white silk gloves, which were probably from the later part of her act. Liza stared at her, then glared accusingly at Jeremy. 'What the hell's going on?'

'Celia left her clothes here, earlier.' He gave her a charming smile, and Liza knew that he wasn't telling her the whole truth.

'I don't believe you.'

Celia walked over to the wardrobe, opened it, and took out a hanger. A clinging white silk dress was hanging from it, in the style of the famous Marilyn dress; Liza knew without seeing it on her that the dress would reveal her curves and leave very little to the imagination.

'One dress, which I wore earlier this evening,' Celia said with a grin.

To Liza's surprise, Celia made no attempt to put it on. She replaced the hanger in the wardrobe, and came to sit on the bed next to them. 'You're new, aren't you?'

Liza flushed, and would have pulled the sheet over her to cover her nakedness, but for the fact that Jeremy stopped her. 'Yes.'

Jeremy stroked the underside of her breast, toying with the nipple; Liza slapped him away. 'Stop it,' she hissed.

'Liza, Liza, Liza.' He tweaked her nipple. 'Don't be so uptight. This is your chance.'

'My chance for what?' Liza knew that she'd made a mistake as soon as the words were out of her mouth. She'd played right into his hands.

He grinned. 'What we were talking about, earlier. At the entertainment.'

Liza coloured hotly. 'I want to go, now.'

'Liza.' He touched her other nipple, which was erect. 'This gives you away. You're excited.'

'No, I'm not.'

'Then how do you explain these?' He rubbed her nipples.

'Perhaps I'm cold.'

Celia had been silent throughout the exchange; now, she chuckled. 'You're digging yourself into a deeper hole, Liza. You've just set it up nicely for us to offer to warm you up.'

Liza swallowed. 'I didn't mean –' she began.

'I know.' Celia's smile was kind.

'But aren't you supposed to be –'

'Downstairs, with Tilly?' Celia finished. 'No. The entertainment changes every so often.'

A horrible thought struck Liza. Was she meant to be the next form of entertainment? She looked at Jeremy. 'There isn't a camera in here, is there, with everything that happens in this room being beamed to a screen somewhere?'

He grinned. 'You have a very suspicious mind.'

'Answer my question, please.' Her face was grim.

'No, there isn't a camera in here. Dizzy isn't quite that sophisticated – in a technical sense, that is.'

Liza realised then that she'd been holding her breath, fearing the worst. She exhaled sharply, and swallowed. 'What do you want of me?'

'Pleasure.' The word was almost purred, spoken in a velvety-smooth voice that sent shivers down her spine. 'Pleasure, for all of us.'

'If we do anything you're not ready for,' Celia said, 'all you have to do is tell us to stop.' She drew the back of her hand down Liza's body, starting at her collar-bone and finishing just below her navel.

The feel of the silk gloves against her skin made Liza arch her back involuntarily; Jeremy smiled. 'You're going to enjoy this,' he promised.

Liza suddenly felt like an innocent virgin. 'I've never –' she began.

'Sh.' Celia pressed one gloved finger against her lips. 'It's going to be fine. Just relax, and leave everything to me.' She stroked Liza's cheek with the backs of her fingers, then dipped her head, pressing her lips very lightly against the other woman's. Liza froze, terrified of both the quickening pulse between her legs and the surge of familiar feelings running through her body – familiar feelings, in a very unfamiliar situation.

Celia didn't seem to be fazed by Liza's reaction; she merely continued kissing her, very lightly, cupping her face and murmuring affectionate endearments. Eventually, Liza found herself relaxing; as if she knew exactly what was going through Liza's mind, Celia deepened the kiss, sliding her tongue between Liza's lips and exploring the sweetness of her mouth.

At the same time, Celia allowed one hand to slide down over Liza's throat, stroking her skin, and moving downwards until she had cupped one breast. To Liza's shame, her nipple grew even harder, tingling under the pressure of Celia's gloved fingers. The silk felt deliciously soft and cool against her skin, in sharp contrast to the hot pressure of Celia's fingers against her flesh. Unable to help herself, Liza arched upwards.

Celia broke the kiss, making a small noise of pleasure in the back of her throat, and began a trail of kisses downwards. She licked the sensitive hollows of Liza's collar-bones, then nuzzled between her breasts, her hair trailing over Liza's skin. Liza closed her eyes, torn between shame at her own behaviour, and being turned on by what Celia was doing to her. She and Celia were 'entertainment', now, performing for an audience of one; without looking at him, Liza knew that Jeremy was sitting on the bed cross-legged, watching them and stroking his hard cock almost absent-mindedly.

But the way that Celia's mouth was working over her skin, her lips and tongue pleasuring Liza's breasts, sent all thoughts out of Liza's head. Sighing, she gave herself up to pleasure, arching her back and sliding her fingers into Celia's dark hair. Encouraged, Celia drew harder on Liza's nipple, and then blew on the wet skin, making Liza wriggle. She did the same with the other breast, teasing the nipple until it almost hurt, then began to nuzzle her way down Liza's body.

She licked round the edges of Liza's navel, making Liza laugh and squirm; then she slid her hands between Liza's thighs, pressing them apart. She lifted Liza's legs, pushing them back to give her the visual access she wanted; then she knelt back on her heels, looking at Liza's glistening and puffy quim. 'Beautiful,' she murmured. 'Pure vermilion. Or maybe not so pure, by the time I've finished with you.' She drew one finger down the musky cleft, and Liza almost cried out with pleasure. The coolness of the silk felt so good against the heat of her intimate flesh; she wanted more, more.

As if Celia could tell exactly what Liza wanted, she pushed one finger into Liza's sex, settling her thumb against Liza's clitoris. Liza moaned, and Celia dipped her head, replacing her thumb with her mouth and sucking hard on the little peak of engorged flesh. At the same time, she added a second finger into Liza's quim, and pistoned her hand back and forth.

'Your gloves,' Liza moaned, her mind switching to the most ridiculously prosaic thought.

'They're washable,' Celia replied with a grin, lifting her head for a moment. Then she resumed working on Liza's quim, licking and lapping and sucking. Liza closed her eyes, focusing on the sensations induced by Celia's clever mouth: it felt so good, so very good, the way that the other woman caressed her. Celia knew exactly where to touch her, and the right pace and pressure and rhythm; although some of Liza's past lovers had been very skilled in the art of cunnilingus, none of them could have matched Celia's expertise.

Liza felt her orgasm rise through her, swirling through her body. She cried out, her internal muscles flexing hard round Celia's fingers; then Celia withdrew her hand and shifted up the bed to kiss her. Liza could taste her own juices on Celia's mouth, and she was shocked to discover that it turned her on even more. She kissed Celia back, her tongue sliding into the other woman's mouth; the next thing she knew, they had rolled over, and she was lying above Celia, deepening the kiss. She was oblivious of the fact that Jeremy was watching them; all she could think about was the sweet perfumed flesh beneath her, and how much she wanted to touch and taste it.

She stroked Celia's exposed breasts, playing with the hard

rosy tips; she wasn't one hundred per cent sure that what she was doing was right, but she hoped that Celia liked more or less the same kind of things that she did. Working on that premise, she squeezed and kneaded Celia's breasts gently, then bent her head to suckle one nipple. It felt strange, yet delicious, to taste a woman's flesh, to feel the rough texture of her nipple beneath her tongue – so different from the hard and almost button-like flesh of a man's nipple.

Liza hooked her fingers into the edge of Celia's teddy, rolling the lace garment downwards; Celia lifted her buttocks to help Liza remove the garment properly. Liza left Celia's stockings in place, and parted her thighs, stroking the smooth white skin above the welts of the stockings. Celia's quim was glistening and puffy with arousal; Liza let one finger drift along the full length of Celia's quim, from the top to the bottom, and Celia moaned, tipping her pelvis and thrusting towards Liza. Liza continued teasing her, touching her very lightly and letting her fingertip skate across the apex of Celia's clitoris.

Celia moaned again. 'Don't tease me.'

Liza smiled, and inserted one finger into the other woman's quim. Her flesh was smooth and wet, like warm velvet pressing against Liza's finger. It was much as Liza's own quim felt when she was masturbating, touching herself intimately: except that, this time, she had power over someone else's body. She pushed her finger in as deeply as she could, withdrawing it slowly, and pushing it in hard again, setting up a teasingly slow rhythm. With her other hand, she spread Celia's labia, and began to work on the hard coral nub of her clitoris. Celia moaned, thrusting towards her, and Liza took pity on her, quickening the pace and adding a second and third finger to give Celia greater pleasure.

At precisely the moment that Celia pushed her head back against the pillows, baring her teeth and flexing her internal muscles sharply round Liza's fingers, Jeremy came, his pearly white semen spraying over Celia's body. Liza rubbed it into Celia's skin, anointing her nipples and smoothing it across her abdomen; then she bent her head, licking the salty fluid from Celia's nipples. Celia sat up, then, cupping Liza's face and kissing her hard.

None of them spoke, but Celia climbed off the bed and went into the *en suite*. Liza had the distinct impression that she was familiar with Jeremy's bedroom. She wasn't sure if they were lovers all the time, or if it was a semi-casual arrangement. Not that it was any of her business, she thought. She had no intentions of getting serious with Jeremy herself, and she knew that what had happened with Celia was a one-off.

Jeremy took her hands, licking Celia's juices from her fingers, and smiling at her. 'Not quite what you expected, hm?'

'Not quite,' she admitted.

Celia came back to join them, her skin still slightly damp from where she'd washed herself, and dropped her gloves on the floor next to the bed. 'Thank you,' she said softly, sitting down on the mattress next to Liza. 'That was good for me.'

'But she didn't quite go all the way,' Jeremy remarked.

Liza flushed. 'I –'

Before Celia could jump in and castigate Jeremy for criticising Liza, he added softly, 'Don't you want to know what she tastes like, Liza? Don't you want to feel the texture of her flesh against your mouth, like a ripe melon just picked from the greenhouse and warmed by the sun?'

Liza's flush deepened.

Celia looked at her, and lifted her hand to stroke her face. 'You don't have to do anything you don't want to do, sweetheart,' she said quietly, her brown eyes sincere. Liza licked her lower lip. Part of her did want to do it; and part of her was afraid.

Jeremy drew his hands down Liza's spine, stroking her skin and cupping her buttocks. 'Think of it as your chance to do something different, something from your wildest dreams. No strings, no pressure, no expectations. Just pleasure. Your chance to go down on a woman and make her come again and again, until she's filled your mouth with her sweet nectar. Your chance to know how a man feels, when he's licking your delectable quim and tasting your arousal.'

His voice was low and husky, and Liza found it hypnotic. She shivered, imagining Jeremy's words becoming reality.

Could she do it? Could she really do what she'd seen Celia and Tilly do in the room below, albeit in a much more private situation?

Slowly, Celia shifted, lying back against the pillows and spreading her legs in invitation. She blew Liza a stylised kiss, and Liza shivered. She could smell Celia's arousal, a scent so similar to her own – a heady, musky aroma.

She knew then that she was going to do it. Slowly, she moved into a kneeling position, between Celia's thighs, and wrapped her arms round Celia's legs. She dipped her head, and drew her tongue along the full length of the brunette's quim. It was her first taste of an aroused woman, and she discovered that she liked the sweet-salt tang. She lapped again and again; as Celia began to move beneath her, weaving her hips sinuously and thrusting her pelvis upwards, Liza made her tongue into a hard point, inserting it as deeply as she could into Celia's sex.

'Oh, yes,' Celia moaned. 'That's so good, baby. Do it. Do it. Fuck me with your mouth. Make me come.'

Liza spread Celia's legs wider, giving her easier access. Celia's hands came up to grasp her thighs, and she held herself open, baring her teeth and grimacing with pleasure as Liza continued to lap at her.

Liza was suddenly aware that Jeremy was kneeling behind her, stroking her spine and moving his fingertips in tiny erotic circles over her skin. She could feel his breath, warm against the nape of her neck, and arched against him, still lapping at Celia's quim. Jeremy kissed the nape of her neck, nuzzling her hair out of the way, then made his tongue into a hard point and licked his way down her spine.

Her moan of pleasure was lost in Celia's intimate flesh, and, as if Jeremy sensed it, he stroked her buttocks, pushing her bottom cheeks apart slightly. Liza stiffened as she felt his tongue probe the puckered rosy hole of her anus; he murmured a soft endearment and turned his cheek to her back, pressing his lips against the base of her spine. 'I don't think that you're quite ready for that, yet,' he said softly. 'Much as I'd like to slide my cock into you, here, feel how hot and tight you are, I won't.'

She relaxed again, relieved, and then she felt his erection pressing against her. Suddenly, she wanted to feel him inside her quim, filling and stretching her. She wriggled slightly, and Jeremy positioned himself between her thighs. He'd obviously put on another condom while she was busy attending to Celia, and she felt the tip of his cock, encased in the slippery latex, move up and down the length of her quim. Jeremy rubbed his cock against her perineum, and then fitted it to the entrance of her sex, and gently eased inside.

He rested his hands on her hips, and began to thrust, taking it slow and steady, pushing into her up to the hilt. Liza gasped as he suddenly moved more quickly, just pushing the thickest part of his cock rapidly in and out. It felt so good, so very good; her tongue worked more rapidly on Celia, who was in turn moaning in delight.

Finally, she felt Celia's quim flutter under her mouth, and then her mouth was fitted with musky juices. Almost at the same time, an answering pulse exploded in her own quim, and she felt Jeremy tense against her, driving in deeply and holding her tightly to him.

When Jeremy withdrew from her, she crawled up the bed to lie next to Celia, who kissed her deeply. 'Thank you.'

Jeremy disposed of his condom, then came to lie on Liza's other side, curling into her. 'That was incredible,' he murmured.

They lay in companionable silence for a while; then, lazily, Celia got up and removed her gloves and stockings. 'I need a shower,' she said, stretching. Her face was lit by a mischievous grin. 'Though I think that it had better be a solo shower, or we'll be here all night!'

Liza chuckled and remained in Jeremy's arms until Celia came out of the bathroom again. To her surprise, Celia didn't replace her lace teddy; she merely stepped into her dress, then came over to Jeremy to have the zip drawn up. 'Your turn,' Jeremy said softly. 'After all, it should be ladies first.'

'Thanks.' Liza went into the bathroom, and showered quickly. The water was hot, the shower gel was sweet-smelling and lathered richly, and the thick fluffy towels were generously sized. It was the perfect pick-me-up, she thought. She returned, refreshed, to see Celia on her knees, fellating Jeremy, who was lying across the bed and groaning. She watched the tableau until they had finished; after his climax, Jeremy sat up and kissed Celia in thanks, then gave Liza a slightly self-conscious smile.

Liza merely smiled back, and then dressed. There was a full length mirror – surprisingly not opposite the bed: she'd half expected Jeremy to want to see exactly what he was dong with his lovers – and she checked her appearance, making sure that she looked like Leila's immaculate chauffeur again, before turning to face Jeremy and Celia. 'I'd better be going,' she said softly.

Celia came over to her, taking her hands and squeezing them. 'It was nice to meet you.' Her eyes glittered. 'You never know, our paths could cross again.'

'Maybe.' Liza smiled, blew a kiss to Jeremy, and left the room. She didn't meet anyone in the corridor, much to her relief; she wondered guiltily whether Leila had been looking for her. She hoped that she hadn't. The last thing she wanted was for *James* to be found wanting, thanks to her selfish neglect of her client. Though Jeremy had assured her that Leila would be busy; if he knew her that well, he was probably right.

She returned to the first room, and poured herself another glass of mineral water. She picked at the buffet, and then retired to a corner, drifting into a daydream while she waited for Leila. Some time later, the writer appeared, putting a hand on Liza's shoulder and smiling. 'Ready when you are,' she smiled.

Liza looked at her client. Her skin was glowing, and her pupils were expanded – all the signs, Liza thought, of good sex. Though quite who Leila had been with, she didn't know. She suddenly remembered Jeremy's comment that Leila swung both ways; she wondered whether her partner had been Dizzy, or maybe the blonde who had been part of the 'entertainment' with Celia. Or had it been one of the more attractive men around the room?

She shook herself. It was none of her business what Leila had been doing. All the same, she couldn't help noticing how Leila's hardened nipples showed through the thin material of her dress – and how Leila was surrounded by the musky scent of arousal. She licked her lower lip. After what had just happened between herself and Celia, she could appreciate why Leila liked women as well as men. And she could imagine just what Leila's skin felt like, tasted like. 'Should I say goodbye to Dizzy?' she asked.

Leila shook her head. 'No need,' she said.

Liza flushed. It was obvious that, whatever Leila had been doing, Dizzy had been involved in some way. Whether they had been together on their own, or whether they'd shared a similar duet for three as she had done, was anyone's guess.

She opened the front door for Leila, then walked with her to the car. She opened the passenger door, letting Leila settle herself in the back seat before closing it again, then slid behind the steering wheel. She glanced in the mirror, then pulled out, and drove Leila back to Holland Park. 'Did you have a good evening?' she asked.

'Oh yes.' Leila's voice was sensual and husky. 'Dizzy's parties are always good for the soul – don't you think?'

Liza flushed deeply. God. Did Leila know what had happened between her, Jeremy and Celia? And if so, how? 'Um – let's just say that I haven't been to a party like that before.'

Leila chuckled. 'No, Dizzy's dos are quite unlike anything else.'

When Liza dropped Leila off at her house, to her surprise, Leila bent forward and kissed her on the cheek. 'Thank you,' she said. 'It's been a pleasure.'

Liza had the uncomfortable feeling again that Leila knew exactly what had happened; on the other hand, Jeremy had assured her that there were no cameras in the room, and she had no reason to disbelieve him. She forced a smile to her face. 'I hope that we can help you again, Ms Swift.'

'Leila. And I'm sure that you can.' Leila gave her a broad wink, which made Liza's face flame, and walked down her front path. Liza waited until she'd unlocked the door and closed it behind her again, then drove home, a thoughtful frown on her face. Leila definitely knew something. Though how?

She suddenly remembered the large mirror on Jeremy's wall. It hadn't been opposite the bed – but if it had been a two-way mirror, it wouldn't have needed to be exactly opposite the bed for the people on the other side of it to have a good view. She groaned. God. No wonder Leila had smiled at her like that. Maybe Leila had watched her, while a lover – male or female – had taken her from behind . . .

She shook herself. There was nothing she could do about it, now.

And then another thought struck her. If this wasn't the first time that Leila had used the services of *James*, who had driven her before? Bryn? And if the assignment had been to take Leila to another of Dizzy's *soirées*, had Bryn experienced the same kind of thing that she just had? The idea of watching Bryn with another woman didn't appeal to her in the slightest; but the idea of Bryn spread across the bed as Jeremy had been earlier, with herself crouching between his thighs and taking his cock into her mouth . . .

She shivered. 'Face it, Hargreaves, you're becoming obsessed with the man. It's about time you did something about it,' she admonished herself sharply. 'And you'd better make it soon.'

Eleven

Bryn came over to Liza's desk, holding a piece of paper that he'd just picked up from the printer. 'What's this?' he asked.

Liza looked up from her desk, and realised what he was holding. 'Our customer services questionnaire.'

'You what?'

'Our customer services questionnaire,' she repeated.

He frowned. 'And what's that, when it's at home?'

She rolled her eyes. 'Exactly what it sounds like. I'm sending a questionnaire out to our customers, to find out how happy they are with our service, and what sort of things they'd like us to do for them.'

'And how much is this going to cost?' His face was set. 'Liza, you can't try to run this place like a multi-national corporation. We don't have the budget to send out questionnaires and that kind of thing. Be realistic, can't you?'

Liza looked back at him. God, she thought, when he was in a bad mood, he looked so incredibly sexy. The set of his mouth was sulky and sensual, and his hair was tousled, as if he'd just run his hands through it: bedroom hair, she thought. She suppressed an insane urge to stand up and kiss him – but only just. Then her brain snapped back into gear, and she digested what he'd just said. 'Bryn, I know what I'm doing. I do have marketing qualifications, you know.'

'Yeah, and you're used to big budgets, not running things on a shoestring. For God's sake, woman, we're in overdraft.'

Her eyes widened in annoyance. She was supposed to be his partner, and yet he didn't trust her to make any decisions. 'This isn't going to cost us a great deal, and if we're going to expand, we need to know what our customers want from us. If they just want lots of short journeys, we need to have more staff; if they want longer journeys, then we can cope with the staff we have. Either way, we'll need to think about whether we're using the right sort of cars. The answers we get back from our customers are going to help; and yes, I do know that there won't be a hundred per cent response rate. There never is, to a questionnaire. As long as we get our main accounts to answer, that's the important thing.'

He stared at her, but made no further comment; he merely dropped the piece of paper on her desk, turned on his heel, and stomped back to his own desk. Liza picked up a pen and started working on her draft, modifying the questions and tidying up the layout of the questionnaire. Half an hour or so later, she stretched, yawned, and looked up. 'Do you want a coffee?' she asked Bryn.

He shook his head. 'I've already had too much today. I'm trying to limit my caffeine intake.'

Bryn, the office coffee-junkie, was trying to cut down on caffeine? Liza was surprised. A niggling thought occurred to her. When a man started being interested in his health, there was usually a woman involved somewhere. Was Bryn seeing someone? But he'd always kept his private life strictly private; he never asked her about hers, either. The most personal he got with her was to ask her if she'd had a nice evening or a nice weekend; but she knew that he didn't want to know the details. A simple yes or no was enough for him. 'Fair enough,' she said equably, and went to make herself a coffee.

Later that evening, Liza went home via Marks and Spencer's, stocking up on cheese, biscuits and canapés. Sally was due to come round for the evening, and Liza felt too tired to cook; unlike Sally, she didn't take pleasure in spending hours in the kitchen. Besides, she wanted to spend her time talking to her best friend rather than messing about cooking.

When she got home, she put three bottles of Chardonnay in the fridge to chill, arranged the nibbles on several plates, and had a shower. Then she dressed in a comfortable baggy sweater and a pair of leggings, poured herself a glass of wine, put a George Michael CD on the stereo, and curled up on the sofa, closing her eyes and letting herself relax to the mellow tones of the music while she waited for Sally.

A few minutes later, the doorbell rang; she answered it, and gave her best friend a hug. 'Hi. Good to see you.'

'You, too.' Sally returned the hug, then handed her a large bunch of irises. 'These are for you.'

Liza smiled. 'My favourites. Thanks.'

'Oh – and these.'

Liza grinned as she took the Belgian chocolate seashells. 'Yum. I'm sure that we can manage these between us.'

'Yeah, we've done that before, haven't we?' Sally said, remembering past girly evenings they'd spent together, drinking wine and eating chocolate and laughing.

'Come in – the wine's chilling, and I've done some nibbles.'

'Thanks to the food department at dear old M&S?' Sally teased.

'Where else?' Liza retorted with a smile. She went into the kitchen, putting the flowers into a vase, then picked up the canapés and headed for the sitting room.

'I see that you've already started,' Sally remarked, as she sat down on the sofa and noticed Liza's half-full glass.

'Only just.' Liza handed her a clean glass. 'Help yourself.'

Sally poured a glass of wine, and lifted her glass in a toast. 'Well, here's to *James* – and may it be a huge success.'

Liza smiled, echoing the toast and sipping the chilled white wine.

'I must say,' Sally remarked, 'you look so much happier and relaxed than you did at Fitchett's, even though you're working longer hours, now.'

'Well, it's different, when you're working for yourself.' Liza smiled. 'I'm really enjoying it. I'm still not that good at routing, and Bryn won't let me anywhere near the engines – especially after I ended up buying us a real lemon – but I'm OK at driving jobs, and the office is a hell of a lot better organised than it was.'

'A lemon?' Sally quizzed, mystified.

Liza rolled her eyes. 'He challenged me to buy us a new car for the fleet. Unfortunately, I didn't pick a good one.'

'You're telling me that he made you go to buy one on your

own, even though he knows that you're not a mechanic?'

Liza chuckled. 'He won't make that mistake again. Anyway, I got our money back, so there was no harm done.' She decided not to tell Sally just how she'd got their money back; although Sally was her best friend, and was more than broad-minded, Liza didn't think that Sally would appreciate what she'd done. And when she thought of it, now, she felt a faint distaste for her actions: it had been sleazy in the extreme. Louis had enjoyed it, and she'd had a temporary kick from it; but she didn't want her sexual life to go down that route.

Sally took a cracker, slicing herself a piece of Brie and nibbling on it. 'So, what's the best job you've had so far, then?'

Liza wagged her finger, grinning. 'The company motto is discretion. I'm not supposed to talk about our clients.'

Sally chuckled. 'Okay, okay. You don't have to drop any names. And I certainly won't become a groupie and start hanging round your offices in the hope of spotting one of my favourite actors – unless you ever get to pick up Ralph Fiennes or Colin Firth, that is, and then I think I'd offer to work for you for nothing!'

'Well,' Liza said, her tongue loosened slightly by the wine that she'd consumed on an empty stomach, 'we have driven a few actors. Actually, my first job was with an actor, taking him to Brighton.'

Sally whistled. 'Was he nice?'

Liza grinned. 'Very nice. Just your type.' One of Sally's favourite fantasy men, although Liza knew that she couldn't tell her. Not without breaking a confidence.

'I don't think I'd have been able to drive him, then. I'd have been too busy looking at him in the rear-view mirror, than concentrating on the road.'

Liza, too, cut herself a piece of Brie. 'I had a bloody hard job concentrating, I can tell you!'

'Oh, yes?' Sally was interested.

Liza decided to throw caution to the wind. It was something she'd kept to herself for so long: and Sally was probably about the only person she could talk to about it. 'This is just between you and me, right?'

'Of course.' Sally rolled her eyes. 'You know I'm good at keeping secrets.'

'I know. Sorry.' Liza smiled. 'Well, he wasn't alone in the back seat, let's put it this way. I think his companion wanted to break into movies, and she decided to use the back seat of my limo as a casting couch.' She licked her lower lip. 'I could see everything that was going on in the mirror. She was obviously a bottle blonde, quite pretty – though too skinny by half – and she just took her top off. He pulled the cups of her bra down, and started working on her breasts.'

Sally swallowed. 'Wow. And they did this in the back of the car, when anyone could see them?'

'The windows of this particular car are dark glass,' Liza said. 'Which is just as well, because they went a hell of a lot further than that. He undid her jeans, and she wasn't wearing anything beneath them – she'd shaved herself, as well. Neither of them were wearing a seat belt, but I didn't dare say anything about it, because I didn't want them to think that I was watching.'

'Did they know that you could see them?'

Liza nodded. 'He caught my eye in the mirror, and winked at me. Then he parted her legs, and started stroking her. I couldn't believe it. I tried to concentrate on the road – but all I can say is that it was lucky it was a straight road. I couldn't help watching what they were doing. And then he blew me a kiss, and went down on her, making her come.'

'He . . . ?' Sally's eyes were wide. 'No.'

'I know. I could hardly believe it, either. And they weren't finished then, not by a long way.' Liza took another sip of wine. 'She undid his chinos, and pulled them down, and gave him a hand job. She had a pretty good technique, considering that she couldn't have been more than eighteen: I don't know where she'd learned it.'

'Probably the casting couch,' Sally said dryly.

'Then she went down on him.' Liza swallowed. 'The worst thing is, Sal, it really turned me on – because I could imagine being in her position, having him use his hands and mouth on me until I climaxed, then repaying the compliment. I don't know how the hell I stayed so calm, or how I didn't crash the car. And then she shifted to sit astride him; he was already hard again, and slipped into her. She started moving over him – and then I saw the police car coming towards us.'

'Oh my God! Did they pull you over?'

Liza shook her head. 'Thank God, no; like I said, the windows were darkened, so no-one could see what was happening – except me, that is. Anyway, she rode him to orgasm, and then they dressed again. By the time I dropped them off at their hotel, they both looked perfectly decent, and no-one would ever have guessed what had gone on between them in the car.'

Sally whistled. 'Do you get many jobs like that?'

'No. Every one's different.' Liza's lips twitched. 'And how.'

'Come on, you can't keep me in suspense.' Sally topped up their glasses. 'Are you telling me that you did something with one of your clients?'

'Er – yes.' Liza bit her lip. 'Well, I'm the only one in the office who can speak French, and it was an all-weekend job. I picked him up from Gatwick, and he was a lot younger than I'd been expecting. Very nice. I suppose you could describe him as a sort of young Sacha Distel. Anyway, the attraction was mutual – and he let me know, in French, because he didn't realise at the time that I could speak French.'

Sally grinned. 'And did you put him straight?'

'Mm. I had to, when he started quizzing me; he'd sussed out that I wasn't just a chauffeuse. So I explained that I was Bryn's partner, and I was driving him because I spoke French.'

'I thought that you didn't believe in mixing business with pleasure?' Sally teased.

'I didn't. He – er – persuaded me otherwise,' Liza said. 'And bear in mind that I'd been celibate for a long while. I hadn't made love with anyone since I split up with Rupert.'

'What about Steve?' Sally reminded her.

Liza smiled wryly. 'Okay. Since Steve, then. Bryn's been completely unreachable. He hasn't even offered to have lunch or a drink with me, and it's been driving me mad. So when my client asked me to pull over in this little wood so he could stretch his legs and admire the view, then asked me if I'd like to join him, I agreed. I needed the break, too – it's a long drive from Gatwick to the Peak District. Anyway, we walked deeper into the woods, and he turned me to face him, pulled off my hat, and kissed me.'

'Good?'

'Very.' Liza took another gulp of wine. 'I told him that I was supposed to be his driver, and I didn't mix business and pleasure; he said that he admired my principles, but then he started touching me. We went back to the car and got the rug from the boot, and then we made love in the middle of the woods.' She shivered with pleasure as she remembered what had happened. 'It was so good, Sally. I didn't care that anyone could have been walking there and seen us. What mattered was the way he was touching me, the way he was kissing me.' She closed her eyes. 'Afterwards, I drove him to Bakewell. He had a "cottage" there – I was expecting a pretty little two-up, two-down kind of place, but it was this large stone house, beautifully decorated and kept.'

'So he spends part of his time in England, then?'

'Yes.'

Sally looked at her friend. 'So are you going to see him again?'

'I don't know,' Liza replied honestly. 'If he has any business trips to England, he'll use our services – and I expect I'll be the one to drive him. But . . . Oh, I don't know.'

'So the episode in the woods was a one-off, then?'

Liza flushed. 'Um. No. He said that there was a separate bedroom for me, if I wanted it, but I ended up staying with him, in his four poster.'

'Very romantic.'

'Mm, it was.' Liza smiled at the memory. 'The next day, he had business on the outskirts of Sheffield. I drove him there, and waited for him in the office. There was another chauffeur there: much more your stereotype driver. You'd have liked him, actually – he had a ponytail, and looked a bit like a Chippendale.'

'Fancied himself, as well, did he?' Sally asked dryly.

'Yep. Anyway, he suggested that we played cards. I told him that I didn't play for money, and that I could only play snap; he decided to teach me blackjack. He was far too cocky, and I thought that he could do with a bit of a lesson. So when he suggested playing for some stakes, I told him again that I didn't play for money. He suggested that we played for clothes, and that we played in one of the offices, in case the meeting finished early.'

'So, what happened?'

'I lost the first four hands.'

'Deliberately?'

Liza chuckled. 'Sort of. I'd already noticed how he reacted if he thought he had a winning hand. Anyway, I won the next eight in a row.'

'Ouch. I bet he didn't take that well.'

'Put it this way, he was wearing just his boxer shorts; he thought that he'd still be completely clothed, by that point, and I'd be naked. He was really annoyed; but, at the same time, he was turned on. His boxer shorts didn't exactly hide anything. Anyway, I lost the next one, to make him feel better – then I won, so he had to take off his shorts.' She licked her lips. 'Obviously, he spent most of his spare time working out. He had a good body. A very good body.'

'Are you sure that you didn't know how to play blackjack, before then?'

'I'm sure,' Liza confirmed. 'You know I pick things up quickly.'

'Hm.' Sally ate a smoked salmon pinwheel. 'So what happened, then?'

'I won the next hand, and suggested that we went onto forfeits. He looked really sulky about it – but I could tell how interested he was, at the same time.'

Sally giggled. 'By his erection?'

'Mm-hm.' Liza grinned back. 'I don't know what got into me, Sal. I mean, I still really fancied Bryn; I'd spent the previous night making love with my client, and knew that the same thing was probably going to happen that night; but I couldn't resist taking advantage of the situation. So I told him to use his mouth on me.'

'And he did?'

'He sulked about it, because he didn't like the idea of losing to a woman; and that made me more determined.' Her lips twitched. 'Anyway, he paid up, doing exactly what I'd told him to do.'

'Good?'

'Very. He gave me an incredibly good orgasm. Then he suggested that we took it to the limit . . .' She flushed with pleasure as she remembered what had happened between them. 'So we did. We made love in the office – and then, when we went to the washroom to clean ourselves up, he took me again, up against the wall. There was a full-length mirror behind him, and I could see everything; I think that turned me on, even more, because I came twice before he did.'

Sally whistled. 'I don't suppose you have any more vacancies for drivers, do you?'

Liza grinned. 'It isn't all like that, you know. There are a lot of very boring jobs, when you're just driving a client from one end of London to the other, and your client spends all his time on his mobile phone or his laptop, paying no attention to you.'

'Did your Frenchman realise what had been going on, when he came out of his meeting?'

'I don't know. He certainly didn't mention it.' Liza shrugged. 'We had a good afternoon, playing tourist, and then he took me out to dinner, to celebrate his deal.' She smiled. 'Then we went to bed, with a bottle of champagne.'

'I don't need to guess what happened next,' Sally said.

'No.' Liza sipped her wine. 'Though not all the jobs are like that. Mostly, it's straightforward chauffeuring. Like I said, there are very few where the clients want to – shall we say, mingle with the chauffeur.'

'So there have been others?'

'Sort of.' Liza wrinkled her nose. 'Though it wasn't the client who wanted to get to know me better, in that case. She'd asked for a female driver, and she wanted me to take her to a private party. I'd expected her to ring me when she wanted picking up again, but she insisted that I went into the party with her.' She rolled her eyes. 'And because she'd wanted me to wear a chauffeur's uniform, everyone thought that I was her lover.'

'I don't know if I dare ask what sort of party it was,' Sally said.

'Not quite what you think. The hostess's cousin, Jeremy, told me that my client swung both ways; that's why he assumed that I was her latest "friend".'

'And you put him straight?'

'Mm. After he'd taken me under his wing and shown me round the party.'

Sally's eyes narrowed. 'How do you mean, shown you round the party?'

'There were several rooms. The one I went into, first, looked perfectly normal: people eating, drinking and talking. Then Jeremy took me into the other rooms.' She looked down at her hands. 'I suppose I should have guessed that it wasn't the average kind of party. My client was wearing a black chiffon dress and a lace shawl – with no underwear. Not that you realised it, until she moved into the light.'

Sally nodded. 'Right.'

Liza looked shame-faced. 'I felt so gauche, Sal. Like a shy teenager.'

Sally chuckled. 'I wish I'd seen that!'

'Well.' Liza shrugged. 'Anyway, she looked really demure, compared with some of the other guests. The women, that is; most of the men were in formal evening dress.'

'This is in the straight room, yes?'

Liza nodded. 'The first room he took me into, there was music playing. People were dancing – but it was a hell of lot more sexy than I was used to. Some of them were even making love as they danced.' She swallowed. 'The next room was darker; there were cushions all over the place, and there was a dominatrix there, beating a man. Jeremy told me that it was just entertainment, for those who liked it.' She toyed with the stem of her glass. 'I always thought that I was pretty broadminded, but I think now that my life's been a bit more sheltered than I used to believe. I mean, the S&M scene just doesn't do anything for me – I can't get my head round how anyone can think that pain's sexy – but, in the next room . . .' Her voice tailed off.

'What happened in the next room?' Sally asked softly.

'More entertainment. People were sitting in a circle, more or less, watching a floor show.'

'A floor show?' Sally prompted.

Liza swallowed. 'Two women, making love. Sal, I always thought that I was a hundred per cent straight. But it really turned me on, watching them; they looked so beautiful. It was obviously carefully staged, because one was blonde and one was brunette, but that didn't seem to matter. It was the way their bodies moved, the way they looked together. Jeremy could tell what I was feeling, too, because he started touching me. I didn't like being a public spectacle, even though most of the audience were engrossed in their partners; so I pulled away. He was sophisticated, I suppose – because he was amused rather than annoyed by the way I reacted. That's when he told me that my client was bisexual and that, because I was in uniform, he thought that I was her latest "friend". I told him the truth, and he said that I was hiding something. We had a row, and then he suggested that we went somewhere quiet and made it up.'

Sally topped up their glasses. 'Go on.'

'He kissed me, and I found myself responding to him. Even though I was furious with him for making me face up to something I hadn't known about myself, I was still turned on, and he was very attractive.'

'The usual Hargreaves type – dark hair and blue eyes, looked a bit intellectual, and had a good body?'

'Mm,' Liza admitted wryly. 'Like I said, he was the hostess's cousin, and he had his own room there. He took me to his bedroom. I felt a bit guilty, in case my client wanted to leave early, but he put me straight about that. So then he undressed me, and we went to bed.'

'Good?'

'Very,' Liza admitted. 'Afterwards, we were talking; and then the door opened.' She swallowed. 'It was one of the women who'd been in the floor show. She said that she'd left her clothes there, earlier; I didn't believe her, but then she took her dress out of the wardrobe to prove it.' She coughed. 'Jeremy started touching me again. I pushed him away, but he told me not to be so uptight – that it was my chance.'

'Your chance?' Sally echoed.

'To make love with another woman, find out what it feels like.'

Sally whistled. 'The direct approach.'

'Mm. I had a nasty feeling that I was about to become the next piece of entertainment, but Jeremy told me that there weren't any hidden cameras. And then she touched me.'

'What was it like?'

'Not what I'd expected. I was embarrassed, at first; but she was very, very good. The way she touched me and kissed me and licked me . . . It was incredible, as though she knew exactly what I liked and where and how. Jeremy was sitting next to us, watching us, and she made me come.

'Then it was my turn, to touch her. I was a novice, really, but I just worked on the basis of what I liked, and hoped that it was the same for her. When she came, so did Jeremy. She went to have a shower, and then Jeremy goaded me into going down on her. As I used my mouth on her, Jeremy took me from behind. I'd never, ever done anything like that before, Sal, and it was incredible.'

'Mm.'

The huskiness of her voice made Liza look at her friend; she was surprised to see that Sally's hardened nipples were clearly visible through her thin sweater. Sally was as turned on by the idea as she had been. 'Yeah, well. After that, I had a shower, and went downstairs to wait for my client. I drove her home, and that was that.'

'No wonder you're enjoying your job so much,' Sally said softly. 'Like I said, I wouldn't mind working for you.'

Liza smiled. 'And, like I said, these assignments are few and far between. Most of the time, the clients are ordinary and want to be driven from A to B while they get on with important business calls, so you're lucky to get more than a minute's worth of conversation.'

'But these other jobs make it all worth it, hm?'

'Yes.'

Sally nodded. 'Dare I ask how you're getting on with Bryn, these days?'

'Pretty much as before. He's unreachable, Sal.' She sighed.

'He accepts me as being his business partner, but he never suggests socialising. If I ask him if he had a nice weekend, he just says "Yes", and changes the subject. He never seems to notice what I'm wearing, whether I'm dressed casually or wearing a business suit and high heels. He treats me almost as if I'm sexless.'

Sally winced. 'Oh, Liza,' she said, her voice sympathetic.

'Yeah, well. It's something that I'll have to live with.' Liza shrugged. 'Anyway, enough about Bryn. I've babbled on about *James* all evening; it's about time that you told me all your news.'

'There's not much to tell,' Sally said. 'No gossip, or anything like that. Though you might be interested to know that Mark's grooming your replacement, in true "dat's my boy" style.'

Liza pulled a face. 'If you'd told me something like that a few months ago, I'd have been spitting feathers.'

'Exactly. That's why I waited until now before telling you.' Sally shrugged. 'He's all right, I suppose, though it's going to take him a while to reach your standards.'

Liza chuckled. 'Flattery,' she said, 'will get you anywhere.' She surveyed the empty wine bottle, and stood up. 'Let's have another.'

'Mm. And then we can work out how to change your situation with Bryn.'

Twelve

Several weeks later, Liza was working on the analysis of the returned questionnaires. Bryn had flatly refused to have anything to do with it, so she was going it alone. Which suited her fine, she thought; the last thing she needed was Bryn interfering and telling her how to do something when she was more qualified than he was, on this point.

She glanced at her watch, and realised that it was almost seven o'clock. So much for an exciting Friday night, she thought wryly. Still, she didn't have any special plans. Sally was already going out on a hot date, and most of her other friends were going out as couples. All she had lined up was a deep bath and an early night with a good book. Since the evening when she'd taken Leila Swift to Dizzy's party, she'd been completely celibate – apart from the occasional night when her desire for Bryn had been too much for her, and she'd resorted to comforting herself with her own right hand.

She looked at the pile of questionnaires. She might as well finish them, she thought, before going home. She stood up, and went to the door of the office, intending to make herself a cup of coffee; at that precise moment, the door opened, and Bryn walked into the office, colliding with her. His hands shot out to grab her elbows, steadying her; he winced at the impact. 'Sorry. I didn't realise that you were still here.'

'That's OK.' She looked up at him, her blue eyes luminous. He hadn't let go of her, and her skin tingled where he touched her. She looked into his eyes, and couldn't help licking her lower lip: the invitation was blatant and unsubtle, she knew, but it was too much for her to resist. Having him so close to her, like this, it would be easy to reach up and kiss him . . .

He returned her gaze, looking tormented; then he bent his

head, and touched his mouth lightly to hers. It was like lighting touchpaper; Liza slid her arms round his neck, opening her lips under his, and he slid his tongue into her mouth, deepening the kiss. His hands slid down her back, moulding the soft curves of her buttocks; then he worked one hand under the hem of her sweater, drawing it up so that he could stroke her back.

Liza was in paradise. Kissing Bryn was as good as she'd dreamed it would be – if not better. The way his mouth moved over hers, and the way he was touching her . . . She wanted it to go on forever. He continued kissing her, his hands exploring her back and caressing her spine. He came to the fastening of her bra, and undid it deftly; then his hands slid round to her front, pushing the lacy garment out of the way so that he could cup her swelling breasts. Her nipples hardened instantly, and he rubbed his thumbs over her areolae.

She arched against him, and he continued caressing her breasts, squeezing them. He let one hand slide down her body, and she parted her legs; he slid his hands between her thighs, cupping her sex. Liza's sex was growing wet and puffy, and she was sure that he could feel how hot she was, even through the thickness of the soft denim. He began to move his hand back and forth, rubbing her; she groaned, wriggling against him, and the sound was enough to break the spell.

Bryn froze, then stepped back, dropping his hands. 'God, I'm sorry, Liza. I don't know what came over me.'

She stared at him mutely, her eyes pleading. Surely he wasn't going to back out now? Not after the way they'd responded to each other. He couldn't do this to her.

Bryn swallowed, flushing. 'It won't happen again, I assure you. I'm sorry.' He turned on his heel and left the room; Liza watched him go, wanting to call him back and pull him into her arms, resuming where they'd stopped. Only her pride stopped her: he obviously didn't want her, which was why he had left. He'd simply forgotten himself – forgotten who she was, maybe dreaming of the woman in his life and the contact between them making him suddenly long for his lover, pretending that Liza was her.

Choking back a sob of mingled anger and embarrassment,

she restored order to her clothes, then gathered her papers. She couldn't work here, this evening. Not now. She couldn't bear the idea of having to face him, after he'd rejected her like that. Not until she'd had time to put a mask over her feelings.

Just as she was about to leave the room, she heard the hum of an engine, and then a roaring sound which suggested that Bryn had driven off at speed. She switched off the light, then locked up the *James* office, and went to her own car. Although she usually took the tube to work, she'd intended to work late that night, anyway, so she'd brought the car with her that morning. Slowly, glad that she was forced to concentrate on the road and didn't have the time to think about what had just happened between her and Bryn, she drove home.

When she let herself inside the front door, she dropped the papers she'd been carrying and her handbag, then leaned back against the wall and sank slowly to the floor. God, what a mess. What a bloody, bloody mess. How could she have let it happen? She should have pulled away in the first place, not let him touch her.

She closed her eyes in misery, remembering the feel of him against her body. The warm, clean musky smell of him; the touch of his hands against her skin; the way his mouth had moved against hers. She traced her lower lip with the tip of her finger, then let her finger drift slowly down her throat. The worst thing was, she was still aroused, her body hungry and unsatisfied.

Leaving her things where they were, she got to her feet, kicked off her shoes, and went upstairs to her bedroom. She knew that she'd hate herself for this, later, but until the craving in her body had died down, she couldn't even think straight. She switched on the bedside light and pulled the curtains, then undressed swiftly, leaving her clothes in a tangled heap on the floor. She pushed back her duvet and climbed onto the bed; then she reached across to her bedside cabinet, opening the bottom drawer and extracting her vibrator. Sighing, she lay back against the pillows, closing her eyes and reliving the moment when she'd been in Bryn's arms.

In her mind, the situation was quite different. He was kissing her and touching her breasts, playing with the nipples and pinching them gently between his thumbs and forefingers, keeping just the right side of the pain-pleasure barrier. His tongue was pushed against hers, and he was kissing her deeply, passionately, as though he wanted to pour himself into her body. He slid his hands down over her abdomen, undoing the button and zipper of her jeans; then he eased one hand under the waistband of her knickers, cupping her mons veneris and sliding one finger between her labia, feeling how warm and wet and ready she was for him.

He inserted a finger into her sex, moving it tormentingly slowly; as she rocked her pelvis, pushing against him and trying to force him to caress her harder, he broke the kiss, laughing, and began a trail of kisses along the sensitive cord at the side of her neck. She arched against him, and he continued rubbing her sex, putting his thumb against her clitoris and teasing the hard bud of flesh from its hood. With his free hand, he pulled at her sweater; she lifted her arms, helping him to remove it, and he pulled off her bra at the same time. He stared at her for a moment, drinking in her beauty, then dipped his head and drew his tongue between her breasts. She closed her eyes, arching back and lifting her rib-cage almost in offering to him. He cupped one breast, stroking the soft undersides with the tips of his fingers, and then took one hard peak of flesh into his mouth, licking and sucking; she groaned with the sheer pleasure of it.

He eased her jeans and knickers downwards, and she wriggled out of the garments, kicking off her shoes. When she was at last standing naked in front of him, he smiled, dropping a kiss on the tip of her nose and placing her hands on her hips, posing her for his pleasure. She grinned, and gave him her best Marilyn Monroe impersonation; he grinned back, and walked round her, studying her as an artist would study his model.

'Perfect,' he pronounced.

He pulled her back into his arms, stroking her buttocks and her midriff. As his hands dipped lower, she widened the gap between her thighs, allowing him the access he needed. He rested the heel of his palm against her mons veneris, and cupped her sex with his fingers; he used his forefinger and third finger to part her labia, then curled his middle finger and drew it very slowly down the musky furrow of her quim. He repeated the action again and again, his finger gliding easily against the warm wetness of her flesh; finally, Liza moaned, and he pushed his finger against the entrance of her sex. He added a second finger, and a third, and pistoned his hand rapidly back and forth.

Just when Liza was on the point of coming, he stopped. 'Not yet,' he told her huskily. He withdrew his hand, holding her gaze and bringing his hand up to his mouth. His fingers were glistening with her musky juices, and he licked them clean, savouring the musky tang with relish. Liza felt herself flush, and he grinned. 'Like the most perfect wine,' he said. 'I want you, Liza. I want you now.'

She stepped towards him, and unbuttoned his shirt, sliding the soft cotton from his shoulders. Although she knew that he didn't work out at a gym – he spent so much time at the business, he didn't have time for anything else – his body was naturally well toned. She let her hands wander over the muscles of his shoulders, then down over his pectorals, stroking his rib-cage and then following the line of hair which arrowed down his midriff and disappeared under the belt of his jeans.

He closed his eyes, tipping his head back and opening his mouth, licking his lower lip; Liza undid the buckle of his belt, then unzipped his jeans, guiding the soft denim over his hips. He was wearing navy blue silk boxer shorts underneath, and the thick rigid outline of his cock was clearly visible through them. She curled her fingers round his shaft, using her thumb and forefinger to rub his frenum through the silk of his underpants; he made a small sound of pleasure, and curled one hand over hers, urging her on.

She hooked her thumbs into the waistband of his boxer shorts and slowly drew them downwards. Bryn helped to remove the rest of his clothes; Liza drew a sharp intake of breath as she saw him, naked, for the first time. He really was beautiful, his body almost as angelic as his face. He wasn't thin, but there wasn't a trace of fat on him, either. She couldn't help reaching out to stroke the clean lines of his sides and buttocks; he made a sound of rough impatience, and pulled her back into his arms, wrapping one hand round the nape of her neck and jamming his mouth over hers.

The next thing that Liza knew, he had walked her over to his desk. He swept the papers aside, not caring that they scattered everywhere on the floor, and hoisted her onto the bleached ash. She rested back on her elbows, and he bent his head, licking the hollows of her collar-bones and covering the whole of her upper body with kisses, tiny butterfly kisses which sensitised her skin and left her craving more. 'Touch me, Bryn,' she urged. 'Use your mouth on me.'

He needed no second bidding. He nuzzled her rib-cage, trailing a line of kisses down her abdomen, and she lifted her thighs, parting them and gripping her legs to open herself to him. She felt him smile against her skin, and then he was kissing her inner thighs, nuzzling her and breathing in the scent of her arousal. She felt so hot, as though her quim were on fire; when he blew gently over her quim, it was as though he fanned the flames, rather than cooling her.

'Don't tease me,' she said, her voice husky and low.

He smiled, then, and at last she felt the slow stroke of his tongue over her quim. She sighed, giving herself up to pleasure, and he began to suck her labia, nipping at them gently with his lips and then pushing his tongue deep into her. He sucked her clitoris, drawing fiercely on the hard coral bud, and she felt her sex pool.

'Make love to me, Bryn,' she said. 'I want to feel you inside me.'

He straightened up, leaning over to kiss her; she could taste herself on his mouth. He rubbed his nose gently against hers, and then, at long last, she felt the tip of his cock pressing against the entrance of her sex. He eased into her, a millimetre at a time; when he was in her up to the hilt, he paused, letting her body get used to the feel of him. Then he began to thrust, pushing in slowly and withdrawing quickly, pulling almost out of her, until Liza was moaning and writhing beneath him. She locked her legs round his waist, pulling him more deeply into her, and drew her hands up to caress her breasts, tugging at her nipples.

When she came, she virtually saw stars, it felt so good, his body pumping into hers and his cock twitching deep inside her. Her internal muscles flexed hard round him, deepening and lengthening the climax for both of them; Bryn stooped to wrap his arms round her, pressing his cheek against hers and breathing in the scent of her hair. They lay locked together until he slipped from her; then, with regret, he stood up, disentangling her legs from him. 'I've wanted to do that for a very long time.'

'And so have I,' Liza moaned, lying on her bed with her quim flexing hard round the vibrator, her legs spread wide and her free hand working madly on her clitoris as she reached a climax. 'So have I, you bastard. And the only way it's going to happen is in my dreams.'

Bryn stared moodily at his empty glass. The bottle of red wine he'd just consumed hadn't helped one little bit. If anything, it had made things worse. His mind kept replaying the image of Liza in his arms. The moment he'd touched her, even though it had only been to steady her, he'd known that he was going to kiss her. He hadn't been able to help himself.

The way she'd looked up at him, her blue eyes so candid and soft – she'd even looked a little vulnerable. When she'd licked her lower lip like that, he hadn't been able to help himself. From the first moment that he'd seen her, when she'd pretended to be a client and then told him who she really was and what she was going to do at *James*, he had itched to kiss her. He'd spent so many evenings since then driving home, fantasising what it would be like to feel her mouth under his. So he'd bent his head, and touched his mouth to hers.

When she'd kissed him back, he'd lost control. His body had worked of its own volition then, his mind switching off from the fact that she was his business partner, and what he was doing was incredibly risky and stupid. His hands slid under her sweater to stroke her back, unclasping her bra, and then he'd cupped her gorgeous breasts, feeling her soft warm flesh against his skin. She'd been aroused, too, her nipples hard and inviting as they pressed against his palms.

He squirmed on the sofa, his erection springing up anew. Even the thought of her delectable mouth made him hard.

He lay back, sliding one hand into his jeans and adjusting his hard cock to make himself more comfortable. God. Why had he done it? He'd really ruined things, now. He'd maintained his control for so long, knowing that he couldn't risk the business by making love to Liza: and the first time he'd touched her, his control had snapped completely.

He licked his lower lip. She'd smelled so sweet, her skin had felt so soft. And the feel of her mouth under his had been incredible. She'd wanted him back, he knew that. The moment he'd slid his fingers over her groin, and discovered just how warm she was – even through the thickness of her denims – he'd almost laughed with the sheer delight of knowing that she wanted him as much as he wanted her. If she hadn't made that little noise of pleasure, who knew what would have happened? He closed his eyes, and undid the button of his jeans, sliding down the zip and pulling down his underpants so that his cock was exposed. He curled his fingers round the shaft and began to rub himself, as he thought of Liza.

If she hadn't cried out, jerked his mind back to reality . . . Then he would have slowly let his hand drift down from her beautiful breasts, gliding over her skin and stroking her midriff, feeling how sweet and soft her skin was. He'd have taken the hem of her sweater and pulled it upwards; and she'd have lifted her arms, letting him take it off properly so that he was free to look at her, touch her. Her bra would have followed suit, and then he would have cupped her breasts with his hands, dipping his head and nuzzling her skin, breathing in her soft powdery scent. He didn't recognise the perfume she wore – it was obviously expensive – but it turned him on in a big way. Even the faintest whiff of it in the office, when she was away from her desk, was enough to make him hard.

Then he would have traced her areolae with the tip of his nose, feeling the skin crinkle under his touch, and then dipped his head back slightly so that he could take one hard rosy peak into his mouth, rolling her nipple on his tongue and sucking hard, tasting the sweetness of her skin. At the same time, he would have caressed her other breast, kneading it gently; as she'd arched against him, he would have transferred his mouth to her other breast, arousing her still further and making her writhe and tilt her pelvis towards him. She would have slid her fingers into his hair, urging him on . . .

Bryn groaned, and began to masturbate more vigorously, his hand moving up and down his shaft at speed. And then he would undo her jeans, sliding them down over her hips. She would step out of them, and stand before him, unabashed and unashamed of her nakedness. She'd be wearing a pair of white lacy knickers, and he'd draw them slowly downwards, dropping to his knees and breathing in the musky scent of her arousal. From there, it would be one short sweet movement to bury his face in her quim, draw his tongue between her labia and taste the sweet-salt evidence of her arousal. Her quim would blossom under his mouth, her sex growing wet and puffy, her labia opening for him like a stylised flower.

He'd feel the heat in her quim rising, and then she'd start to move, rocking her pelvis and sliding her fingers into his hair again, her fingertips digging into his scalp as her pleasure grew. He'd continue to lap her, taking her to the limit – and then he'd feel her quim flutter over his mouth, and his mouth would be filled with her musky nectar.

When the aftershocks of her climax had died away, he'd stand up again, and she'd slide her hands round his neck, drawing his face down to hers and kissing him deeply, tasting herself on his mouth. She'd start to undress him, then, removing his sweater and sliding her hands over his skin, feeling his muscles and making him itch for her to touch him more intimately. Then, at last, she'd undo his jeans, pushing them down. He'd help her to remove his clothes, and then he'd be naked beside her, his cock rising hard and heavy from the cloud of hair at his groin.

She'd smile at him, then, a slow and coquettish smile – and then she'd drop to her knees, drawing a trail of kisses over his midriff and making her tongue into a sharp point as she traced the outline of his cock against his abdomen, just millimetres away from touching the thick shaft of flesh. She'd tease him until he was groaning, almost begging her to take him; and then she'd cup his balls with one hand, ringing his shaft with the other, and dip her head to take the tip of his cock into her mouth.

He'd close his eyes in an agony of pleasure, stroking her hair and tilting his pelvis so that she could take him more deeply into her mouth. As she fellated him, he'd be moaning her name, telling her how much he loved her and how beautiful he thought she was – how he loved everything about her, from her stubbornness to her mind to the mischievous glint in her eyes when she bantered with one of the lads or one of her favourite clients.

She'd continue to work him with her mouth, teasing his frenum and stroking his balls until he could feel his orgasm approaching and, although he'd warn her that he was near the edge, she'd still continue sucking him, taking his seed into her mouth and swallowing every last drop of the salty fluid. Then she'd stand up and give him another of those come-hither smiles, placing her hands on her hips and raising one eyebrow. She'd beckon to him, then turn round and stand by her desk, her hands gripping the edge of the bleached ash and her buttocks wriggling invitingly at him. He'd have a perfect view of her quim, glistening from her recent climax; and he'd be hard again in an instant, wanting to bury his cock deeply within her warm sweet depths.

He'd walk over to join her, wrapping his arms round her waist and holding her close to him, pressing his cheek against her shoulder and maybe touching his lips slightly to her skin. He'd tell her how much he adored her, how much he wanted to make love with her; and then he'd straighten up again, sliding the tip of his cock to the entrance of her sex and pushing in. She'd feel so good, so very good, her internal muscles flexing round the thick shaft as he eased into her. He'd place his hands on her hips, and start to thrust, pushing in deeply and then withdrawing slowly, circling his hips to change the angle of his penetration and give her greater pleasure.

She'd begin to make small noises of pleasure as he continued to thrust into her; then, at last, he'd feel her quim rippling round his shaft, her internal muscles clenching him sharply as she reached her orgasm. At the same moment, he'd reach his own climax, and his body would pour into hers. He'd hold her close, whispering her name and murmuring sweet endearments; and then, when he slid from her, he'd turn her round to face him, cupping her face and telling her how much he adored her . . .

Bryn groaned, and white silky fluid spattered his abdomen as he climaxed. He squeezed his eyes even more tightly shut. 'Oh God, Liza,' he murmured. 'What have I done? And how the hell am I going to face you, now?'

Thirteen

The following Monday morning, Liza walked into the *James* office. She'd spent most of the weekend rehearsing what she was going to say to Bryn; but saying the words to an imaginary Bryn in the familiar surroundings of her own home was quite different from saying them to the man himself in the office.

She'd been such a fool. She'd virtually thrown herself at him, even though he'd made it very clear that he wasn't interested in her. He saw her purely in the role of his business partner, and she'd been completely stupid to hope otherwise. The man was a workaholic, and that was probably why his first marriage had broken up. He wasn't likely to make the same mistake again – even if it was to have an affair, rather than risk the commitment of marriage.

Grimly, she made herself a cup of coffee, and headed for her desk. She switched on her computer, and was buried deep in the rest of the questionnaire analyses by the time that Bryn walked in.

'Good morning.' He nodded coldly at her.

'Good morning.' She didn't dare ask him how his weekend had been. He looked like death warmed up, she thought, as if he hadn't had much sleep. And that was probably due to her – he'd been lying awake, wondering how the hell to deal with the adolescent behaviour of his business partner. Well, she'd show him that she could be as adult about it as he was. 'There's some coffee in the kitchen, if you want some.'

He shook his head. 'Thanks, but I don't have time, this morning.' He picked up a file from his desk, and disappeared.

Liza watched him as he left the room. In some ways, it was easier not having to face him; in others, it was making things worse. They couldn't avoid the subject forever – could they?

Of course not, she told herself crossly. They'd have to talk about it sometime. The question was, when? And what the hell would she say to him?

She spent an uncomfortable morning alone in the office; she was glad that she had the questionnaires to finish analysing, because it helped to keep her mind focused on something else. Even so, she was aware that she was listening out for Bryn's return, and she was annoyed with herself for it. What did she expect him to do? Come back into the office, sweep her into his arms, and declare undying love for her? She pulled a face at herself. 'Grow up, Hargreaves,' she told herself roughly.

Bryn didn't return at lunchtime, or in the afternoon; Liza thought about leaving him a note, but decided against it, and merely left the office, asking Steve on her way out whether he'd lock up for her. The next day followed a similar pattern, with Bryn leaving her alone in the office and merely greeting her with a cold 'good morning'.

When the same thing happened on the Wednesday, Liza decided that they really had to talk. It was obvious that Bryn was avoiding her, and she was beginning to think that there was more to it than met the eye. He was quite capable of being civil to her, so the fact that he was avoiding her meant that he, too, felt strange about what had happened between them. In fact, Liza thought, it was beginning to look as if her attraction to Bryn was mutual. That would go a long way to explaining his behaviour – he was avoiding her because he couldn't trust himself not to repeat that little episode.

On the Thursday morning, Liza was ready for him. Just as Bryn was about to leave the room, she coughed loudly. 'Bryn.'

He turned round to look at her. 'What?'

'We need to talk.'

'About what?'

She sighed. 'Bryn, you haven't been here all week. We're partners in a business, if you remember.'

'I have to go out.'

'I think it can wait for five minutes. Come and sit down.' She stood up, walking over to the door and closing it. Bryn's eyes narrowed, but he dragged his chair over to hers, and sat down.

Liza sat next to him. 'Bryn,' she began. The phone shrilled, interrupting her; she rolled her eyes. 'What timing,' she murmured dryly. When Bryn was about to pick up the phone, she shook her head. 'Leave it. They'll ring back.'

'What's so important that you're prepared to lose business?'

She met his gaze without flinching. 'Friday night.'

The phone stopped ringing, and he exhaled sharply. 'Look, I've apologised for that. It won't happen again.'

'I want to know why.'

His eyes narrowed. 'Why what?'

'Why you kissed me.' Her colour rose. 'And I want the truth.'

'I don't know.'

She noticed that he hadn't been able to meet her eyes. She smiled to herself; it looked like her theory was right. Bryn felt the same about her as she did about him. So there was hope, after all. 'Bryn,' she said softly, placing her hand over his. 'Talk to me.'

'There's nothing to say.' He shook her hand away.

Her gaze dropped; his erection was clearly visible. Again, she smiled to herself. He was too damned stubborn to admit it, but her touch affected him. 'I think that there is.'

This time, he met her eyes. 'Such as?'

'Don't pussyfoot, Bryn. You know exactly what I mean. We have to talk – about us.'

'There is no us.'

'After Friday, I think that maybe there should be.' She reached up to touch his face, curving her fingers round his jaw. 'Bryn. I—'

He pulled her hand away. 'Liza, as you said, we're partners in a business. There's no room for anything else.'

'Why not?' Her eyes narrowed. 'Look, you told me that you'd been married before. I haven't asked you any of the details, because it's none of my business, but if you worked with your ex-wife and it all went sour over work, don't think that it always has to be that way. There's no reason why we can't mix business and pleasure.'

Bryn scowled. 'I never mix business and pleasure.'

'That's what I always used to think – but you have a lot to learn,' she said softly. 'Bryn, we'd be good together. I've been thinking about it ever since Friday – and from the look of you, I'd say that you've been losing sleep over it, too.'

Bryn stood up. 'I don't have time for this, Liza. We have a business to run.'

As he left the room, Liza propped her elbows on the desk and rested her face in her hands. Maybe she'd come on too strong. But she'd been so sure that he felt the same way. There was a possibility that she'd made a mistake, but she doubted it. Bryn just wasn't going to admit to his true feelings, or do anything about them. Which meant that until he was ready to make a move, she had to pretend as well. That, or work on a strategy to make him change his mind: and she'd have her work cut out with that.

By the time that Liza got home that evening, she was in a foul temper. Why was Bryn being so bloody stubborn about things? The way he'd kissed her, the way he'd touched her – he'd been just as affected by it as she'd been. She'd replayed their conversation in her head time and time again since that morning, and she'd come to the conclusion that he'd spent the previous months holding himself on as tight a rein as she had. Now she'd admitted to him that she found him attractive, why the hell was he still avoiding her?

The phone rang; part of her was tempted to leave her answerphone switched on to take the message, and maybe call whoever it was when she was in a better frame of mind; on the other hand, it might be Sally or one of her other friends. And she could certainly do with the company to cheer her up. She snatched up the phone. 'Hello?'

'Liza. Sweetheart.'

Her jaw set as she recognised the voice. 'Rupert. What do you want?'

'Hey, that's not a very friendly thing to say.'

'I'm not in the mood for being messed about. Why are you ringing me?'

'Would you believe, I've missed you? Liza, I've called you several times. I've left messages for you – and you've just ignored me. Look, I know I upset you, and I want to apologise. I've had a lot of time to think about things, and I'd really like to see you.'

'Maybe I don't want to see you.'

'Liza, you were right. I was a selfish bastard, and I needed to grow up. Look, I know that maybe things won't ever be the way they were again between us, but I'd like to think that we could still be friends. Why don't I pick you up and take you out to dinner? You can tell me all about your new job, and how you're enjoying running your own business.'

She thought about it. Although there was no way she wanted to renew her relationship with Rupert – despite what he'd just said, she doubted that he really meant it; he had probably just been stood up by another girlfriend and didn't want to waste the restaurant booking – it would do her good to go out, and try to forget Bryn the Unreachable. 'Okay.'

'Really?'

He sounded shocked, and she grinned. 'Were you expecting me to say no, then?'

'Well – yes,' he admitted. 'But I'm glad that you'll see me.'

'What time?'

'I can be there in an hour, if that suits you?'

'That's fine. See you then.' She replaced the receiver, and walked thoughtfully into the bathroom, putting the plug in the bath and adding liberal quantities of expensive foam bath oil before running the water. This evening could turn out to be a complete waste of time; but Rupert could be charming company, in the right mood, and that was exactly what she needed. An attractive man to be charming her.

She smiled wryly. There were a number of other men she could have called. Jeremy Walker, for starters. Or she could have phoned Leila Swift, and suggested that they went out on the town together. She would certainly have had a diverting evening with either of them. But at the same time, she knew that she didn't really fit in with their more decadent lifestyles. With Rupert, at least he was on her level. She didn't feel out of depth, with him.

* * *

When Rupert arrived, exactly on time, Liza was dressed to kill. She had piled her hair on top of her head in a sophisticated style which managed at the same time to look as if she'd recently got out of bed after a lengthy love-making session; she was wearing full make-up; and her little black silk dress was one of Rupert's favourites.

His eyes widened as he looked at her. 'Wow. You look fantastic, Liza.' He leaned forward to kiss her cheek.

'Thank you.' She smiled back at him.

'Ready to go?'

She nodded, sliding a lacy wrap round her shoulders and grabbing her handbag. She set the burglar alarm and closed the door behind her; then she allowed him to escort her to his car. 'So where are we going?' Rupert named a small and very expensive restaurant in Mayfair. She raised an eyebrow. 'You've obviously been doing some good deals, lately.'

He grinned. 'Yeah, it's bonus time again. I haven't done so badly.'

Liza was impressed. The old Rupert would have boasted about exactly how much he'd made, and what a fantastic dealer he was. Maybe he really had changed.

'So how's the business, then?' he asked, surprising her again. Rupert had always preferred to talk about himself; the fact that he was showing interest in what she was doing meant that either he was up to something, or that he really had grown up. She was inclined to think that it was the latter.

'Fine. I'm really enjoying it – now I'm my own boss, I really don't think that I could go back to the rat race. Certainly not to a place like Fitchett's, anyway.'

'I'm glad it's all working out for you.' He smiled at her. 'I only hope that you don't have your professional hat on at the moment.'

'Hm?' Liza didn't quite follow him.

'I'm driving you. If you were sort of mystery shopping . . .'

She grinned. 'If you're angling for a job, Rupert, you'd also need to be interviewed by my partner. And I definitely don't have my professional hat on, tonight.'

'Good. You often used to bring your work home with you,

because you hated it so much,' he mused. 'You certainly look a lot happier, now.'

'I am.' And I'd be even happier if Bryn would only admit what he really felt about me, she thought. She tried to push the idea from her. It wasn't fair to Rupert. He'd asked her out, that evening – whatever his real motive had been – and it was only fair that she should concentrate on him, not on Bryn.

They drove in companionable silence the rest of the way to Mayfair. Liza had been to the restaurant Rupert had chosen, when she'd worked at Fitchett's, and she knew that the food was good; she smiled as he ushered her through the door. This was going to be just the kind of evening she needed: good food, good wine, good company.

'By the way, this is my bill. No strings attached,' Rupert murmured as the waiter left them to read the menu.

Liza looked at him. His blue eyes were sincere: he meant it. She decided to accept with good grace. 'Thank you.'

The food was as good as she remembered it, and Rupert was good company, amusing her with anecdotes about his City firm and people they both knew. She had almost forgotten about Bryn by the time that Rupert drove her home – particularly as she'd drunk more than her fair share of a bottle of champagne. Champagne, which Rupert had told her with a grin, should also be celebrating her new job as well as his bonus. She'd flushed at that, remembering how she'd smashed the bottle of champagne on his kitchen floor, the last time that she'd seen him, but he'd squeezed her hand and said that he'd deserved everything he'd got, and to forget it.

Rupert parked the car, and escorted her to her door. She was feeling relaxed enough to turn to smile at him. 'Come in for a coffee.'

He smiled back. 'Thank you. I'd like that.'

He followed her into the kitchen, and watched her as she made the coffee, tipping coffee grounds into the cafétière and adding boiling water. She poured them both a mug, then looked at him. 'Do you still take your coffee the same?'

He nodded. 'I know I ought to be healthy and give up sugar, but I just can't.'

She added two sugars to his coffee, and milk to her own,

handing him a mug. 'Let's go and sit down.'

They went into the sitting room, and Rupert sat on the sofa. She went to the stereo, putting on her favourite Dire Straits CD. As the first bars floated into the air, Rupert smiled. 'I love this one.'

'Me, too.'

They lapsed into silence, and Liza kicked off her shoes, going to sit on the sofa next to him and curling her legs under her. She closed her eyes, sipping the coffee and listening to the music. It was almost like old times, she thought, then smiled wryly to herself. No. They had both changed. Rupert seemed to have grown up, and she . . . Yes, she had learned a few things about herself, too.

Rupert reached for her hand, curling his fingers round hers and rubbing her palm with his thumb. Liza opened her eyes and looked at him; he flushed, and dropped her hand. 'Sorry. I really meant it when I said "no strings". I suppose I was just thinking about old times.'

'Me, too.' The words were out before she could stop them.

He was very still. 'Liza. Perhaps I ought to go.'

Part of her knew that his suggestion was sensible; but part of her was still so angry with Bryn that she was in the mood to do something crazy – anything to release the tension. Rupert found her attractive still, and she'd drunk enough champagne to want the release of good sex. Why should she deprive herself, on the account of someone who wasn't going to give her what she needed? She smiled. 'Like you said, no strings. Let's go to bed.'

His eyes widened. 'Liza. I didn't ask you out just because I wanted to go to bed with you.'

She spread her hands. 'Are you telling me that you don't want to make love with me?'

He winced. 'No, of course not. I'm not saying that at all – but you're drunk.'

'Tipsy,' she corrected. 'I'm fully compos mentis, believe me. I know exactly what I'm saying and doing. I don't want to be your girlfriend again – I think we've both moved on, and that's a good thing – but we were always good together, in bed. And, right now, I'm in the mood for making love. With you.'

She reached up to cup his face, drawing her thumb along his lower lip. His mouth opened involuntary, and he drew her thumb into his mouth, sucking gently. Liza felt the familiar flood of pleasure well up inside her, and smiled. Yes, this was exactly what she needed. This was the best way to forget Bryn and his coldness – by making love with someone who knew her body well, and knew exactly how to coax the best response from her. 'Come to bed, Rupert,' she said softly. She stood up, holding out her hand; Rupert took it, and stood up, letting her lead him to her bedroom.

She'd left the curtains closed earlier, when she'd changed before dinner; she switched on the bedside light, and smiled at him, moving into his arms. He slid his hands down her sides, moulding her curves to his, and bent his head, touching his lips to hers. Her mouth opened beneath his, and he deepened the kiss, sliding down the zipper at the back of her dress at the same time.

She stepped away from him for a moment, and the silk dress fell in a rustle to the floor. The dress was fully lined, so she hadn't been wearing a slip; she was wearing a black lacy bra, matching knickers, and her favourite lace-topped hold-up stockings. Rupert stood with his hands on her shoulders, just looking at her; Liza smiled in pleasure as she saw the dark flush of desire staining his cheekbones and the fact that his pupils had enlarged, making his blue eyes seem nearly black.

Slowly, he let one hand slide down her throat, stroking her in the hollows of her collar-bones and then dipping one finger into her cleavage. 'Mm, I'd almost forgotten how good you feel,' he said huskily. He traced the edges of her bra, noting the way her breasts were beginning to swell and her hardened nipples were clearly visible through the thin black lace of her bra.

With intense concentration, he pushed the cups downwards to reveal her breasts properly, and slid his fingertip over her areolae, noting the way the skin puckered beneath his touch. He took his time, and Liza wriggled impatiently, wanting him to touch her more intimately. She reached up to loosen his tie and unbutton his shirt; he helped her to remove his clothing, not caring that it ended up in a crumpled heap on the floor. Then he slowly pulled her knickers downwards. She stepped out of the black lacy garment, and put her hands behind her back to unclasp her bra; Rupert shook his head. 'Leave it,' he told her quietly. 'I love seeing you like this. You look so lewd and wanton and desirable, with your bra all askew and your stockings on.'

Liza grinned. 'I'm glad you're in the mood for playing.' Her gaze travelled down his body. Rupert still looked good, his body firm and well toned; she'd forgotten how good his erect cock looked, too. Rupert had been endowed with quantity as well as quality. She trailed her hands down his body, and he closed his eyes as her fingers curled round his cock.

'Oh, Liza. I've missed you.'

'I've missed you, too.' It wasn't strictly true. She'd taken her pleasure with several other men since Rupert – although not with the one man she really wanted. And yet a part of her had missed the nights she'd shared with him, the comfort and warmth and desire.

'Let's make up for it now.'

She smiled, and pushed the duvet back; Rupert picked her up, laying her on the bed. 'Mr Macho,' she said.

Rupert didn't miss the slightly sharp note in her voice. 'Just indulge me, this once,' he breathed.

Liza shook her head. 'I was hoping that you were going to indulge me.'

He raised an eyebrow. 'Like how?'

She grinned. 'Wait and see.' She turned on her side, facing him, and reached up to kiss him, sliding her tongue into his mouth. Rupert kissed her back, stroking her breasts and then sliding one hand between her legs; she was already wet, and when he pressed his fingertip to her sex, he slid easily inside.

She made a small noise of pleasure, and stretched out, widening the gap between her thighs and closing her eyes. Rupert continued to thrust his finger in and out, adding a second and teasing her clitoris with his thumb. She came almost instantly, her internal muscles contracting sharply around his fingers; he smiled, rubbing his nose against hers and then withdrawing his fingers, lifting them to his mouth and licking the gleaming musky juices from his skin.

Liza smiled, curling her fingers round his cock and squeezing gently. She nuzzled his cheek, and bit his earlobe. 'Rupert, I want you to do something for me,' she commanded huskily.

He recognised the glint in her eyes. Liza was in the mood to play – and he remembered just how good it was when Liza decided to play. 'Of course.'

She rolled him over onto his back, then leaned over to open the top drawer of her bedside cabinet. She extracted two black silk scarves, and attached one to each of his wrists, tying him to the wrought-iron headboard. She tested the bonds; they held. 'Not too tight?' she asked softly.

Rupert shook his head. 'That's fine.' His cock twitched with anticipation, and Liza saw a small bead of clear moisture form in its eye. She grinned, and moved down the bed, dipping her head so that the ends of her hair tickled his abdomen. Again, she encircled his shaft with her fingers, lifting it slightly, and touched the tip of her tongue to the eye of his cock, lapping the tangy fluid from it. She licked his glans, her tongue smooth and swirling over it; then she retracted his foreskin, holding it back.

She looked up then, her eyes glinting with mischief. 'Do you like that?' she enquired.

Rupert groaned. 'You know I do.'

'Good. Though I haven't finished with you, yet. Not by a long way.' She shifted again, so that she was sitting astride him with her back to him, and placed her ankles inside the crook of his knees. She held the root of his cock with one hand, pulling the skin back with her other hand, then began giving him quick sharp strokes, spacing them at one per second. Rupert cried out with pleasure, and she quickened the rhythm for half a dozen strokes, before resuming the slow masturbation. She repeated the actions again and again; just when Rupert was near to coming, she stopped him, squeezing just below his frenum to delay his orgasm. Then she shifted so that she was kneeling astride him, backing up towards his face so that her quim was within reach of his mouth, and bent her head, taking the tip of his cock into her mouth.

He lifted his head, stretching forward as far as he could, and slid his tongue between her labia, savouring the sweet-salt tang of her arousal. His rhythm matched hers as she continued to fellate him; he flicked his tongue over her clitoris, exciting her still further, and then pushed his tongue as deeply into her as he could. Just at the moment when he came, he felt her quim ripple over his mouth. She swallowed the creamy fluid, then shifted round to lie beside him, cradling into him and resting her cheek on his chest.

'Aren't you going to untie me?'

'Not yet.' She lifted her head; her eyes were sparkling. 'I haven't finished with you, yet.' She cupped his balls, stroking them softly; as his cock hardened again, she smiled to herself. This was exactly what she wanted, what she needed. This was what she'd wanted Bryn to do to her.

Bryn. Her smile faded. Why couldn't she get him out of her mind? It had been a mistake even to think about him; now that she had, this was impossible. But supposing it had been Bryn, not Rupert, lying beside her . . . She closed her eyes, knowing that she wasn't being fair to Rupert, but unable to stop the fantasy from taking over.

She moved to straddle him, rubbing her quim against his hard cock so that he could feel how hot and wet she was, the evidence of her recent orgasms. He groaned, and she leaned forward, kissing him deeply so that their juices mingled in their mouths. Then she shifted herself slightly, easing her hands between their bodies and guiding his cock into her sex. She lowered herself on him, and leaned back slightly to increase the sensations of the way his cock filled her. She lifted one hand to her breasts, stroking the hard nipples and squeezing the creamy globes of flesh; she rested the palm of her other hand on her mound of Venus and parted her labia with her middle finger, seeking and finding her clitoris.

As she raised and lowered herself over him, she rubbed her clitoris, using a rapid figure-of-eight movement. Her intimate flesh was wet and slippery beneath her fingers, and she rubbed herself harder. Her movements quickened as her arousal grew; she could imagine Bryn lying there, watching the way she pleasured herself while she rode him. His beautiful sensuous mouth would be open, his lower lip moistened by his tongue. He'd be longing to touch her himself, with his hands and his mouth, except that she'd tied him too tightly for him to be able to slip from his bonds.

His eyes would be black with desire, and he'd be completely helpless; all he could do was enjoy the way her warm wet flesh was wrapped round his cock, the way she rode him. She'd lean back still further, shifting her hand from her clitoris to stroke his perineum; her finger, wet from her juices, would slide easily against the puckered rosy hole of his anus, her finger pushing against the tight channel. He'd resist her at first, and then he'd let himself relax, allowing her to penetrate him as he was penetrating her.

She'd continue to ride him, the pace of her movements over him matching the way that her finger slid in and out of his forbidden portal. He wouldn't be able to stop himself crying out with pleasure as his climax surged through him and his cock twitched inside her, filling her. The movement of his body within hers would be enough to trigger her own orgasm, and it would go on and on and on . . .

At that precise moment, Rupert cried out, and she felt his cock throb inside her. She, too, climaxed; though she had to bite her lower lip to stop her crying out Bryn's name and, when she opened her eyes, she was careful not to let it show in her face that she felt she was with the wrong man. She withdrew her finger, and leaned forward, kissing him tightly on the mouth. 'Thank you.'

'My pleasure.' He looked enquiringly at her. 'Do you think you could untie me, before my circulation vanishes completely?'

She smiled ruefully, and climbed off him, shifting up the bed to untie his bonds. He rubbed his wrists, shook his hands, then knelt up and pulled her close to him, stroking her back and kissing the curve of her shoulder. 'If that's what a new job does for you, you should have done it a long time ago,' he told her.

She tensed. 'Rupert – I thought we'd already agreed, no ties.'

He nodded. 'If that's the way you want it.'

'I do.' She stroked his face. 'Though I'm not throwing you out, just yet.'

'I'm glad to hear it.' He kissed her lightly. 'Because I think that, this time, you should be the one tied up . . .'

Fourteen

He kissed her deeply; Liza found herself responding. The next thing she knew, she was lying on her back, propped up by pillows, with the silk scarves attaching her wrists to the bedstead. He reached into the drawer, removing another two scarves, and tied her ankles to the foot of the bed. Then he smiled, climbed off the bed, and sauntered out of the bedroom.

'Rupert?'

'I'll be back in a minute,' he called, his voice filled with suppressed mischief.

Liza's eyes widened. His clothes were still in her bedroom, and it was unlikely that he'd leave without them, so he wasn't going to tie her up and abandon her. But what the hell did he have in mind?

She soon found out. He returned to the bedroom, carrying a glass of ice-cubes. 'I thought that these might be . . . a little diversion,' he said.

Her eyes narrowed. 'A bit *9½ Weeks*, isn't it?'

He shrugged. 'No. Because I'm not going to blindfold you – and I'm not going to drip ice-cold water into your navel.' He licked his lower lip, and sat down on the bed beside her. 'But I promise you this, Liza – you're going to enjoy yourself. A lot.'

A pleasurable shiver ran down her back. She'd forgotten just how inventive Rupert could be. Whatever he had in mind, she was sure that he was right: she'd enjoy it. She settled back against the pillows, and smiled at him, closing her eyes. 'Promises, promises,' she drawled.

He bit her lower lip, and she opened her eyes in surprise. 'What the–?'

He grinned. 'That's better. I want you to watch this. In

fact . . .' He climbed off the bed again, and moved her cheval mirror to the foot of the bed. 'Can you see yourself, or do you need some more pillows?'

Liza swallowed. 'I can see myself.' A woman with hair the colour of winter wheat, lying on pale apricot sheets which served to highlight the paleness of her skin, with her wrists and ankles tied to the wrought-iron bedstead by black silk scarves. Her blue eyes were glittering with intense desire, there was a flush across her cheekbones, her mouth was full and red, and her nipples were dark and erect. The way he'd tied her, with her legs wide apart, meant that her quim was clearly visible through the ornate wrought ironwork, and it was glistening with her recent climax. Her thighs were slightly sticky with Rupert's seed: in all, she looked lush and wanton.

'It's a beautiful sight,' Rupert said, as though he had read her mind and agreed with everything she'd thought. 'A woman ready for pleasure, ready to be taken to the limit and beyond.'

She licked her lower lip. 'What did you have in mind, then?'

'This.' He sat beside her, and took one of the ice-cubes from the glass. He drew it over her areolae, making her cry out at the shocking change in temperature; he smiled. 'And that was pleasure, not pain. Look at the way your nipples are standing up, dark and erect. Like raspberries. It makes me want to take one into my mouth and roll it on my tongue – but not yet, not yet.'

She shivered with anticipation. Was he going to trail the ice-cube over her midriff? Or was he going to bring it up to her mouth, trace the curve of her lip with it?

In the end, it turned out to be neither. 'Because where I really want to use that ice-cube is here. Here, in your lovely, warm, wet, glistening cunt.' He moved swiftly, sliding the ice-cube along her quim; she yelped.

'You bastard! That's cold!'

'Ice usually is,' he told her, his eyes glinting with amusement and desire. 'I love the contrast, Liza, between the warmth of your flesh and the coldness of this ice-cube, between your softness and its hardness, the way it tastes of nothing and you taste of pure ambrosia.' He continued stroking the ice-cube up and down her quim; the heat of her sex was melting the ice-cube, and the sensation of water dripping over her was at once disconcerting and arousing.

She closed her eyes, and he dripped water onto her midriff, making her jump and open her eyes again. 'I want you to watch this, see what I'm doing to you,' he reminded her softly.

She nodded. 'Sorry.'

'That's okay. Now, where was I?' He popped the ice-cube into his mouth, crunching it. 'Mm. It tastes of you.' Then he took a second ice-cube, putting it into his mouth briefly to blunt the sharp edges, and pushed it against the entrance of her sex. Liza watched, fascinated and horrified and excited, as it slid into her. 'I could pack you with ice, and then fuck you back to warmth again,' he mused. 'Or maybe not.' He retrieved the ice again. 'Mm, see how hot you are, how you've already melted it.' He rubbed it across her clitoris, and she jerked. He smiled, and continued rubbing her. 'Like an ice-cold cock rubbing against you, isn't it? Do you like it, Liza? Do you like the way the cold makes your pretty little clit even harder, so it almost hurts when I rub you? And yet it makes you want more, doesn't it? It makes you want me to rub you and rub you and rub you, until you're screaming as you come.'

Liza swallowed. 'I—'

'Tell me what you want, Liza,' he said, his voice still soft and melting like honey.

'I – I want you to rub my clitoris. I want you to make me come.'

'With the ice?'

She nodded, unable to speak.

He smiled, then. 'I wish I'd thought of putting your vibrator in the freezer, filling you with a proper ice-cold cock. But we'll just have to make do with this.' He began to rub her clitoris in earnest, using the ice-cube skilfully.

She could see everything that he was doing to her, as well as feeling it, and it heightened her excitement. Yes, she thought, this was exactly what she needed. An inventive lover who'd take her mind off her problems. Rupert was doing one hell of a job of taking her mind off things; the way he was touching her, teasing her with the coldness of the ice, was driving her almost insane with desire.

She cried out as her orgasm swept over her, shockingly fast, her internal muscles flexing sharply; Rupert smiled, and removed the ice-cube, placing it in her mouth to stop her saying any more. Then he shifted to kneel between her thighs, and guided the tip of his cock to her still-quivering sex; he pushed into her, then began to thrust, taking it hard and fast. Liza cried out again; this time, when she closed her eyes, he made no objection, merely pumping even harder into her.

When she came, this time, she was almost sobbing, it was so strong. Gently, Rupert withdrew from her, untied her swiftly, and pulled her into his arms, holding her close. 'Better?' he whispered against her ear.

She nodded, not trusting herself to speak.

'I think you needed that, sweetheart.' He stroked her hair. 'And so did I.'

Liza nuzzled into him, filling her senses with his warm familiar smell, and drifted into sleep.

The next morning, she woke to find herself lying on her side, an obviously male body curled behind her with his arm under her breasts, pulling her back into him. For one heart-stopping moment, she thought that it was Bryn; then she remembered the previous night. Rupert.

'Sleeping Beauty awakes, then?' he whispered in her ear.

'Mm.' She wasn't quite sure how to face him. She'd been tipsy, the previous evening, but she could remember everything that had happened – including the way he'd played with her, with the ice – and she knew that she hadn't made any rash promises to him.

'I would offer to make you a coffee,' Rupert said, 'but I'm not that familiar with your kitchen.'

She turned round to face him. 'It's sweet of you, but I don't really have time for a coffee. I really ought to be getting to work – and you always used to start pretty early.'

'Work can wait.' He rubbed his nose against hers. 'Liza–'

She pulled away. 'No ties, remember. We agreed.'

'I know.' His blue eyes were candid. 'But it's a nice way to start the day. And to seal the fact that we're friends, now.' He drew his hand down her side, tracing her curves and then squeezing her buttocks gently. His hand came up to cup one breast, and his thumb rubbed across her nipple, a smile crossing his face as he felt the flesh harden and peak under his touch. 'Mm. Liza.' His voice was husky.

Part of Liza knew that she ought to push him away and get to work; but her body was enjoying the way he touched her, and she could still remember the way he'd pleasured her, the previous night. She closed her eyes and tipped her head back, letting him kiss her throat and move down to nuzzle her breasts. He rolled her onto her back, and took one nipple into his mouth, sucking fiercely on the rosy flesh; then he moved to the other breast, sensitising that nipple, too. She gave a small murmur of pleasure as he continued his trail of kisses downwards, outlining her navel with the tip of his nose and then nuzzling her, parting her legs and crouching between her thighs.

She tilted her pelvis as she felt his stubble-roughened cheeks graze her inner thighs; she could feel his breath warm against her quim, and it made her sex grow liquid with desire. He held her labia apart, just looking at her for a moment; then he let his mouth traverse the intimate folds and crevices of her quim, exploring the ground he'd once known so well. Liza slid her hands into his hair; again, the treacherous thought slid into her mind that it could be Bryn licking her so thoroughly, not Rupert. She gave herself up to the fantasy and relaxed, letting his mouth go exactly where he wanted.

He sucked the hard bud of her clitoris, making her writhe beneath him; then he pushed his tongue deep inside her, savouring her arousal. He brought her to a rapid climax and then lifted his head again, wrapping her legs round his waist and pushing his cock into the entrance of her sex.

Liza cried out as he penetrated her. He stayed there for a moment, letting her body grow used to his, and then he began to thrust, taking it deep and slow. He carried on for twenty strokes, then speeded up the rhythm, pushing just the fattest part of his cock rapidly into her and making her cry out with pleasure. Then he resumed the slow thrusts, raising her to a higher peak. Her orgasm splintered through her, and she turned her face to the pillows, baring her teeth and trying hard not to call out his name.

Her climax tipped him into his own orgasm. He lay quietly within her, keeping his weight on his hands and knees; when her flesh had stopped rippling round him, he withdrew, kissing the tip of her nose. 'I feel set up for the day, now,' he said softly.

'Yes,' Liza agreed hollowly. Rupert's body had slaked part of her desire, but she knew that the moment she saw Bryn again, the fever would burn hotly again, out of control. But that was something she'd have to learn to deal with, until she worked out a way to crack Bryn's stubbornness.

He kissed her lightly. 'Is it okay if I have a shower?'

'Of course.' She glanced at the crumpled heap of clothing on her bedroom floor. 'Um, I think your colleagues might notice if you go to work wearing those, though.'

'Perhaps I could borrow an iron?' She looked at him in shock. Rupert was actually saying that he'd iron his own shirt, not expecting her to do it for him? He grinned. 'Okay, so I hate ironing. But I can't expect you to do it for me, can I?'

'You really have changed.' The words were out before she could bite them back.

He grinned. 'You could say that. And it's all down to you. When you left me, I did some hard thinking.'

'Rupert – look, don't take this the wrong way, but I really don't think that it would work between us, now.'

'There's someone else, isn't there?'

She flushed. 'No.'

'Meaning that there is someone, but it's not working out between you, yet.' Rupert stroked her face. 'All I can say is that the man's an idiot, if he lets a woman like you slip through his fingers.'

She winced. 'I don't want to talk about it.'

Rupert nodded. 'I'll have my shower, then,' he said.

'And I'll iron your shirt,' Liza added, feeling guilty.

'There's no need, sweetheart.' He smiled at her. 'I'll do it, while you have a shower – and then I'll leave.'

She nodded. 'I did enjoy last night, though. All of it.'

'Me, too.' He leaned forward to kiss her lightly. 'Any time you're at a loose end, call me.'

'Thanks. I will.' She meant it, too. Rupert as a lover, with no strings, was a very pleasant idea indeed, something to soothe the pain of the way that Bryn rejected her.

He smiled at her, and headed for the shower. In the meantime, she grabbed her dressing gown and went downstairs, setting up the iron and ironing board. She had intended to iron his shirt, but he was already out of the shower when she returned to the bedroom.

'It's all in the kitchen,' she said.

'Thanks.' He nodded. 'Take care, Liza.'

'You, too.'

He didn't kiss her goodbye, simply smiled, and left the room. Liza headed for the shower, turning the water up as hot as she could bear it and washing her hair as well. By the time that she emerged, her hair wrapped in a towel, Rupert had gone, leaving her a note to say that he hoped everything worked out well for her.

'You're a prize bitch, Hargreaves,' she told herself wryly. 'You should have just let him go, last night – not invited him to bed with you.' Still, it had happened; there was no point in dwelling on something that she couldn't change. Sighing, she dried her hair, dressed, and left for work.

To her annoyance, Bryn completely ignored her that morning, not even saying hello or making a comment about the fact that she was late. She gritted her teeth. Two could play at being childish, she thought; and, in a battle of wills, she wouldn't be the one to crack first.

She was in a bad mood all day, being abrupt with the drivers and even with a couple of clients – clients whom she disliked, but was always scrupulously polite to when they called. Bryn spent very little time in the office; and the brief time when he was there, he studiously ignored Liza. She itched to slap him, shake him – anything to get a reaction from him; but she managed to maintain her cool. Just.

The next day was as bad, and she spent the weekend seething over his behaviour. When he managed to avoid her on the Monday and Tuesday as well, she snapped. She left the office without telling him where she was going or leaving him a note, and headed for the shops. Several hundred pounds' worth of shopping later, she felt slightly better – but she was still furious with him. And at a complete loss as to what she should do next.

When she got home, she dropped her bags in the hall and picked up the phone, dialling Sally's work number.

Sally answered almost immediately. 'Marketing department, Sally Reynolds.'

'Hi, Sal, it's me.'

'Liza! Hi, how are you?'

'I've been shopping and spent a small fortune, but I'm still in a bad mood. I was wondering, do you fancy going out for a meal, tonight? I thought that Chinese might be nice.'

'Then we can go back to mine to sink some wine, and you can tell me what's bothering you, hm?'

Liza chuckled. 'That transparent, am I?'

'Considering how long I've known you, yes.' Sally laughed back. 'Mark's away this afternoon, so I can leave on time. Shall we meet outside the Haagen Dasz shop in Leicester Square at about seven?'

'Sounds perfect to me. See you then.'

Liza replaced the receiver, then decided to spend the rest of the afternoon pampering herself. She ran herself a long bath, adding liberal quantities of aromatherapy oil, then moved her portable CD player to the doorway of the bathroom and put on her favourite Vivaldi cello concertos. She poured herself a glass of Chardonnay, took the box of white Belgian chocolate praline shells she'd bought earlier that afternoon into the bathroom, and stripped off, piling her hair on top of her head. Lying back in the bath, inhaling the gorgeous citrussy scent of the aromatherapy oil, sipping wine, eating chocolates and listening to music, made her feel slightly better.

Sod Bryn Davies. He really wasn't worth it, she told herself savagely. The only thing was, her body still remembered what it had been like to be touched by him, and it craved more of the same. Angrily, Liza ate another chocolate, following it with a sip of wine. It didn't help much; in the end, she gave in, lying back against the bath and closing her eyes. If he was there in the bath beside her . . .

* * *

Her imagination supplied the rest. Bryn was kneeling on the carpet, wearing only his jeans. He was holding a bar of soap, washing his hands, and then he began to smooth the creamy foam over her skin, moving his fingertips in tiny erotic circles. He concentrated on her arms, his hands gliding up and down and paying attention to the crease of her elbows, the sensitive skin of her inner wrists, her palms and her fingers, washing them one by one and running his finger and thumb up and down them as though he were giving her a shiatsu massage.

Then he sluiced her skin clean, and urged her to lean forward so that he could work on her back and shoulders. He lathered his hands again, smoothing over her shoulders and loosening the knots of tension. He worked down her spine, his hands moving in spider's-feet fashion, and then worked his way up either side of her spine, still moving his fingertips in small circles. Again, he sluiced her clean.

By this time, Liza was aroused, longing for him to touch her more intimately. She looked up at him as she lay back against the bath, her eyes pleading; he simply smiled, and picked up her left foot, working round her ankle and the sole of her foot. He washed her thoroughly, paying attention to every bit of skin; although she was usually ticklish, she found it incredibly relaxing and sensuous. He worked his way up over her calf, then the back of her knee; Liza waited in anticipation as he moved up towards her thigh. She wanted him to touch her sex – but he didn't. He merely finished washing her leg, rinsed away the lather, and picked up her other foot, working on that in exactly the same way.

Liza had to bite back a moan of longing as he lowered her legs again. Her midriff was next, and she willed his hands to shift higher, work on her tingling breasts, or to dip lower and ease the nagging ache in her sex. Cruelly, he did neither. He worked on her throat instead, his fingers moving to just below her collar-bones and no lower. She arched up, her breasts taut and needing release; finally, he took pity on her, cupping the creamy globes and squeezing them gently. He'd already aroused her so much that, to her shock, she climaxed as soon as he touched her nipples, her quim flexing hard. She cried out, and he bent his head to kiss her gently.

'That okay?' he asked.

She nodded, unable to speak. It had been more than just okay . . .

Liza opened her eyes. Her quim was still flexing from her fantasy. Although she hadn't inserted a finger into herself or even touched her clitoris – she'd merely touched her nipples – she had experienced a powerful orgasm. 'Oh hell,' she said softly. This was getting too much for her. After the night she'd spent with Rupert, she should have felt completely sated for a few days; and yet still, the thought of Bryn drove her to touch herself, stroke her body to a climax. She had to do something about it. But what? Still, maybe Sally would have some good ideas.

She finished washing herself, drained the glass of Chardonnay, and hauled herself out of the bath. The CD had finished playing; she pressed the play button again, filling the air with music, then finished her toilette, smoothing body lotion into her skin and unpinning her hair.

Not bothering to put on a dressing gown or wrap a towel round herself, she walked into her bedroom. She'd spent quite a bit of money on new underwear that afternoon, having learned during her teenage years that wearing good underwear always made her feel better, and she put some of it on, liking the smoothness of the silk and lace against her skin. She sprayed herself liberally with perfume, then slipped into a comfortable pair of trousers, adding a cashmere sweater and taking a tailored jacket from her wardrobe.

She put her hair into a complicated knot and did her make-up, then surveyed herself in the cheval mirror. 'You'll do,' she told her reflection. Thanks to the make-up, the shadows under her eyes were no longer visible; no-one would guess that she had anything on her mind. She pulled a face at herself, grinned, and switched off the stereo. Then she went downstairs, set the burglar alarm, locked the door behind her, and set off for Leicester Square.

She arrived at the place where she'd agreed to meet Sally at five to seven. Two minutes later, Sally joined her, hugging her and kissing her cheek. 'Hi. Okay?'

'I suppose so,' Liza replied. 'How about you?'

'With Mark away, so I could get right on top of things at work – brilliant.' Sally smiled at her. 'I'm starving.'

'Me, too.' Liza spread her hands. 'Let's hit Chinatown.'

They walked through the streets to Chinatown, and Liza picked one of the more upmarket restaurants. 'This is on me,' she said.

'Don't be daft. We'll go Dutch, as we usually do,' Sally said.

'Don't argue. I'm in spend mode.'

Sally whistled. 'You really are having a bad time, aren't you?' She'd been party to some of Liza's shopping expeditions when Liza had been at her most unhappy at Fitchett's, so she knew just how much money Liza could blow in an afternoon, when she was in that sort of mood. 'Want to talk about it?'

'After dinner,' Liza said.

They went into the restaurant, and Liza scanned the menu greedily. 'I don't know about you, but I could go for the full works, tonight.'

'Suits me fine.' Sally sniffed the air. 'Something smells gorgeous – and I bet it tastes even better!'

Eventually, they chose bang-bang chicken, crispy duck, five-spice prawns, crispy seaweed, Singapore noodles, and sesame prawn toasts, as well as tiny spring rolls and prawn crackers. Liza ordered a bottle of Chardonnay to go with it, and she and Sally sat chatting while they waited for their meal to arrive.

'So how was your hot date, then?' Liza asked.

Sally wrinkled her nose. 'Lukewarm, really. I prefer my men to have a little more finesse.'

Liza nodded. 'I know what you mean. Never mind.'

'Men. Who needs them?' Sally quipped.

The food was as good as it had smelled, and both Liza and Sally eyed the remains of their meal regretfully. 'I'll burst if I eat another mouthful,' Sally groaned. 'Though, in other ways, I could quite happily eat it all over again.'

Liza grinned. 'Same time, same place, next week?' she teased.

'Don't tempt me.'

Liza paid the bill, then they headed back to Islington, to Sally's flat. 'Coffee or wine?' Sally asked as she closed the door behind them. Then she laughed. 'Silly question. I think you need the latter.'

'Yes.'

Sally took a bottle of white wine from the fridge, and poured them both a glass. They went into the living room, and Sally put on a Suzanne Vega CD. 'Right, then. Spit it out.'

Liza sighed. 'It's Bryn.'

'What happened?'

'The other week, I was working late. I was just going to get myself a cup of coffee, and I thought I was on my own. As I walked through the door, I collided with him – and we ended up kissing.' She pulled a face. 'Then he backed away, apologised, and left. I thought about it all weekend, and I came to the conclusion that he feels the same way about me as I feel about him.'

'So what's the problem?'

'He spent the next few days avoiding me. I tackled him about it, and he wouldn't admit how he felt. He's been ignoring me, ever since.' She grimaced. 'And then, Rupert rang me, the other night. He asked me out to dinner – no strings.' She shrugged. 'We had a good time. He's changed; he's grown up a bit, I suppose. Though, before you say it, I'm not intending to go back to him. It wouldn't work. I spent the evening fantasising that it was Bryn with me, not him.'

'Ouch.' Sally was sympathetic.

'Anyway, I asked him in for coffee. I'd drunk too much champagne, and I was still furious with Bryn for being so bloody difficult and stubborn, so I suggested that we went to bed.'

Sally raised an eyebrow. 'Did it make you feel better?'

'Yes and no. His technique's good, and I've always enjoyed sex with Rupert – but I kept seeing Bryn's face. In the morning, I woke up, convinced that I was in Bryn's arms; but it was Rupert.'

'So what happened?'

Liza shrugged. 'We parted on good terms. I was late into work, and Bryn didn't say a single word to me. He's been refusing even to speak to me. I've been a complete bitch to everyone in the office, and I nearly lost a key account. That's why I decided to spend this afternoon shopping, to try and get it out of my system.'

'And it didn't work,' Sally finished sympathetically.

'Not at all.' She grimaced. 'Sally, I've got to do something about the situation, but what?'

Sally was thoughtful. 'Hm. Do you know that he definitely feels the same way about you?'

Liza nodded. 'When I tackled him about it, I put my hand over his. I could tell that he had an erection, and his pupils had dilated. He reacts to me in a physical way, Sal. He feels that same weird tingle when we touch.'

'Then why is he backing off, do you think?'

'Well, he's divorced. I don't know if his ex-wife was part of the business, and *James* came between them – I haven't asked him, and it's none of my business – but that's the only thing that I can think of. He says he won't ever mix business with pleasure.'

Sally sipped her wine. 'Well, you could give up *James*. Then he wouldn't be mixing business with pleasure.'

Liza shook her head. 'No way. I want to stay part of the business.'

'Can you afford to buy him out?'

'No.'

'Well, then. The only thing I reckon you can do is have a huge row with him, then seduce him.'

Liza laughed. 'Sal, he won't even talk to me. How the hell am I going to have a row with him?'

Sally grinned. 'I'm sure you'll find a way.'

'Yeah.' Liza stared glumly into her glass. 'If it doesn't work –'

'Then you'll have to give up. But it's worth a try, isn't it?'

Liza nodded. 'You're right. I'll give it a try.'

Sally lifted her glass in a toast. 'I'm not going to wish you luck – you don't need it. When you set your mind on doing things, you always succeed. So just go for it!'

Fifteen

The following morning, Liza dressed with great care, doing her make-up and wearing her most sensual perfume. She'd slept badly, spending most of the night rehearsing the lines she wanted to say to Bryn in her mind. It hadn't worked well last time, but that was no reason for her to assume that she'd have the same problem this time. It wasn't exactly a row that she was planning to have with him, but she was going to make it very clear to him how she felt.

She was the first to arrive in the office, and she brewed herself a coffee, making it stronger than usual. She drank it black, for once, needing the shot of caffeine to her system; and then she settled back to wait for Bryn. She couldn't concentrate on her work, so she spent her time playing patience games on the computer, and losing badly.

'Come on, come on,' she murmured, glancing at her watch. 'Don't say that you're going to be late. Not today. I can't handle it.'

At last, she heard the rattle of the key in the lock – she always left the front door locked when she was alone in the office, on Bryn's insistence that it was safer for her – and he walked in.

'Good morning,' she said.

He looked at her; something in her face made him reply, rather than ignoring her as he had done for the previous few days. 'Good morning.'

His voice was curt, but at least he'd spoken to her, she thought. 'Look, Bryn, we need to talk.'

'About what?'

The coldness of his tone annoyed her; she decided to go straight for the shock treatment. If he didn't want her as a person, he needed her in one respect. 'The business. Whether I continue to be a partner here or not.'

He stared at her, shocked. 'How do you mean?'

'Sit down.' Liza walked over to the office door, closing it and locking it. At his surprised look, she added, 'I don't want us to be disturbed.'

'What's going on, Liza?'

'You tell me.' She looked levelly at him. 'I've been here for several months, now. I think it's time that we reviewed my position in the firm. You haven't said whether you're happy with the work I've done, or not.'

He shrugged. 'You're my business partner. You can't tell a duff car when you see one, but you're doing all right.'

Her eyes widened with anger. 'All right? Just all right? Oh, come on, Bryn. Everyone else in the firm likes me and works well with me; I've improved our cashflow; I've negotiated a decent overdraft at better terms than we had before; and I've brought in more new business. How can you say that that's just all right?'

'Okay, then, you're doing well.' He spread his hands. 'What else do you want me to say?'

Liza swallowed hard. This was going to be make or break. 'When I first came to see you, you said that you'd like me to do what Gramps did – be your sleeping partner and let you run the business. I've been thinking about that.'

'So you want out?'

She shook her head. 'Far from it. I like working here. In fact, as you haven't been around much for the past week or so, and I've found out that I can cope pretty much on my own, I'd like to make you the same offer.'

His face flushed with surprise and anger. 'You what?'

'I want you to be my sleeping partner.'

He shook his head in disbelief. 'You can't mean that! I set this firm up in the first place. How the hell can you even consider cutting me out of *James*?'

She shrugged. 'You don't listen very hard, do you?'

He frowned. 'I don't follow you.'

She came to sit on the edge of his desk, holding his gaze with her own. 'There's more than one type of sleeping partner.'

'What do you mean, Liza?'

She sighed. 'This isn't working, is it? Look, it's cards on the table time, Bryn. Almost from the moment I met you, I was attracted to you. Like you, I didn't want to mix business and pleasure. I wanted to prove to you that I could pull my weight as part of *James*. Now, I have, and after what happened between us, the other night . . . I figure that you must feel the same about me, or you wouldn't be reacting like this.'

'Like what?'

'Avoiding me, ignoring me – and don't deny it, it's obvious that you've been trying to keep out of my way.' She licked her lower lip. 'Bryn. We can't go on like this, pretending that nothing happened between us. Either we get it out of our systems, or—'

'Or what?'

'Or I'll be forced to withdraw my half in *James*.'

His eyes narrowed. 'You wouldn't do that to me.'

'Try me.' She stared levelly at him. 'So are you going to admit it, and make our relationship a partnership in every sense, or do I walk out?'

'I–'

She could see the uncertainty in his face; she decided to make the decision for him. She leaned forward, and touched her lips to his, very gently.

At first, he didn't respond; she cupped his face in her hands, and nibbled gently at his lower lip. He gave a small tormented moan, and opened his mouth, giving her the access she wanted; she deepened the kiss, pressing her tongue against his.

He remained still, and she slid off the desk to stand between his open thighs, caressing the nape of his neck with one hand and unbuttoning his loose cotton shirt with the other. She pulled the soft cotton from the waistband of his jeans and pushed the garment from his shoulders, still kissing him. Then she broke the kiss, and rubbed her nose against his. 'Bryn.' Her voice was low and husky with arousal.

He curled his fingers round her wrists. 'Liza. We're in the office. Anyone could walk in.'

'They couldn't. The door's locked.' She gently shook her

hands free, and walked over to the office window, closing the blind to give them complete privacy. 'No one is going to interrupt us.'

'I didn't intend—'

She stopped him, pressing her forefinger against his mouth. 'Sh. Not just now. I think there's something more important that we both need, don't you?'

It was as though her words allowed his control to snap. He stood up and pulled her into his arms, squeezing her buttocks and pressing her body hard against his. She could feel his erection pulse against her, and her blood sang with pleasure. She'd been right. He felt the same way – and what had been waiting to happen between them for so long was finally going to happen.

He kissed her deeply, his tongue plunging into her mouth; she slid her hands round his neck, pushing her hands into his hair and revelling in the crisp clean feel of it. He slid his hands under the hem of her sweater, stroking her back and undoing her bra; Liza shivered. This was where it had all gone wrong, last time.

But this time, it was different. Bryn broke the kiss, gently disentangling her arms from his neck, and slowly removed her sweater, dropping her bra on top of it. He drew one finger down her cleavage; she noticed that his hand was shaking. 'You're just how I imagined you to look,' he said huskily. 'Your skin so soft and creamy, your nipples so dark, your breasts so perfect and soft and round. And your perfume – it's been haunting me for weeks.'

She smiled. 'Time to exorcise it, then.'

He shook his head. 'I'm not so sure that I can exorcise it.' Before she could ask him what he meant, he bent his head, kissing her throat; she tipped her head back, and his mouth shifted downwards. He cupped her breasts, nuzzling her cleavage and breathing in her perfume; then, at long last, Liza felt his mouth close over one hardened nipple, licking and sucking and grazing the sensitive tissue with his teeth. She stifled a cry, not wanting to break the spell, and then he squeezed her breasts gently, rubbing his thumb over her other areola. He pulled back slightly, breathing over her wet nipple, and she shivered as desire lanced through her. God, she wanted him so much. She wanted him right now.

But Bryn was in no hurry. He began a trail of kisses along her midriff, nuzzling the soft underside of her breasts in a way that made her arch her back and dig her fingertips into his scalp, urging him on. She whimpered, and he slid one hand between her thighs, rubbing along her quim with the base of his thumb. Liza closed her eyes in bliss as he continued to rub her; he was still taking his time, exploring her body with his mouth. At last, he undid the button of her jeans, sliding the zipper downwards. She waited for an agonising moment as he teased her, nuzzling her skin; at her impatient wriggle, he chuckled against her skin, and began to pull her jeans downwards. When the soft denims were at her ankles, she kicked off her shoes and stepped out of the clinging garment. Bryn slid his hands down her thighs. 'God, you're so very lovely,' he breathed. 'I can't believe this is happening. That it's real.'

'Oh, it is. Believe me.' She bit his shoulder. 'See?'

'Ouch!' He bit her earlobe, in revenge. 'You're not dreaming, either, then?'

'Nope.'

Again, he slid his hand between her thighs, rubbing her quim through the thin stuff of her knickers. The silk was no barrier to him; he could feel how hot she was. She gave a strangled cry as he pushed the gusset of her knickers to one side, and slowly drew his finger between her labia. She was already wet, ready for him; he smiled, and continued to rub her, holding her open with one hand and exploring her intimate contours with the forefinger of his other hand.

When he touched her clitoris, she nearly came; he rubbed his cheek against her midriff, and then plunged one finger deep inside her. She rocked her pelvis, wanting more; he dropped to his knees in front of her, and buried his face in her groin. Her blood was pounding, and she thought that she was going to pass out. 'Oh, Liza,' he murmured, and then at last she felt the slow stroke of his tongue along her intimate flesh. She cried out, her internal muscles flexing sharply within seconds, but he didn't stop. He continued licking her, bringing her to another climax, and another. By the time that he lifted his head again, she was shaking, barely able to stand.

He stood up, pulling her against him and kissing her so that she could taste herself on his mouth. 'I've wanted to do that for weeks,' he said.

'I wanted you to do it, too,' she told him huskily. 'I want you, Bryn. I want to feel your cock inside me. I want you to fuck me to Paradise and back.'

The phone rang; he lifted the receiver, cut the line, and left the receiver off the hook. Liza's eyes widened in shock. 'That could have been business.'

'I don't care. Whoever it is, if they want to talk to us, they'll call back, later.' His echo of her words to him, the last time she'd tried to tackle him about what was happening between them, was deliberate.

She smiled. 'Make love with me, Bryn. Let's make this a real partnership – not just work, but our bodies as well. I want to be with you. I want to make love with you. Right here, right now.'

'Not so fast.' He met her gaze. 'First of all, I want to know – did you sleep with Alain Joubert?'

She nodded. 'Though that's not why he recommended us to his business associates, if that's what you're thinking. It was the fact that I took him for a cup of coffee when I met him from the plane, and stopped partway through the journey to his cottage to let him stretch his legs.'

'He sounded sophisticated, when I spoke to him on the phone. I thought you probably slept with him.'

His voice held an odd note; she stared at him in wonder. 'Don't tell me that you were jealous?'

'Just a bit. I was trying to stop myself thinking of you, at the time.' He toyed idly with her breast, rolling her nipple between his thumb and forefinger and making her arch against him.

'Perhaps you can tell me something, then. Did you ever drive Leila Swift to a party?'

He nodded. 'How did you know?'

'The way she said your name. The fact that she seemed so familiar with you.' She raised an eyebrow. 'You did more than just drive her to a party, didn't you?'

He grinned. 'I think that it's my turn to ask you if you were jealous,' he teased.

She undid the button of his jeans, sliding the zip downwards and then pushing the denims over his hips. 'You haven't answered my question,' she reminded him, curling her fingers round the shaft of his cock and rubbing him gently through the thin cotton of his underpants.

'Yes. She asked me to wait inside, and I ended up dancing with her. It seemed only natural for us to leave the room together, via the patio doors; then we found a secluded place in the garden.' He licked his lower hip. 'I don't think I'd better ask what happened to you, when you drove her.'

She flushed. 'No. But it probably isn't what you think.'

'Oh, Liza.' He bent his head to kiss her again. 'This is going to make things bloody difficult, you know.'

'It's not.'

'No?'

'No. We can keep our professional life as it is – and be together in private, as well.' She sighed. 'It's been driving me crazy. I'm used to getting what I want, Bryn. Having you so close and yet so untouchable was so frustrating. I tried to forget you in other people – but it didn't work,' she admitted. 'I kept thinking about you, when they were touching me, seeing your face instead of theirs. And I haven't slept properly for weeks.'

He smiled wryly. 'You've given me quite a few sleepless nights, too,' he said. 'Every time I closed my eyes, I started fantasising about you. And I couldn't afford to do that.'

She uncovered his cock, touching him skin to skin, and he shivered. 'Alain told me,' she said softly, 'that mixing business with pleasure could give even greater satisfaction.'

He looked thoughtful. 'Jane thought that I spent too much time on the business, and not enough time on her. That's why she divorced me – although she was the one having the affair, not me.'

She stroked his face. 'Bryn, that's not going to happen between us. First of all, we're partners in this business, so work pressures affect us both the same; and secondly, if I think you're working too hard and neglecting the private part of our partnership, I won't whinge at you. I'll just – let's say, distract you.'

He grinned as she stroked his buttocks. 'Like you're doing now?'

'Exactly.' She grinned back. 'So are you telling me that you haven't had a serious relationship since your wife?'

He nodded. 'I haven't been celibate, so I won't pretend that I haven't made love to another woman since then; but I just haven't wanted to get involved in anything long-term. That's why you drove me crazy – because I knew that you were different. I had to fight you.'

'So that's why you weren't keen on me joining the firm.'

'That, and the fact that yes, I did think that you were a spoilt little rich kid who'd get bored within a week.'

Her eyes glittered. 'I hope that you've changed your mind about me, now.' She squeezed his cock.

'Oh, yes,' he breathed. 'This firm needs you – and so do I. Make love to me, Liza. I can't hold out any more.'

She needed no second invitation. She helped him remove the rest of his clothes, then pushed him back against his desk. 'I want you here,' she told him softly. 'I was fantasising about something like this, the other night. After you kissed me, touched me – and walked out.'

'I had to walk out. I couldn't trust myself not to leap on you – and I wasn't sure how you felt about me.'

'You could have asked me.'

'And if you hadn't felt the same – it would have meant that you'd leave, and *James* would go under. I couldn't risk it.'

'I told you how I felt. At least, I tried to,' she amended. 'But you were the male equivalent of the Ice Maiden. You wouldn't even listen to me.'

He sighed. 'I'm sorry. I was going through hell myself, at the time.'

She pressed her face to his chest. 'I wanted you so much. I kept fantasising about you. Especially after you'd touched me.'

He bit gently at her neck. 'And did you touch yourself, when you fantasised?'

She nodded. She couldn't quite tell him that she'd been driven to use her vibrator. 'I couldn't help myself.'

'You made yourself come.'

She nodded. 'I needed the release, Bryn. I was so frustrated.'

He smiled slowly. 'Guess what. So did I.'

She looked up at him, her eyes widening in surprise. 'You – you masturbated, over me?'

He nodded. 'Though we weren't quite like this, in my fantasy.'

'What did you do?' Her voice was a whisper.

'I drove home, furious with myself for losing control and touching you, when I'd promised myself that you were off limits. Then I sat on my sofa and sank a bottle of red wine, thinking that it would help me to forget you.'

'And did it?'

He shook his head. 'Far from it. I kept remembering how soft your skin was, how you'd smelled and tasted. I wanted you so badly. I started wondering what would have happened if I hadn't hauled myself back from the brink – if I'd continued to touch you and kiss you, the way I wanted to. In the end, my cock ached so much, I undid my jeans and brought myself off. I haven't masturbated like that for years, but I couldn't help myself.'

Her eyes glittered. 'And what were you doing, in your mind, as you touched yourself?'

He smiled. 'In my fantasy, you were bending over the desk, wiggling your beautiful bottom at me, and I took you from behind, sliding my cock into your warm wet welcoming depths.'

She smiled back at him. 'We can do that, later. Right now, I want you here.' She patted the desk, and he pushed his paperwork aside, lying prone on the bleached desk. She climbed onto the desk, straddling him; her quim rested lightly on his cock. She pulled the gusset of her knickers aside, feeling his cock push against her moist labia; she groaned, and began to rock over him, letting the tip of his cock brush against her clitoris.

'God, Liza. I don't know how much of this I can take,' he told her huskily. 'I want you to make love with me, Liza. I want you to ride me. I want you to fuck me.' He cupped her breasts, his thumbs lightly stroking her still-erect nipples. She tipped her head back, closing her eyes in pleasure, and he raised his upper body, bending his head to one breast and licking her areola. He didn't take it into his mouth, however; he just breathed on her skin, making her whole body tingle.

'Bryn, don't tease me,' she murmured. 'Taste me. Touch me properly.' She shivered in the agony of waiting; and then, at last, he licked her nipple again, the tip of his tongue circling her areola and then flicking rapidly across the hard peak of flesh. Her clitoris seemed to twitch, in sympathy; she made a small noise of pleasure, and he began to suck. All her nerve-endings seemed to ripple, wave after wave of sensation concentrating round the spot where Bryn's mouth touched her skin, then pulsing outwards to arouse her whole body.

He eased one hand between their bodies, stroking her midriff and then pushing his hand between her thighs; the second that his finger touched her clitoris, she cried out, the sensation was so good and so sharp. She wanted it to go on forever, just this one moment of pure pleasure.

He nuzzled against her skin, and continued to rub her, bringing her almost to the edge of orgasm. Before she climaxed, he lifted her slightly, positioning the head of his cock at the entrance to her vagina. She lowered herself gently onto the rigid muscle, feeling her internal muscles contract sharply round him as he entered her.

'Oh, God,' she moaned. 'You feel so good.'

'So do you. Warm wet velvet, peaches and cream. Soft and smooth and wet and tight. I could stay inside you forever.' He tilted his chin, and she bent her head to kiss him, tasting her earlier climax on his mouth and revelling in the sweet-salt tang.

He sank back onto the desk, his hands sliding down her body to support her over him; Liza almost laughed with the sheer joy of it, and began to move, lifting herself gently upwards and then slamming down hard, grinding her pubis against the root of his cock. She moved her lower body in small circles, flexing her internal muscles round him; as she bore down on him, he tilted his pelvis, pushing up so that he was enveloped by her soft flesh to the hilt.

She could feel how aroused he was, how his balls had lifted and tightened; she continued to move, her body weaving over his, until she felt the surge of her climax running through her veins. At precisely the moment that her orgasm exploded within her, she felt his cock throb inside her, and she heard him cry out her name.

She closed her eyes, bending over to bury her face in his neck, breathing in his sharp masculine scent; he stroked her spine, holding her close. 'Liza. My beautiful, beautiful Liza,' he murmured.

Eventually, he slipped from her. She climbed off him, and sat down in his chair. 'So. What happens now?'

'What I'd like to happen now,' he told her, sitting up, 'is to take you home to bed. I don't care whether it's my place or yours – I just want to spend the rest of the day making love with you, in comfort.' He flexed his shoulders. 'That desk is definitely too hard.'

Her lips twitched. 'Considering that you whinged at me for not answering the phone during a few brief minutes, the other day, I'm surprised that you're considering abandoning the office for a whole day.'

'Yeah, I know.' He slid from the desk, and bent to kiss her. 'We've got a business to run.'

She looked faintly disappointed. 'And that's it?'

He shook his head. 'Oh, no. When we finish, tonight, I'm going to drive you out to Hampstead Heath, and make love to you under the stars. Then we're going to eat – and then we're going to spend the rest of the night making love.' His lips twitched. 'And then – well, tomorrow's another day. But as long as I wake up with you in my arms, I don't care.'

She smiled back at him. 'That makes two of us, then.'

'Mind you, there's a condition attached.'

Her eyes narrowed. 'Which is?'

'You stay in the office, from now on – or you only drive our female clients, and not ones like Leila, either.'

'I'm an equal partner in this firm. I'll do my share,' she told him, lifting her chin.

He grinned. 'In that case, I'm looking forward to talking to you over the radio, next time you're driving an ultra-respectable client. Because I'll rig your car so that your passengers can hear exactly what I'm saying to you – every proposition I make, in loud and lurid detail.'

'You wouldn't.'

'Try me.'

She grinned. 'As they say, what's sauce for the goose.'

'Meaning?'

'Meaning that I could get your car rigged, the same way. Anything you can do, I can do better,' she teased.

His lips twitched. 'I think that this is going to be one hell of a partnership, Ms Hargreaves.'

'I'll drink to that – later tonight. We'll have champagne.' Liza licked her lips, thinking of exactly what she was going to do to Bryn, later, with the champagne.

His eyes met hers. 'Celebrating the start of a true partnership . . .'

A Message from the Publisher

Headline Liaison is a new concept in erotic fiction: a list of books designed for the reading pleasure of both men and women, to be read alone – or together with your lover. As such, we would be most interested to hear from our readers.

Did you read the book with your partner? Did it fire your imagination? Did it turn you on – or off? Did you like the story, the characters, the setting? What did you think of the cover presentation? In short, what's your opinion? If you care to offer it, please write to:

The Editor
Headline Liaison
338 Euston Road
London NW1 3BH

Or maybe you think you could do better if you wrote an erotic novel yourself. We are always on the look-out for new authors. If you'd like to try your hand at writing a book for possible inclusion in the Liaison list, here are our basic guidelines: We are looking for novels of approximately 80,000 words in which the erotic content should aim to please both men and women and should not describe illegal sexual activity (pedophilia, for example). The novel should contain sympathetic and interesting characters, pace, atmosphere and an intriguing plotline.

If you'd like to have a go, please submit to the Editor a sample of at least 10,000 words, clearly typed on one side of the paper only, together with a short resume of the storyline. Should you wish your material returned to you please include a stamped addressed envelope. If we like it sufficiently, we will offer you a contract for publication.

More Erotic Fiction from Headline Liaison

SEVEN DAYS

Adult Fiction for Lovers

J J Duke

Erica's arms were spread apart and she pulled against the silk bonds – not because she wanted to escape but to savour the experience. As the silk bit into her wrists, a surge of pure pleasure shot through her, so intense that the darkness behind the blindfold turned crimson . . .

Erica is not exactly an innocent abroad. On the other hand, she's never been in New York before.This trip could make or break her career in the fashion business. It could also free her from the inhibitions that prevent her exploring her sensual needs.

She has a week for her work commitments – and a week to take her pleasure in the world's wildest city. Now's her chance to make her most daring dreams come true. She's on a voyage of erotic discovery and she doesn't care if things get a little crazy. After all, it can only last seven days . . .

0 7472 5094 4